Withdrawn

Point No-Point

Point No-Point

A ZIZA TODD MYSTERY

DAVID WILLIS
McCULLOUGH

VIKING

VIKING
Published by the Penguin Group
Viking Penguin, a division of Penguin Books USA Inc.,
375 Hudson Street, New York, New York 10014, U.S.A.
Penguin Books Ltd, 27 Wrights Lane, London W8 5TZ, England
Penguin Books Australia Ltd, Ringwood, Victoria, Australia
Penguin Books Canada Ltd, 10 Alcorn Avenue, Suite 300,
Toronto, Ontario, Canada M4V 3B2
Penguin Books (N. Z.) Ltd, 182–190 Wairau Road, Auckland 10, New Zealand

Penguin Books Ltd, Registered Offices: Harmondsworth, Middlesex, England

First published in 1992 by Viking Penguin,
a division of Penguin Books USA Inc.

1 3 5 7 9 10 8 6 4 2

LIBRARY OF CONGRESS CATALOGING IN PUBLICATION DATA
McCullough, David W.
Point no-point: a Ziza Todd mystery/David Willis McCullough.
p. cm.
ISBN 0-670-84184-6
I. Title.
PS3563.C35293P65 1992
813'.54—dc20 91–21832

Printed in the United States of America
Set in Garamond No. 3

"Death is a warning."

—The Reverend T. L. Daise, Jr.
New First Baptist Church
Edisto Island, South Carolina

Point No-Point

PROLOGUE

HILLSIDE AND RIVERSIDE

He had been on the waterfront before. He had roamed around with his friends, thrown a few stones, broken a few windows, stood on the rotting bulkheads, and pissed into the Hudson, but he had never been there alone.

The place looked bigger than he remembered and in worse condition. He had made his first visit there back in the seventh grade. For social studies class they had been taken on a walking tour around the old and empty factory buildings, but never inside. Local history. Know your community.

An old guy who used to work in one of the mills had talked to them about the good old days during the war—W.W. II, he called it—when all the factories had been busy, when they all had their own baseball teams, and when everyone made good money. An old lady from the historical society talked about the good old days before that, when there were sugar mills all along the river and the marble quarries were still in business. People even came up from New York City on steamboats to watch illegal boxing matches on barges just offshore. Once, one of the boxers was killed, she said, punched to death, and there had been a big scandal.

That's what Dennis Morland remembered most about that day: the old man really coming alive—even remembering old scores and great catches—when he talked about the factory baseball teams, and the old lady trying to act shocked, trying to get the kids to act shocked, because one guy had beaten the brains out of another guy—"in front of all those people"—right there in Quarryville.

But this time Dennis was alone. He had crossed the railroad tracks and climbed through the rusted fence to get a good look at what was there. Besides the blue knapsack that carried his schoolbooks, he had brought a small notebook and his mother's disc camera that fit into his pocket. No one knew he was there. He almost felt like a spy.

He had come down after soccer practice to scout—the word made him smile—*scout* the place out. With luck he would get into a building or two before it got dark, get a good look. He might even think of some way to use the waterfront for a community project. He had—or would have in time—the required merit badges, all twenty-one of them, to become an Eagle Scout. (Then, if he ever flipped out, the newspaper headlines could read—as they always did—EAGLE SCOUT SLAUGHTERS FAMILY.) All he needed now was a community-service project.

Dennis Morland knew he was famous for being a good kid. He was president of his junior class, next year's editor of the school paper, a good-enough first-string soccer player, Honor Society member. His form of rebellion was the Boy Scouts.

Quarryville-on-Hudson had its own caste system. Riverside boys, the grandsons of the old man who remembered the good old days of W.W. II, were on the football team. Hillside boys, the grandsons of the historical society lady, played soccer. No one but the social dregs in either part of town would join the Scouts. Scouts weren't even the class clowns. They were the kids you passed in the halls and vaguely recognized, but whose names you couldn't quite remember.

He told himself that what he liked was the outdoor stuff, the hikes, the canoe trips. He wouldn't admit it, but what he really liked was the order, the rules. He loved the idea of having books to tell him exactly what steps he had to take—what clearly defined tests he had to pass—to move from Tenderfoot to Second Class to First Class, Star, Life, and finally Eagle. He even loved the look of the tidy little merit-badge pamphlets that told him exactly how to master Physical Fitness or Bird Study or Citizenship in the Community. And this is what he most hated to admit; he loved the uniform that could only be worn in exactly the way the book said.

Marching made him uneasy at first. They had a scoutmaster, a harmless-enough old guy, who liked to march them around the church basement barking "Column left, column right, to the rear, MARCH!" at them, and what a scraggly, gawky, inept bunch they were, skipping around, falling over each other trying to keep in step. But once they had been in a parade in Manhattan, on Fifth Avenue, not their troop alone but the entire county Scout district in one unit, thirty-two across. The nearest band was so far away that all they could hear were the drums. Every now and then an adult would yell, "Line it up over there," but the sound around them came mostly from shoes hitting the pavement, the rustling uniforms, the snapping of the flags. Time fell away. Dennis could not explain it. How could it be pleasure if he couldn't remember it? But before he knew it, the parade was over. He had never been aware of the crowds on the sidewalk. No one they passed would have noticed him. They had marched over fifty blocks, and he felt a calm he had never known before.

His friends, his real friends, never talked about the Scouts. They never asked questions. His fellow Scouts never tried to be his friends at school. They all knew the rules. The caste system was preserved.

Today he was alone as a secret Scout, a spy. The wind off the river was sharp and cold. His hair was still wet from playing soccer and he could feel it stiffen around his ears. Every now and then the wind caught a loose piece of sheet metal tacked over a broken window and made it rumble like thunder. Most of the waterfront construction had taken place in the 1920s and 1940s. Low, flat-roofed rectangular brick buildings and a few dull aluminum-colored cubes were broken up here and there with long lines of connected Quonset huts. The narrow factory streets, now overgrown with weeds and littered with trash, were either paved with uneven hexagonal asphalt blocks or they doubled as railway sidings. Most of the windows close enough to the ground to climb through were boarded up or tinned over. Whoever was breaking into the buildings could ignore the windows, since the doors were ripped off their hinges.

Dennis looked through a few doorways. What he saw was almost always the same. Light, from skylights so clear he knew the glass was gone, spilled down onto huge, empty rooms. All the machinery had been ripped out, leaving great rusted bolts sticking up from the floors. A few buildings that had been converted into warehouses before they were abandoned were filled with empty pipe racks. Huge puddles of rainwater covered many of the cement floors, and next to them, like campfires near a mountain lake, were black smudges of ashes and charred scrap wood.

He pulled out his camera and took a few pictures. On the walls were faded signs left over from the factory days (NO SMOKING, 117 DAYS WITHOUT AN ACCIDENT, BUY BONDS) and in fresher spray-can graffiti, names of rock groups, names of lovers Dennis didn't recognize, a few QUARRYVILLE SUCKS, and—of course—RIVER RATS.

Did the River Rats actually exist? Everyone said so, but Dennis thought it strange that no one had any firsthand stories about them. Everyone knew someone who had had a run-in with the gang, although the Rats didn't actually seem to live in Quarryville. Vandalism was always blamed on the River Rats. So were most daytime burglaries. There was even a legendary battle between the Rats and a mob of Riverside kids so bloody the local cops had been afraid to break it up, but the story was about older brothers and uncles. No one Dennis knew had been there.

He finished taking the last picture, the fifteenth, and put in a new film disc. The plan forming in Dennis's mind as he moved from building to building was for a massive photographic project. He would map the whole waterfront on a grid, figuring out when the light would be best to photograph each part of each building. Every kid in the troop would have a camera and be assigned specific areas to shoot at specific times. Twenty-five kids, twenty-five cameras, twenty-five rolls of film. It could all be done on one or two bright and sunny weekends. And in the end he would have a complete photographic record to give to the village library or the historical society. Maybe there could even be a big exhibit called "The Waterfront Today" that would accompany historical pictures of the place.

He was approaching the southernmost edge of the factory area, where a much older-looking building was surrounded by a protective cyclone fence. The sun was beginning to slip behind the Palisades on the other bank of the river. It was still a long time to sunset, but now everything was in shadow and the wind felt sharper than ever.

Dennis followed the perimeter of the fence searching for an opening. The building inside the fence looked like a church. The boarded-up side windows were tall and narrow and came to a point on top. The steep copper roof was studded with rows of sharp points that looked like arrowheads. Near the peak on the front wall was a round window, like the rose window in a church. The one tall chimney could have been a bell tower with its thin arches and heavy lintels. The brick walls were not flat but broken up from time to time with buttresses topped with red sandstone.

All fences on the waterfront have holes in them, Dennis thought. It was only a matter of searching until you found one, and he found a narrow slit next to the ground and squeezed through it. All locks on the waterfront are broken, although this one—on a door solid enough for a cathedral—had been carefully put back into place to look as though it could still keep people out. He removed it and pushed open the heavy door.

Inside was another huge room, but this one was not empty. There was dirty glass still in the skylights and gray light too dim for photographs filtered down. Oversized pieces of heavy iron machinery were still in place. He could hear water dripping somewhere, but there were no giant puddles on the sooty floor. There was, though, a faint smell of smoke. Along one wall were a number of tall wooden crates, some of which had been broken open. Maybe to see what was inside, but more likely to use the crates for fire wood. Several charred circles were over near what might once have been an open forge of some kind. Discarded cans of beans and ravioli lay near one of them.

The homeless, maybe? He knew they were a serious problem. One of the churches in town distributed food in the city, and he had helped them out a couple of times. He had seen people in old clothes sleeping on cardboard in the back hallways of Grand Central. He had smelled their urine as he walked by. Once, sitting on the stairs, waiting for a late train back from the city, he and a friend of his had been offered sandwiches and juice by a bored social worker. The idea of being mistaken for the homeless seemed like a great joke.

But it wasn't really funny, and now they were even here in Quarryville. Maybe, he wondered, his project should have something to do with them. Not a soup kitchen, but something.

He looked up into the dusty light. There were high round windows at each end of the building, and the brightest spot in the room was up among the rafters. He looked through his camera's viewfinder and clicked off a shot he knew would not come out. The rafters were metal by the look of them, but fancy with all sorts of curves and decorations that looked something like vines and leaves. Dennis was again reminded of pictures he had seen of churches in Europe. It was almost beautiful, he thought, a funny idea. Who ever heard of a beautiful factory?

There was a sound from over in the corner, beyond the crates. He held his breath. Rats, he thought, real ones with four legs. Then there was a shuffling sound in another corner. The River Rats? His first thought was to run. But maybe it *was* the homeless. "Hello?" he said. He realized it sounded like a question. "Hello," he said, louder, as though he meant it. ("Sound off as though you got a pair," the old scoutmaster would sometimes yell at them.) "Hello!" he shouted.

No one answered, but someone was behind him.

"Hel . . . ," he began to say as he turned. Then he froze and said, just once, "Don't."

1

&

"Don't," Whooten said.

It sounded like a shout to Adele, even—of all things—an order, and she froze before her hands even touched the heavy gold-leaf picture frame. She could not remember the last time someone had shouted at her in her own house. Or—taxi drivers aside—anywhere else.

"It's bad luck," Whooten said, this time sounding almost apologetic. He glanced over at Fogle as though he were looking for agreement. Fogle ignored him. He had a briefcase full of papers in front of him and seemed to be searching for something he had mislaid. "You should never straighten a picture when someone else is in the room, Adele. It's bad luck." He turned to Fogle again. "It is."

For well over an hour the three of them had been sitting in the drafty fireside inglenook of Aladdin Baraclough's old studio, a "space"—as Whooten called the room—recently registered as an architectural landmark with the National Institute of Historical Design. The sun had long since set. If they had turned their heads—which they hadn't—they could have watched it through the room's twenty-seven windows, dropping behind the Palisades on the other side of the river. It went, as usual, with all the well-worn garish splendor

Baraclough—Adele's great-grandfather—had spent a life-time trying to preserve on canvas.

There was, of course, no fire burning in the shoulder-high Gothic fireplace that Baraclough had designed wide enough to accommodate Yule logs (the insurance company had long ago insisted that the flue be blocked off), and the barnlike room was becoming downright chilly.

They had been talking about the law. Rather, Fogle was talking about lawsuits, legal actions, and dispositions, ex-plaining them, one after another, as Adele and Whooten tried to pay attention. First, there was the case they were—that is, she was—bringing against a Connecticut mail-order house that had stolen the patented design of the Baraclough rustic wrought-iron garden bench (ads for it appeared in *The New Yorker, Smithsonian, Preservation,* and Lord knows where else). Then came all the legal documentation that Fogle said they needed to get approval for their—rather, for her—riv-erfront project. The process involved everyone from the county board of health to the state office of environmental something-or-other to—and here Fogle's voice became es-pecially ominous—the Feds.

Adele's attention had long since begun to wander as Fogle went on and one about RIFS, PCBs, PRPs, the DEF, and environmental and archaeological impact statements. At one point she interrupted to say all she wanted to do was turn an old iron foundry into a museum. His response had been a "dear Adele," a shake of his head, and an understanding smile. Then he went back to an important document called the SEQRA and an Order of Magnitude Estimate.

That was when she noticed that one of the paintings on a wall full of paintings opposite her was crooked. Was it "Pic-nic on Verdrietege Hook"? All she could see of it in the shadows was its mottled gold frame. But it wasn't simply tilted, the sort of thing that can happen during a serious dusting (although the studio had not been given a truly serious dusting in months), it was noticeably off kilter. She got up to set it right.

That meant threading her way through the carefully preserved clutter that fanned out from the inglenook: the high-backed couches, the twin Morris chairs, the genteelly tattered Persian carpets (Turkey carpets, her mother always called them), the hammered copper tray, on legs, from some Moroccan marketplace (still holding cracked paint boxes and earthenware vases jammed with dried-out and encrusted brushes), the outsized black walnut easel, which held what was said to have been her great-grandfather's last painting, an almost impressionistic oil sketch of the Palisades left unfinished for nearly ninety years.

As she walked she turned on three heavy wrought-iron floor lamps (one of the profitable sidelines of the now defunct Baraclough foundry), and the rich light shining through the honey-colored cut parchment seemed to warm the room. She could now see that the painting was indeed "Pic-nic." She hated it. She had hated it since she was a child. It showed an ill-at-ease group of thoroughly unpleasant-looking people (most of them men in bulky uniforms, the women in more skirts and bows than could ever have been fashionable) sitting in a riverside grove, holding but not actually eating what looked like fried chicken. In the background a black servant was keeping a fractious horse from bolting the scene. Adele had always felt a certain sympathy for the horse.

"Don't," Whooten called out as she reached toward the painting.

"Bad luck?" she asked. She had still to touch the frame.

"Jesse James was shot straightening a picture," he said. "In the back."

"Or so some would have you think," said Fogle, who had made a successful sideline out of making remarks like that.

"Dead," Whooten said.

"Jesse James was a bank robber," Adele said, "which I

suspect had more to do with his getting shot than did straightening a picture."

"He was also standing on a chair," said Fogle. "Or at least so they say." Fogle's syndicated column, "Or So They Say," regularly disproved assumed facts, such as the notion that the North won the Battle of Gettysburg or that George Washington was the first President (he was actually someone named Hanson) or that Gertrude Stein ever wrote "A rose is a rose is a rose."

"I never straighten a picture when I am not alone," Whooten said.

"And he has yet to be shot in the back," said Fogle.

"Exactly," said Whooten.

"James Garfield was shot going to an alumni meeting," Fogle said. "Maybe that's bad luck, too."

"What college?" asked Whooten.

"Williams."

"I suppose that's better than being a bank robber," Adele said.

Whooten snickered.

She shot him a glance. Adele had not altogether forgiven Whooten for shouting at her in her own house, no matter how well-intentioned he was. He was a curiously turned-out little man. The first time she met him, two years ago, when Fogle brought him (quite improperly) to a board meeting of the Lower Hudson Valley Victorian Society, she gasped in surprise at the way he looked. She was embarrassed, of course. Later, she suspected she reacted just as she was supposed to.

If seen only in a snapshot with a plain backdrop that gave no hint of perspective (the sort of photograph he always used for publicity purposes), Whooten looked tall and gangling. Lincolnesque, Adele thought, crag-faced, straight-haired Lincoln before he grew the beard. Face-to-face, he was a perfectly made miniature whose feet never touched the ground when he sat in an ordinary chair. Adele also suspected that the highly polished boots he always wore, with their curious fretwork of leather straps and hooks, were meant to call attention to his dangling feet.

But he was a wonderful architect. Or was he a designer or a decorator? A builder of stage sets? All of the above, Adele thought. The giant octagonal room they stood in attested to that. She never would have recognized it as being part of the house she had grown up in. He had created it—re-created it—mostly by taking away things that had been added since her great-grandfather built it in the 1870s. Into the trash heap went temporary walls, false ceilings, several different ineffectual heating systems, a gimcrack bathroom, a kitchen. He had layers of cracked linoleum pulled off the floor—each layer releasing the musty, long-buried smell of cat pee—and brought up from the cellar the old Turkey carpets, the easel, old Baraclough litter, and now the place looked as though it hadn't been touched since the old man died in 1910. His next job—if they could ever get the permits to begin work —was to turn the old foundry down on the riverfront into a Baraclough museum.

The painting was still crooked. She sensed the two men watching her (was this some sort of secret test they had made up?) and decided, for now, to leave it alone.

"Chicken," said Fogle.

"Wise," said Whooten.

She reached up quickly and with both hands slid the painting along its hanging wire. "There," she said. "Done and finished."

"Too much," Fogle said. "Now it's hanging too far the other way. Let me." He reached up.

"No." It was a proprietoress's "No" and it went unchallenged.

The two men suddenly became intensely interested in the painting. Fogle was about as tall as Whooten looked in his photographs. He had the kind of tight, curly blond hair that turned gray early, but the effect of the hair against what Adele thought was suspiciously tanned skin made him look younger than he probably was. They never discussed age, the three of them, but they were all about the same, she thought, somewhere in the late forties. And how would she describe herself? When young, a tomboy (is that word still used?), a better jock than her brothers, late brothers now. As a wife she had been matronly, seeming older than she was, looking older than now, the sort of person who fits easily and unobtrusively into committee photographs. As a widow who ran every day for forty-five minutes she liked to think of herself in terms of larger-than-life actresses, Vanessa Redgrave, perhaps, Colleen Dewhurst, on bad days Maureen Stapleton.

"This depicts more people than I've ever noticed in a Baraclough painting," Whooten said about "Pic-nic," as if politeness required him to say something after looking at it so intently.

"It's his only group portrait," Adele said. "Whoever commissioned it refused it when it was finished."

"I can see why," Fogle said. "It's god-awful."

Without allowing a moment's silence, Adele said, "That sort of negative comment"—spacing her words out carefully—"is not welcome in this house."

"Sorry," Fogle said easily and without any noticeable regret, turning his attention to a watery sunset-behind-the-ruins scene hanging above "Pic-nic." "It's simply that portraiture doesn't seem to have been his forte."

Aladdin Baraclough was not, in fact, the worst of the Hudson Valley School painters. He came along late and his name was never, even at the height of his popularity, a household word, but he had always had a small circle of admirers. His considerable financial success, though, came not from the pictures he had turned out like clockwork right up to the day of his death, but from the park benches and ornamental iron-work he designed and produced at the foundry and casting works he built just upstream from his home and studio in Quarryville-on-Hudson. Except in such places as Savannah, Charleston, and the Garden District in New Orleans—where his entwined sunflower fence was especially popular—surviving examples of Baraclough ironwork had become rare in the United States, but the *zócalos* and public parks of any Mexican town that once had dreams of grandeur back at the turn of the century were still lined with heavy Baraclough benches decorated with allegorical and biblical scenes.

A few years before, soon after Adele first met Fogle, the Metropolitan Museum in New York had its big Hudson River School exhibition. The show put an official seal of approval on the art dealers' claims that those almost forgotten nineteenth-century landscape painters were indeed again fashionable, collectible, and worthy of high prices. A group of six Baraclough oils was included, arranged above the very same rustic garden bench whose design was later stolen by the mail-order outfit Adele was suing.

They were small pictures, hung in one of the dead-end side galleries with a selection of his sketches for ornamental iron-work, as though they might have been footnotes or even a sly curatorial joke. Laughter, indeed, was often heard in that gallery, caused perhaps by a series of views of Aztec ruins sitting in the shadow of Storm King Mountain. The most admired—and reproduced—in Baraclough's day was a scene after a summer downpour, in which a flaming eagle with the tail feathers of a giant parrot soared over the ruins, which were braced by a pair of smudged magenta rainbows. The lavish catalogue, in which the Coles and the Churches and the Cropseys were given full-page color reproductions on heavy laminated stock, presented Baraclough's "Mexique-Hudson Perdu Suite" in black and white and only slightly larger than postage stamps.

But Aladdin Baraclough *was* included, and that was enough for Adele and the newly formed Baraclough Foundation Trust to convince a third-floor Madison Avenue art dealer —known chiefly for painted tin windup toys and curiously pristine patchwork quilts—to mount a concurrent Baraclough show, with a stunning catalogue underwritten by the Trust. It was a sellout. Collectors—lacking available Coles, Churches, and Cropseys—settled for Baracloughs.

Thanks to judiciously timed sales of forgotten paintings, the Trust was now actually making a good deal of money. The Trust, of course, had its trustees: a lawyer, a utility-company president, an art historian, a local college professor, a priest (Fogle convinced Adele that Jesuits were the new "hot items" on official boards, hotter than bankers). Their names appeared on the letterhead, but the working Trust consisted of one person, Adele Baraclough Bloodhorn, and two people whose names were not on the stationery, Fogle and Whooten. They served, as Whooten often said to Fogle, at madam's pleasure.

Fogle looked at his watch.

"We should be getting back to the city," Whooten said. "Busy day tomorrow."

"Yes," Fogle said. "Why don't you go on, then. I really want to make sure Adele understands the fine point of this legal stuff. One more time should make it clear."

Whooten looked at Adele first, then Fogle. "I'll have the car."

"Fine."

"We rode up together."

"The train station's only two blocks away. There's one an hour. I'll be fine."

"You know it's bad luck to leave through a different door than you entered. Maybe the same's true of transportation. Come in a BMW, leave in a BMW."

"I think," Fogle said, "that you may be getting too caught up in this good luck/bad luck business."

Whooten looked again at Adele, waiting for her to suggest that he stay for another cup of coffee, maybe a drink of something for the road. She smiled and leaned forward, ever so slightly, awaiting a good-bye kiss.

He did as expected, a quick peck, a wave to Fogle. He said something about finishing off the final sketches for the foundry renovation project. They might be something worth putting on display at the studio open house in two weeks. Adele and Fogle headed back toward the fireplace, and he left the octagon, heading for the front door—the way he came in—through the original Baraclough cottage.

There was an almost Quaker plainness to the older building, really quite unusual for the time just after the Civil War, when it was built. No interior fancy work of any kind. No moldings around the ceilings; no chair rails; no jigsaw work on the banisters. The fireplaces—in a town crowded with marble quarries—were undecorated slate painted white. When Whooten renovated the house for Adele he had emphasized its starkness. All the rooms were painted a near-gray. None of the pictures on the walls made you take a second look, none—except for three childhood sketches— were by Aladdin Baraclough. He removed the bits of fake Hudson River Gothic woodwork that someone—Adele's parents, probably—had stuck outside around the front porch and roof to make the place look like a typical storybook cottage. He would have torn the whole porch down, but Adele drew the line.

His purpose was to increase the sense of surprise when one walked from the thoroughly ordinary house into Aladdin's studio. In the daylight the room shimmered as the sun poured in through the twenty-seven tall windows. The walls of exposed brick—all shades of red, orange, and black set randomly—rose up three stories that felt more like ten—before they nipped in to support a ring of green and red clerestory windows topped with an oxidized copper cupola.

Whooten stood in the darkness of the house's tiny dining room and looked back into the golden light of the octagon. Never again, he thought, would he work on so wonderful a room as this. The wall of the inglenook and the high-backed horsehair couches blocked his view of Adele and Fogle, but he could hear their voices. And not just Fogle's voice explaining legal matters. They were having a conversation.

He tried not to listen, but he didn't try very hard.

In the corner opposite the inglenook was its single most dramatic object, a steep, glistening-black, iron spiral staircase wide enough to climb two abreast and decorated with panels depicting all the scenes and designs once available in the Baraclough foundry catalogue. It rose one story to a small balcony and what had been Aladdin's bedroom, now, he believed, Adele's.

Adele and Fogle had begun laughing, the two of them. Whooten could hear that distinctly, and he left as quietly as he could.

"That's absurd," Adele was saying.

"It's far out but I think it may be the solution to everything," Fogle said as he joined in the laughter.

"I haven't reached this stage in my life to become an iron-monger." She was no longer laughing.

"Hear me out before you slam the door. What are our current problems? We are suing someone for stealing your property, your family's copyrights, and patents. We, on the other hand, seem about to spend a fortune on legal bric-a-brac just because we want to turn a fine old riverfront building into a museum."

"That's the point: a museum of the art of Aladdin Baraclough. Not a new ironworks. The paintings are the point.

You yourself said a museum would do wonders to encourage interest in the old boy."

"And keep the auction prices right up there where they should be. And we can still do that. But we can do more by using their laws and zoning restrictions against them."

"Whooten's architectural plan is a gem," Adele said.

"Of course it is . . ."

"Saving the old foundry intact as a museum. Stripping a few nearby buildings to their bare ribs and framework . . ."

"Ghost memories, he calls them."

"Ghost memories of lost buildings, yes. Beautiful lawns right down to the river. Flowers. And underneath everything, below ground, the Aladdin Baraclough Gallery of Art and Design."

"Genius personified," Fogle said. "But think how much more of an attraction an actual working, fire-breathing foundry would be. 'Nothing musty about the Baraclough Museum,' they'll say. It'll be something for the whole family to see. We can have a little iron workshop, tasteful, of course, right on the spot. And get this—this is the beauty part—by keeping it a foundry we don't lay ourselves open for every kind of environmental investigation they can think of."

"You're losing me."

"There's a loophole."

"If I wanted loopholes I would have hired a lawyer. You are supposed to be above that sort of thing."

"Here it comes: the site is still—*still*—zoned as a foundry, and if you reopen it as a foundry-museum, what can they say? Except for the odd bit of vandalism, the place is just as it was when it shut down after World War II. Everything's still there. We could go into business making authorized, original Baraclough benches, fences, light poles. We have all the old designs; the old molds and castings are still down there in crates. Thanks to your father, the copyrights were all renewed. You have the wherewithal—"

"Stop it."

"Think about it."

"It doesn't bear—"

"Look at all the fancy magazines—*HG, Architectural Digest, Country Living, Metropolitan Home*—everywhere you look ironwork is a big deal."

"This is absurd. The point of all this, as I was trying to say, is *not* to put the Baracloughs back into the iron business. That was the cross my poor great-grandfather had to bear. It's the paintings we're highlighting, especially the late ones when he stopped being interested in Mexican ruins."

"We'll still have paintings in the new gallery. Keep some here. Open the studio as a museum."

"This is my home. Having it open once a year to raise money for local charities is bad enough."

"We could make a big deal out of getting in. Like they do at the Barnes Collection outside Philadelphia."

"This is my home."

"Of course it is."

"I would have thought better of you." She laughed again, a teasing, almost mocking laugh.

She took away the dirty coffee cups and brought out clean ones with fresh coffee.

"Delicate cups," Fogle said.

"My great-grandmother's flowered Wedgwood."

They stared at each other.

"Tell me about your new book," she said, looking away.

"Just an anthology, bits and pieces of old columns. Thomas Edison never invented anything. Neither did George Eastman. Walt Disney couldn't draw. Homer was a woman. The Underground Railway never existed. Mozart didn't die young but came to America and became a church organist in Vermont. The usual sort of thing."

"You've done this before."

"Twice, paperbacks. Stores put them next to the cash registers and people buy them without thinking too much about it."

"You believe it all?"

"Most things that most people believe simply aren't true. I just raise questions others have raised and always give my sources. History, after all, is only what people believe it is."

They stared at each other. Neither one of them had tasted the coffee.

"Messing up Whooten's lovely design with a sooty foundry would be such a shame," Adele said. "I won't have it."

"You're fond of Whooten. I've noticed that."

"A charming boy. So talented."

"Hardly a boy."

"Well, of course . . ."

"You watch him a lot, do you realize that? When we are all together, you tend to keep your eyes on Whooten."

"When I speak to someone I look at him. When he speaks I look at him. Or her."

"Not always."

"Oh, I think—"

"No, often when I say something you watch Whooten to see his reaction."

"He's an intelligent man whose reactions are to be respected."

"And such a sensitive face," Fogle said. "He doesn't even have to speak to express himself. You've noticed that."

Adele did not answer at once. Fogle had set aside his coffee cup and stood up. "I suppose," she said, "if you say I watch his reactions, I probably do. I'm not aware of it." She left her chair and brushed invisible crumbs from her Black Watch skirt.

"A handsome man, really," Fogle said. "In spite of his size. Very well proportioned. You've noticed." He reached out and took her hand.

"No doubt you've wondered about his sexuality," he went

on, "given that aspect of him some thought." They walked toward the spiral staircase. "Probably the way little girls might think about boy dolls. Did you ever have a boy doll?"

"Just an Andy to go with my Raggedy Ann. My mother made them both."

"But you looked. You checked underneath his little blue pants."

"They were sewn so you couldn't look."

"You tried."

They had started up the stairs, turning past cast-iron panels depicting the Raising of Lazarus, the Labors of Hercules, the Triumph of Industry over Poverty, the Four Seasons, the Seven Continents, Washington's Farewell, the Execution of Maximilian, Henry Hudson Sailing Past Manhattan Island, Leda and the Swan, Bolivar in Glory, the Opening of the Erie Canal, Liberty Enlightening the World.

"But then," he continued, "we grew up in the days before anatomically correct playthings, although I suppose even now Ken and Barbie can't be stripped of their underwear."

"I wouldn't know," Adele said. They passed wrought-iron sheaves of wheat, corn stalks, sunflowers.

"Barbie clearly has breasts," he said, "but do you suppose there is even the tiniest little bulge between Ken's legs?"

"You'll have to ask the little girls down the block." She dropped his hand and began to caress the back of his neck as they crossed the narrow balcony into her bedroom. The only light came from the moon shining through two tall Gothic windows with leaded Persian roses at their peaks.

"I'm sure they know," he whispered, "just as you know there's a perfect little bulge in Whooten's pants, perfect thighs (perhaps those trousers are a bit too tight to be fashionable these days), perfect little feet under those socks."

"A perfect little boy doll," she said.

"Perfect," he said. Her bed was still unmade from the night before. They didn't bother straightening it out. The tangle of sheets mixed with the tangle of their clothes. "But tiny."

"A working model in perfect proportion," she said.

"If he put his mouth here," Fogle said, "could he—do you suppose—reach here?" They pushed aside the duvet. "If his knees were here, say, and yours there, just like that, do you possibly imagine that he could ever do this with his hands? Reach there? Or here?"

"If I rolled over here," she said, "do you suppose he could . . . ?"

"Never," Fogel whispered, "never."

"Never?"

"Could his tiny body, at the same time, without ever once moving, touch here and here and here? Perfect as he is?"

"It is perfect."

"Perfectly formed."

"Perfect."

"But not like this, or this. And he could never do this."

"And if I did this," Adele said, shifting her weight, "would he break? Or this, would he cry out for me to stop? Would I lose him forever if I tried this? What would happen with those tiny fingers? Could they hold on? Would they just slip away? Lose their purchase?"

"Perfect," he said, "perfect."

They burrowed through the covers, entangling, disentangling, seeking and imagining perfection, finding it.

"Ah!" Adele called out, throwing her head so her silver-frosted hair spiraled down her back, "spent."

"No," Fogle whispered, catching his breath. "Not spent, invested."

2

Ziza Todd, Ziza Todd, Lamb of God, Eyes of God, Wrath
of God, Rotten Cod, Pretty Odd, Ziza Todd . . .

Maybe she could call it a mantra, Ziza thought. That
sounded too sixties-ish, too Taos and Woodstock, but calling
it a mantra at least glossed over the sheer egotism of running
and mentally repeating, over and over, her name and its variations. Ziza Todd, Ziza Todd. The rhythm was so natural she
couldn't avoid it. Other runners claim to have eye-opening
mystical insights as they trot along. Ziza found she got into
well-worn mental ruts. Jingles from TV commercials were a
great danger, old camp songs, old songs in general.

While she was still at the seminary she often ran with a
fellow student, a man who claimed to have an interesting past
he didn't really want to talk about other than to let her know
he had one. After the third mile he would chant aloud: Up
the hill, Up the hill, Down the hill, Down the hill, All the
way, All the way, Air Borne, Air Borne, Rang-er, Rang-er,
Up the hill . . .

In her more macho moods, she still tried that one. For,
literally, a change of pace—although she certainly wasn't a
Catholic—she would sometimes begin the Rosary even
though those "now and at the hour of our death"s slowed
her down more than she liked. But what came naturally,

without even thinking about it, was Ziza Todd, Ziza Todd
and then the damn variations: Silly Sod, Harold and Maude,
Alien Pod, and all those things ending in God.

Today, running along a wide and well-worn hillside trail
that had not yet become routine, the old, familiar litany was
almost reassuring. It was only her second morning in Quarryville, her second time running along this path high above
the river. They called it the Aqueduct, which called up in
Ziza memories of high school Latin textbooks with photographs of great, incredibly fragile-looking Roman structures
with their tall stone arches. But this aqueduct, which once
brought water to New York City from an old reservoir
upriver at Croton, was buried underground and the path
above it was now an unbroken public trail thirty-five miles
long from the Bronx to northern Westchester.

On her first day she had run south toward Yonkers, and
after passing the usual assortment of unfashionably 1930s
suburban houses she crossed the Quarryville village line and
ran behind a barricade of high-rise apartment houses and
condos (Neo-Mussolini, Ziza thought) that blocked out all
sight of the river and the Palisades beyond. Every mile was
marked by tall stone ventilators that looked like giant chess
pieces, pawns.

Then to her surprise, just as she had assumed she was
coming to some urban area, she entered a deep and enchanted
woods. Gothic stone balustrades overgrown with vines ran
along what must have been the carriageways of a great estate.
A cluster of Corinthian columns rose out of a tangle of half-
grown maple trees and supported an impossibly heavy cornice
and nothing else. A grand staircase guarded by stone lions
that had long ago lost their heads divided into two on a formal
landing—now a ruddy grove of sumac bushes—and made its
way down to the Aqueduct. The broken steps were covered
with discarded beer cans.

A little beyond the ruined staircase, squat in the middle

of the running trail, sat a classical Greek temple the size of a rich child's playhouse. The spaces between the stained-cement columns had been filled in with cinder blocks, and crashed into the back was a rusted-out Dodge Dart. Someone had painted RIVER RATS on its roof.

Ziza had stopped cold. She didn't run in place. She just stopped, caught her breath, and looked around. Below her on the right were the railroad tracks and beyond them the gray river. Far off in the distance she could see the tops of the towers of the George Washington Bridge. The oversized toy Parthenon smelled of stale urine. Here be dragons, she thought, turned and headed back toward home.

This morning she ran north from Quarryville on the Aqueduct, past suburban houses, behind small-town business districts, and high school athletic fields, through the well-maintained grounds of former estates that had been taken over by research centers and religious organizations. The great surprise of that first day's run was not the ruins—that was the sort of thing Ziza expected to find hidden away in the Hudson Valley—but the fact that when she headed back toward Quarryville she felt she was heading for home.

It certainly didn't seem like home, the dusty, unfurnished house that came with her job. In fact her job had yet to actually begin. The title sounded impressive enough: Director of Religious Education for the Quarryville-on-Hudson Community Pulpit. What it meant was that all the Protestant churches in town—there were four of them, counting St. Hubert's Episcopal, which was empty—had decided to combine their different Sunday schools into one, and she was to run it.

The search committee that interviewed Ziza and eventually hired her kept referring to the proposed consolidation as "integration," which made it all sound rather high-minded and lofty. But low attendance at most of the churches was the real reason, and having one Sunday school instead of three, Ziza knew, had more to do with saving money than creating, as the prospectus said, "a unified Christian experience for the youth of Quarryville."

Ziza Todd, Ziza Todd, Throw a Rod, Aging Bod.

Running about twenty-five yards ahead of her was a man in a royal blue sweatsuit with JUST ASK ME in Day-Glo letters across his back. It was the second time she had seen him, the second time in two days, and she wondered what his game was.

Just Ask Me, Just Ask Me. Just Ask Me, What?

But of course the reasons Ziza gave the committee for wanting the job were just as clouded as theirs for offering it. Can you be burned out at twenty-nine? Ziza had begun to think so. Since graduating from divinity school in Rochester she had been involved in what her mother called social work. First she had been an assistant minister, one of three, in a big downtown church in Albany. The fashionable neighborhood where the church had been built a hundred and fifty years before was now on the edge of a slum—although no one used that word when "inner city" could be substituted for it—and Ziza had been put in charge of "community outreach."

That meant the morning hot breakfast program for the homeless, the neighborhood pantry that distributed groceries to welfare families, and Meals on Wheels for the elderly. Before long it dawned on her that she would have been better prepared for the ministry if she had gone to the Cornell hotel school and studied catering. She began to look for a job in which she would be more involved with people than canned goods and found it in a place called Childtown. The name sounded like a toy store and its setting—a nineteenth-century railroad baron's estate in the foothills of the Adirondacks—was idyllic, but it was an isolated community for disturbed and problem children, the last refuge for kids, poor kids usually, that everyone else had given up on.

She stayed there for more than three years, and when the end came, it came over something utterly routine. She was restraining Ezra. Over the last year she spent a lot of time restraining Ezra. One of the premises of Childtown's director was that children losing control of themselves needed to push against a force stronger than themselves, a force that was also comforting. Ezra, who was seven, was often out of control. He had been born a heroin addict. He was also said to have inherited AIDS, although medical records were kept secret from the staff, and Ziza had spent hours, sometimes entire days, sitting behind him, her arms around him, pinning his arms firmly against his sides, his tiny butt between her legs, rocking slowly from side to side in a rhythm that was often calming, listening to him scream at her, calling her every filthy name he could imagine. And for a seven-year-old he could imagine quite a few.

As she rocked and made soothing noises she was actually thinking of what she had accomplished over the past three years. Precious little. Her time had been spent among screaming children who seemed no better off for anything she or anyone else at Childtown did. They had kept the children alive and off the streets, but what else?

She had no personal life. She was almost thirty and was getting, she thought, close to the time when her red hair and freckles were not going to interest anyone anymore. The night before at a staff meeting a married woman who was pregnant for the first time said her great fear was that after the baby was born and she was able to hold it for the first time he would open his eyes, look at her, and start screaming, "Don't touch me bitch, fuckin' keep your hands off me, shit!" They all laughed. That was what Ezra was shouting now, and Ziza broke into tears.

It made no sense. She had not cried since her first week on the job, when a group of ten-year-olds started throwing rocks at her and she could do nothing to stop them. "Don't touch me, bitch!" Ezra screamed, and she obeyed. She let him go. He spun loose, tumbled over her legs, and ran across the lawn in search of something to attack. Nothing was handy. No trees, no rocks. A picnic table was nearby, but too far away for Ezra. He had no interest in escaping. He turned back on Ziza, kicking at her, clawing. She kept clear of his snapping jaws, grabbed his arms, turned him so he faced away from her, and pinned him in the position they were in before. "Fuckin' cunt bitch faggot," Ezra said.

She rocked him, her forehead pressed against the back of his neck, her tears soaking into his T-shirt. Of such is the kingdom of heaven, she thought. Suffer the little children . . . The next morning she called her seminary's alumni placement office and told them she was looking for a new job.

The man in the JUST ASK ME sweatshirt was keeping the same pace as Ziza. He seemed no closer or farther away than he was five minutes before. She decided to catch up with him and ask a question. Something would surely come to mind. Something on the order of, Why do you wear that silly shirt? Or, What's Quarryville's dirty little secret? One of America's favorite illusions, after all, is that every small town has a dirty little secret. Half of American literature is built around that notion. She speeded up. No more leisurely Ziza Todd–Ziza Todds. Now it was simply Todd-Todd-Todd-Todd.

She had already learned about one little secret, two, actually, and a mystery. Someone named Marcie was an ordinary fuck, and someone named Becky wasn't. The mystery concerned a boy named Dennis. He had dropped out of sight and no one—no one—had ever pegged him as a potential runaway.

Ziza had learned all that last night, Friday, when on her first day in town she had been invited to a party. The word "chaperone" was not actually used but that was obviously the idea. One of Quarryville's traditions seemed to be that rather than always having high school dances in the gym, they were sometimes given in private houses, Quarryville's classes being small enough and Quarryville houses (at least some of them) large enough for the whole thing to work out just fine.

Bob Bramer, one of the members of the search committee, offered the invitation. "A good chance to get to know some of our fine young people informally" is how he put it. His daughter, Anne, was a junior, and she had talked her parents into volunteering their house for a dance. The "usual practice," he said, was to invite a few adults to "balance out the crowd."

Ziza's first reaction when she walked in the door was that she hadn't been surrounded by so many white faces since before she had gone to work at Childtown. Then other reactions flooded in: how excessively polite everyone seemed, how well dressed these kids were and how careful they were to disguise that fact, how everyone seemed to be making a point of obeying the rules—and there were a lot of them—when in fact the major one, the ban on drinking, was clearly being broken somewhere. "We kind of blink on that one," Bob Bramer said. "Better to have them stashing six-packs out under the rhododendrons than shooting up in the bathrooms, right?"

Other rules were followed to the letter. Dancing only in the huge basement rec room (a term Ziza hadn't heard since her own high school days), no smoking indoors (which gave everyone an excuse to wander out among the rhododendrons), girls' bathroom in the basement, boys' on the first floor, one customer at a time, no browsing through the refrigerator or kitchen cabinets, no one allowed above the first floor.

"Except us, of course," Bob Bramer told her. "I've found that it's only necessary to walk through the party once every hour or so. Show the flag, that sort of thing. So you're welcome in the TV room. I've rented enough cassettes to keep us all amused. A John Ford festival. *Red River, Rio Bravo, She*

Wore a Yellow Ribbon, and, for a change of pace, *The Quiet Man.* Adult bathroom is off the master bedroom."

The adults consisted of the Bramers (Mrs. Bramer stayed in the kitchen, making popcorn, she said, but actually defending her refrigerator from browsers), a couple too old to have children at the party—Ziza never did get their names—who watched every minute of the film festival in uncontested silence, and Ziza, who tried to do more than just show the flag on her visits downstairs. She introduced herself, let the kids act as though they really were on their best behavior, and half-wished someone would invite her out to the rhododendrons for a drink. Mostly, she listened.

When Dennis Morland's name came up, which it did frequently, she could sense their uneasiness. They dropped their guard. Things were happening that were not supposed to happen. Police had come around the high school asking questions, and not just the village police. Dennis had not been seen since Monday afternoon soccer practice. He never got home. The phrase everyone used was "It's not like him."

Ziza went upstairs and headed through the darkened master bedroom toward the light in the bathroom beyond. Inside, the door closed, she sat down and became fascinated with the reading material piled next to the toilet: *Advertising Age, Women's Wear Daily,* a paperback Calvin-and-Hobbes anthology, *The Collected Poems of Stevie Smith,* and *The New York Review of Books.* Not to mention *The Quarryville Weekly Spy,* which, Ziza noticed, had her eight-year-old college graduation picture on the front page: YOUTH PASTOR BEGINS DUTIES.

She was reading what the paper had to say about her Childtown experience when she began to hear a conversation going on in the bedroom. It was all the "fucks" that caught her attention.

"An ordinary fuck, is that what he wants?" a girl asked.

"Well, I don't know," a boy said.

"An ordinary fuck, if that's what he wants, he's gone to the right place with Marcie."

"Well . . ."

"One thing you can say about me is that I'm not just an ordinary fuck. Becky is not just an ordinary fuck."

Becky, Ziza thought, had clearly found her way to the rhododendrons.

"Sure, I guess," said the boy.

"You can tell him that. Tomorrow you call him up and tell him Becky's not just an ordinary fuck."

"Sure, I can do that, if you really want."

"Not an ordinary fuck."

"Well . . ."

"She looks like him. Notice that? Marcie looks like him. I can't stand boys who go out with girls who look like them."

"No," he said, always agreeable.

"Marcie's sick that way, you know. About people who look like her. All WASPs are like that. They just want to go out with people who look like themselves. Once she even wore her brother's jock, you know that?"

"Well, look . . ."

"She told me all about it. Took it right out of the clothes dryer hot. Tell him tomorrow. He looks nothing like me. Call him tomorrow. Tell him, tell him Marcie wears her brother's jockstrap and that she's just an ordinary fuck."

"I don't think you—"

"You know, Rich, I can talk to you, *really* talk to you. Call him and tell him . . ."

Ziza flushed the toilet. It seemed a diplomatic way of letting them know they were not alone. There was a silence, then a scrambling sound. The bed creaked (Ziza had not pictured the conversation taking place on a bed) and footsteps rushed down the hall. She gave them time to get away and opened the door. Getting informally acquainted with the youth of Quarryville, she thought.

Todd-Todd-Todd-Todd.

Now, on the Aqueduct, she had almost caught up with the JUST ASK ME man. She was breathing hard after her sprint. He must have heard her and looked back to see who was gaining on him. He had that unhealthy, scrawny, bearded look of people photographed at the finish line of the New York Marathon. Stitched onto his baseball cap was MONTY, and as he turned further and waved she could see that MONTY was also printed across his chest in the same Day-Glo color as JUST ASK ME. The man was obviously some sort of nut.

He waved again as though he recognized her, but before he could say anything he looked beyond her, over her shoulder, and his smile vanished. Ziza slowed down and looked back. A police car, its light bar blinking away, was bouncing along the Aqueduct toward them. The siren growled once, and a woman runner who had not heard it coming up behind her jumped to one side. Just as the car reached Ziza it growled again, an animal warning her to keep her distance.

When it came alongside Monty, the car stopped and a policeman jumped out. There seemed to be some scuffling around and Monty ended up in the backseat. The door slammed. The policeman hopped behind the wheel, and the car spun into a U-turn heading back in the opposite direction, this time its siren wailing full blast.

Ziza had stopped running to watch, and the woman who had jumped out of the way of the police car caught up with her.

"Was that an arrest?" Ziza asked.

"Doubt it," the woman said. In spite of the chilly weather she was wearing shorts. She must have been almost fifty, Ziza thought, but she had legs worth showing off. "That was the new mayor," she said.

"In the police car?"

"Running. Our own Monty 'Just Ask Me' Monteagle. It's

nice to know there's something he does that's worth calling out the cops for."

Ziza noticed that, unlike herself, the woman was not at all out of breath. Her metallic hair was as immobile as a Buick hood ornament.

"You're the new youth minister," the woman said. It wasn't a question. "You look better than that baby picture they ran in the *Spy*. I'm Adele Baraclough Bloodhorn." She extended her hand.

Now there, Ziza thought, was no name to run to. "Ziza Todd," she said.

"We'll have tea," Adele said.

"Fine. I'm living at the old Episcopal parsonage, St. Hubert's."

"This afternoon. Four o'clock. The studio."

"The studio?"

"You know where it is. Everyone does."

3

&

"You found him?"

"Me?" The driver did not slow down but turned to look back at the mayor as though he were being accused of something. The squad car bucked its way across the ruts of the Aqueduct and with each bump his head hit the ceiling, pushing the polished visor of his policeman's cap farther down on his forehead.

"Not you personally, of course, Wasco."

"What does that mean? *Of course.*"

The near falsetto *of course* sounded nothing at all like the way Monty had said it. He had been in office more than a month now and still found that it was hell being commander-in-chief to someone you had gone to high school with, especially—and this was true of just about everyone on the fifteen-man police force—someone who had been a class or two ahead. Football players, most of them.

"Forget it and slow down," Monty said.

"He was dead."

"I was afraid of that."

"Bashed in the head . . ."

"Oh, my God."

They were off the Aqueduct now, heading uphill on one

of the residential streets, and Wasco did indeed slow down, although he had not turned off the siren.

"The Walker found him."

"Miss Gatewood." She was one of Quarryville's familiar sights, an old woman who either for her health (that was the rumor) or simple compulsion seemed to spend every waking hour, rain, shine, or blizzard, walking around town and not speaking to a soul. Monty always thought she looked like those photographs of Greta Garbo the *New York Post* used to run every few months, with the old girl all bundled up and wearing dark glasses waiting in a movie line somewhere on the East Side.

"She found him in the Meadow," Wasco said.

"The *Meadow*. Couldn't be."

"On the edge, under some bushes."

"She couldn't."

"Could and did. He's still there."

"It's impossible. When did he disappear? Almost a week ago. You couldn't lose a body on the Meadow for that long. Not unless half the kids in town are in on it."

"Well, *boss*"—Monty didn't like the sound of that *boss*— "what can I tell you?"

Below the top of the hill they turned into the elementary school parking lot. Wasco killed the siren without being asked, although he didn't bother slowing down for the traffic bump. They followed a driveway around the side of the building and then cut across the empty playground. Just behind the jungle gym was an overgrown road that curved through the woods.

Wasco made the turn, but only just. The old road—it was once the driveway to some millionaire's long-gone country house—was blocked with other cars, most of which had names on their doors and lights on their roofs. Wasco growled the siren once, perhaps in defiance of the vehicles blocking his way, perhaps warning the others that the mayor had ar-

rived. Then they both got out and walked uphill toward the
clearing. Coming from each car they passed was the pleading
squawk of a two-way radio begging to be answered.

"Kinda takes you back," Monty said. "I don't think I've
been along here in five years."

"I get here two, three times a month," Wasco said. "Shit,
some Saturdays in the spring two, three times a night, chasing
kids out."

"I guess some things never change."

"Shit." Wasco kicked a stone out of his way for emphasis.
"Kids coming back here used to be a big secret. Now they
tell their parents they're going off to the Meadow and the
parents say, 'Have a nice time.' It's a tourist attraction, these
days. Kids come from Yonkers, Hastings, Dobbs Ferry. Some
nights there's a guy with a keg of beer selling tickets and
stamping hands. It's a regular penny social."

"Something to get on top of," Monty said, patting the side
of his sweatpants, automatically looking for his notebook.

"The only justice," Wasco said, "is that no one gets laid
here anymore. Too much else going on."

The Meadow was smaller than Monty remembered, and a
fresh growth of quaking aspens crowding in on the edges was
making it even smaller. Still, it was about the size of a baseball
diamond, maybe a little larger. The grass was well trampled
and about where the pitcher's mound would have been was
a large rock outcropping, the Pulpit. At least that's what kids
called it in Monty's day. Someone had managed to spray
RIVER RAT across the front of it before running out of paint
or rock.

Set back in the trees and looming over everything, like the
towering keep of a green metal castle, sat the village water
tank, the highest spot in town. At the top, a red light flashed
away day and night. That was Monty's most vivid memory of
the Meadow, lying next to someone who didn't seem to really
want to be there, watching the light high above him in the

darkness blinking on and off, counting off the time before one of them had to be home.

The Meadow had never been busier in daylight. The Quarryville volunteer ambulance had been pulled up next to the Pulpit. Its back doors were open and the volunteers in their bright yellow slickers were standing around, waiting to be allowed to get to work. The far side of the Meadow was crowded with more waiting people. Most of them were in uniforms of one branch of the police or another. State policemen were there, county cops, parkway policemen, even a game warden. They had heard the call over the police band and turned up, needed or not. Those not in official uniform seemed to be in the unofficial, rumpled-sports-jacket-and-gray-slacks uniform of plainclothesmen.

Wasco fell behind as they entered the clearing, and the mayor in his Day-Glo JUST ASK ME sweatshirt and MONTY baseball cap crossed the Meadow alone. All conversation stopped. Someone called out, "Hi, Monty." Someone else swallowed a laugh.

"Chief Malfadi here?" he asked, all business.

"At a police chief's conference in Albany," Wasco answered, still a couple of paces behind him.

"Fill me in," Monty said. "Anybody." He kept walking through the crowd until, like everyone else, he was stopped by the orange plastic scene-of-the-crime tape that had been strung up in a square. Inside it, like a referee in one of those old prints of nineteenth-century outdoor boxing matches, the medical examiner bent over a fallen body.

Monty ducked under the tape. "Anybody," he repeated.

"Not fresh meat," said one of the men with the examiner.

The M.E. himself was more professional, too professional to actually look at the mayor. "Male Caucasian, middle to late teens, date and time of death to be determined (probably three to five days), cause to be determined (probably a blow to the head)." Then he did look at Monty. "Friend of yours?"

The body was obviously Dennis Morland. Everyone there knew that. He was stretched out in an unnaturally formal way with his hands crossed at his waist. His eyes were closed and his hair even seemed to be freshly combed. He was wearing a JUST ASK MONTY campaign button.

"He's been moved, of course," said Monty.

"You want me to talk about lividity?" asked the examiner.

"No, but the boy obviously hasn't been lying here three to five days."

"Couldn't possibly talk about lividity until there is a proper laboratory examination. But I'd speculate that you're right in judging the crime to have been committed elsewhere. Just don't quote me on that." He paused and shifted out of his official tone of voice. "He was one of your people? In the campaign?"

"A lot of kids worked for us. There are a lot of buttons floating around."

"Was he?"

"I don't remember."

"I suppose not." The M.E. stood and made a vague gesture toward the body. One of the men with him whistled through his fingers and waved toward the ambulance, where the volunteers jumped into action.

"Wasco!" Monty shouted.

"Yo." He was standing just outside the tape.

"See to it that all the right things are done, the police business, whatever it is."

Wasco looked as though he could have come up with some wise remark, but instead said, "I'll try to get Malfadi back from Albany."

"I'll call the parents."

"Notifying the next-of-kin," Wasco said, supplying the proper terminology. "This is something, you know? Mayor a couple of months . . ."

"One . . ."

". . . and you have the first real murder I've ever heard of in this town. The Chief's going to kill himself for missing this."

ða   ða   ða

"It's over, done, taken care of. I moved him."

"What?"

"I got thinking about him down there all alone, and I moved him."

"You should've let sleeping dogs lie."

"It wasn't right him lying down there."

"Out of sight, out of—"

"But when they did find him, and they would, then what?"

"River Rats. Everyone blames everything on the River Rats."

"Trouble. So I moved him out of harm's way, where he's sure to be found."

"That's all?"

"That's all what?"

"You just moved him, that's all? Nothing else?"

"Why do you ask something like that?"

"You just moved him, right? No extra touches?"

"Out of harm's way."

"And that's all."

"Just about."

"Just about?"

"One little joke."

"God help us. What was it?"

"A joke so little no one will even notice it, much."

"Much? How much?"

"I gave him a button."

"What?"

"One of those JUST ASK MONTY buttons."

"You're mad."

"Mad, bad, and dangerous to know."

"That's all?"

"I combed his hair, cleaned him up a bit."

"That's all?"

"He seemed like a nice kid."

"That's all?"

"Just about."

ఈ   ఈ   ఈ

Monty wanted to get out of his running clothes before going to see the Morlands and asked Wasco to drive him back to the Village Hall. He was—just temporarily, until things settled down a bit—living in his office, which was certainly a good deal more comfortable than the one-room apartment above the A&P that he used to call home.

As they pulled up to a battery of red lights at the intersection that everyone in town called the Star (six roads came together and the one you were on never had a green light), Monty saw Wasco reaching for the siren switch. "Wait for it," he said. "I'm in no rush for this job." Wasco sighed in a way that suggested he, at least, had more pressing matters that needed doing.

He drummed his fingers on the steering wheel and then suddenly stopped. "Look at that," he said.

"Where?"

"Over by the church."

"Which one?" Each of Quarryville's five Christian churches was located on one of the Star's corners. Parking on Sunday morning was pure hell.

"Over there. Not Sacred Heart."

Monty suspected Wasco didn't know one Protestant church from another, but he saw where he was pointing.

"It's the first time I ever saw her talking to anybody," Wasco said.

The Walker, Miss Gatewood, was busily explaining something to the young red-haired women who looked as though she had been out running. "Who can pass up telling about finding a dead body?" Monty said. "Who's the girl? She looks familiar."

"The new preacher," Wasco said. "Her picture was in the *Spy*. You were waving at her when I picked you up on the Aqueduct."

"Right." Then, as though what Wasco said suddenly explained everything, he said "Right" again. "Come on, two birds with one stone, let's get over there."

Wasco growled the siren a couple of times as they cut through the intersection and pulled up next to St. Hubert's. The Walker gave them one look and sped off down the sidewalk. "Miss Gatewood!" Monty called after her, jumping out of the car. Without looking back, the old lady raised her hand, made a motion that looked as though she were erasing a blackboard, and kept right on walking.

"She was telling me about the Morland boy," Ziza said. "If that's what you gangbusters are trying to find out."

"I'm Monty Monteagle." A smile and an offered hand-shake.

"So I see." She shook his hand but didn't smile.

"Reverend . . ."

"Ziza Todd."

"You know Miss Gatewood well?"

"Not at all, but she knew who I was from the newspaper and thought maybe I could do something to help the boy's parents. Have you told them yet?"

"Well, no. In fact, I was hoping . . ."

"I'll do it."

"The Morlands will appreciate it."

"I suspect it's you who'll appreciate it more."

"What I mean is that it's a time when a woman's touch can mean a lot. He was their only child."

"It's a time . . . Look, I better get over to their house before they hear some really god-awful version of the whole thing from someone else."

"We can give you a lift."

"Miss Gatewood said they live just around the corner. I don't think it's an occasion that'll be helped much by police cars and flashing lights."

She wasn't going to give him an inch, he could see that. It was that damn Wasco's fault, him and that fucking siren.

"Maybe we can run together some morning," he said as she walked away from him. "Might help fill you in on life in Quarryville, my old hometown." She didn't respond, just kept walking, faster if anything. "His name was Dennis," he called after her. "You keep calling him 'the boy,' but his name's Dennis."

She stopped and turned. "Thank you," she said. She might even have smiled.

He waved. She nodded. He would be running with her before next weekend, he thought.

Wasco had stayed in the car. "I have a message for you," he said. "From"—he deepened his voice to sound like an announcer on a high-class car commercial—"*the village manager.* She told me to take notes on what she said."

Monty groaned. Lillian Meservey, village manager. Mayors may come and go but there is always Diamond Lil, with the highest salary in the budget.

"Number one: she has been monitoring the police calls and is keeping abreast—"

"Her word?"

"Yes, *sir.*"

"You didn't laugh."

"No, *sir.*"

"Keep reading but stop trying to mimic a southern accent. You're no Lillian Meservey."

"—is keeping abreast of all developments on the killing

and feels that you are misallocating your time on this matter. This is a police situation and should be left to Chief Malfadi—now en route from Albany—and his boys. Her word.

"Number two: your complete attention is required on the waterfront development matter. You have an appointment with Adele Baraclough Bloodhorn at two (fourteen hundred hours) today. Her place. Be prompt. Expect lawyers. Take notes.

"Number three: she had added new addresses to the list of suitable rental properties for a mayor and wishes you would consult it.

"Number four: she reminds you again (repeat again) that it is against the law to dwell and cook in a municipal office."

"I don't cook."

"And number five: she (Miz Meservey) will not be available for conference until Monday A.M., but will see you then, earliest. Her word."

"Wasco, take me home."

"Home?"

"Village Hall."

"That's a municipal office, not a dwelling."

"Drive, and blow the siren all you want."

4

People always talked to Ziza, talked too much sometimes. If there were an empty seat next to her on a train or a bus, it would be grabbed by someone who was dying to pour out his—or more often her—life story. All the other passengers would be sitting in stony, isolated silence, reading, looking out windows, sleeping. Ziza would hear congested tales of abortions, disputed wills, missing fathers. Was it, she wondered, some sort of character flaw or weakness in herself that drew these people to her?

If, she sometimes asked herself, *if* she had a stronger personality of her own, would she still find herself so honestly interested in other people's lives? Would she still have asked the key question that always encouraged the talker, catching her breath after running through the story once, to get into the real meat of what had happened? More to the point, if she had a life of her own would she have been listening carefully enough to know what question to ask?

And why—this was what she asked when she was really feeling sorry for herself—did she never run into anyone—a stranger on a train, a college adviser, anyone—who showed the slighest interest in hearing, really hearing, her own story?

If she tried baring her soul, Ziza found, she inevitably chose to mention some incident that immediately reminded her

restless listener of something far more interesting in her—
or more often his—experience. Soon Ziza would hear
herself—damn fool—asking that key question that got the
monologue really rolling. And more often than not she was
fascinated by it.

When Miss Gatewood stopped her with the terrible news
of a dead body abandoned in a field, Ziza sensed she was
meeting someone who was unaccustomed to idle conversation. Words came from her in bursts. She kept repeating that
she had recognized Ziza from her picture in the paper, as
though the conversation needed a justification. The police
car spooked the old woman, but before she hurried off, she
grabbed Ziza's sleeve. "We'll speak again," she whispered,
her voice cracking. "Yes, we will," as though Ziza had been
ready to contradict her.

"Call me," Ziza said.

The woman drew closer. "We'll meet by chance," and she
was gone, waving her hand behind her at the idiots in the
police car.

Ziza had no trouble finding the Morlands' house. They
seemed to be expecting her. Mrs. Morland was at the front
door before Ziza had crossed the wide front porch. Mr. Morland was waiting inside. The portable television set in the
living room was on, but the sound was turned off, Saturday
morning cartoons in a house without children. A radio was
playing somewhere, probably in the kitchen, an all-news station from the sound of it.

Ziza introduced herself. The Morlands showed no sign of
surprise or curiosity. They were younger than she expected.
Ziza was reaching the age when she noticed how young parents of teenage children could look. They were waiting for
bad news, and Ziza gave it to them as quietly and directly as
she could.

Dennis's body had been found. He had been dead for some
time. From the look of him he didn't seem to have suffered.

She used the word *instantaneous,* a sportscaster's term that somehow seemed grotesque in the context of death.

Both Morlands spoke at once. "How?" she asked. "Where?" he asked. They were still at the front door. Ziza wondered if she should have asked them to sit down before telling them. People on TV were always big on getting people to sit down before telling them bad news.

"A blow on the head, or so it seems." She was basing all this on what Miss Gatewood told her. She hoped the old lady was reliable. Ziza realized she should have asked more questions of the mayor in his silly sweatshirt. "They found him at the Meadow a few hours ago."

"What a stupid place to be," Mr. Morland said. He had put his arm around his wife, but she did not act as though she had noticed.

"Hit on the head," she said. "At the Meadow? Had there been a fight? They say there's a lot of drinking up there."

"Dennis never gets into fights," said Mr. Morland. "He could always talk his way out of it."

"It didn't look like a fight," Ziza said, hoping she was right. "Is there anyone you'd like me to call?"

"Everyone knows by now. It's Quarryville. For days the phone's been ringing off the hook. This morning, no calls. We could tell they all knew something and no one wanted to be the first to tell us. Who got you to come?"

The question sounded sharper than he probably intended. "We appreciate your coming," Mrs. Morland said. "I'll make tea. Coffee?"

"No, no," Ziza said. "Nothing, thank you." She turned to Mr. Morland. "The mayor, he had been up at the Meadow with the police and ran into me at the church. I volunteered."

"That simple sonofabitch . . ."

"John," Mrs. Morland said.

"Is he still there?" Mr. Morland asked. "Dennis. At the Meadow? I have to see him."

"No," said Mrs. Morland.

"I'm sure they've taken him away," Ziza said. "My visit's not official. Someone else will be coming, someone in uniform. They'll take you to identify the body. You'll be able to see him. Be with him."

"Bureaucrats," Mr. Morland said. "Papers to sign."

There was a sound of people coming up the porch steps. Neighbors, having met first somewhere else, were arriving as a group. Through the front window Ziza could see that they were all the Morlands' age or older. They were the parents' friends, not Dennis's. Most of the women were carrying platters covered with aluminum foil. The men, following along behind, carried the heavier casseroles. Ziza wondered when all that baking had been done.

She opened the door. "I'll call you again," she told the Morlands as the first of the neighbors filed in. Many of them had obviously been crying. The Morlands were not. They were busy acting as unexpected hosts. Their tears, Ziza thought as she headed back to St. Hubert's, would come later.

She was late, of course, or she was about to be, for a meeting scheduled to start at eleven and then turn into what Bob Bramer had called a "working lunch." It was to be her first get-together with the other ministers of the Community Pulpit and they would, Bramer said, be "hammering together the S.O.P." of the new joint Sunday school. She had met them all before during the job interviews when they were on their best behavior. But this would be the beginning of a day-to-day working relationship, and being late for the hammering together was no way to begin.

She dashed into St. Hubert's stark, white—and completely unfurnished—parsonage. Rather, the gray walls would have been stark and white if they had been painted in the last thirty years. Still, the glass-brick windows caught and held the bright morning sunlight. The chrome banister she raced past as she headed upstairs for her shower was still silvery.

The parsonage may have stood empty for a decade but it was still the most modern-looking building Ziza had seen in Quarryville. Its architect, she had been told by everyone who talked to her about the place, not only had studied at the Bauhaus but had also—"And this should especially interest you, Miss Todd"—been a woman. No one, though, seemed to remember her name.

Ziza already had laid out what she was going to put on. All new, never before worn outside her bedroom: gray wool tailored slacks, a salmon-colored Oxford-cloth shirt with a rounded collar that would just peek over a smoky crew-neck sweater ("heather mist" is what the catalogue called the color), and the kind of shoes no one would ever notice. All in all, it was standard-issue L.L. Bean with a leavening touch of Land's End and a hint of Tweeds for class, Ziza's notion of what the Westchester woman wore on a Saturday morning.

Her cross was always a question. It was modest, a silverish Ethiopian cross on a chain. She liked to wear it but was afraid it made her look like one of those with-it, feminist nuns who were always protesting something their bishops had done. (Wonderful, brave women, but they had a Christian *look* Ziza wanted to avoid.) As her hair dried she tried it on, took it off, put it on again, and then gave herself another swipe of lipstick to avoid the nun look. She grabbed her battered purse and a clipboard and headed outside for the meeting at First Presbyterian Church.

Her parsonage was tucked behind St. Hubert's Church, a round stucco-and-glass pillbox now almost completely hidden by a circle of yew trees that had been allowed to grow wild. The front walk she rushed down was crowded over with ivy. Directly across the street was the red-brick First Presbyterian Church, with the tallest steeple in town.

She heard their voices rumbling down the long, dark hallway as soon as she entered the building. They were waiting for her in the minister's study and had left the door open.

She heard Dennis Morland's name mentioned first and then the Meadow. They were loud, clear voices accustomed to being listened to. Now that she was there, she did not rush toward the light coming through the distant doorway. She'd be damned if she'd arrive breathless, panting, late for school. When she finally made the turn into the sunny room she was still not as calm as she hoped but was glad to see that she wasn't the last to arrive after all.

Three men sat there. H. Roger Swain of First Pres. was behind the desk, clearly the man-in-charge. Squeezed onto a small leather couch in front of what looked like a fake fireplace stocked with real birch logs were Dale DeSousa of Trinity Baptist and Bob Bramer. She hadn't expected Bramer, since he was a layman, but he seemed to have made himself Ziza's unofficial Big Brother. Ray Rickert of Mt. Zion Methodist was missing.

They went through the social dance Ziza expected from men who wore suits. They began to get up with exaggerated slowness. She said, "Please, don't get up." They got up all the faster. Without actually shaking hands, they made hand-shaking motions toward her. She was offered a comfortable-looking floral wing chair next to the fireplace. She took it. They sat. Coffee? Please. H. Roger Swain poured from a thermos. Bob Bramer presented the cup to Ziza before she could get out of her chair. Dale DeSousa went through an elaborate charade of looking for cream and sugar before Ziza said black was fine.

Then silence.

"I'm afraid you're welcomed to Quarryville by terrible tragedy," H. Roger Swain said.

"Dennis Morland," Ziza said.

"You've heard?" asked H. Roger Swain.

"That's a small town for you," said Dale DeSousa.

"The mayor told me . . ."

"That twerp," said Bob Bramer.

"I ran into him this morning."

"The voice of reform," said Bob Bramer. "Just Ask Monty."

"Actually, Miss Gatewood was telling me about it when the mayor interrupted."

"The *Walker?*" Dale DeSousa asked. "Spoke?"

"She found the body . . ."

"In the Meadow," they said in unison.

"Disturbing, very disturbing," said H. Roger Swain. Ziza pegged him as a forty-year-old who pretended he was fifty, fifty-five. "Although the new youth program is not scheduled to get under way for another month, Ziza, you should dedicate some serious time to ways we can serve our young people on this. We are going to have some very, very unsettled kids on our hands."

"I'm devoting most of tomorrow's service to it," Dale DeSousa said. He seemed to Ziza to be an authentic fifty-five-year-old who was wearing it well.

"Dennis, of course, grew up at First Pres.," H. Roger Swain said. "Belonged to our Scout troop, practically an Eagle. I wouldn't say his parents are pillars of the church, but they're members, good solid people if not active churchgoers. I'll be seeing them as soon as this meeting's over. I do not think we should drag it out, especially since our colleague from Mt. Zion has found himself too busy to attend."

"A bad sign," said Bob Bramer. Both H. Roger Swain and Dale DeSousa shot him looks that would have shut him up for the rest of the meeting if he had noticed.

"All in good time, Bob," said H. Roger Swain, "all in good time."

"I think," Ziza said sweetly, perversely enjoying the fact that she was about to twist a knife, "the Morlands are fine now, but when the shock wears off . . ."

"You *think* they're fine?" asked H. Roger Swain.

"They were when I saw them this morning."

"You saw them?"

"I told the mayor, who didn't seem to want the job, that I'd tell them about Dennis."

"You?"

"They were prepared for the worst."

"And they got you?"

"I was handy."

"I'm sure you were."

"I fear," Dale DeSousa interrupted, "we have much to cover this morning."

"Indeed," said H. Roger Swain.

There was a chilly silence during which Dale DeSousa re-filled everyone's coffee cup. "To work, to work," he said with good cheer.

H. Roger Swain picked up a thick manila file from his desk and opened it. "Point one," he read, "venue." He obviously had a Standard Operating Procedure that didn't need hammering together and went on reading aloud from his prepared notes.

Bob Bramer, a member of First Pres., agreed with everything. It was mostly housekeeping details. How costs would be divided. Where the classrooms could be located for the different age groups. How the interchurch board that ran the program would be constituted. Who would deal with purchasing matters.

From time to time Dale DeSousa "raised a question," as he put it. Not for himself ("It all seems fine to me") but for what he understood to be Ray Rickert's position. ("If Rickert has gripes, let him show up here himself," Bob Bramer said.) Ziza listened and every now and then wrote something down on her clipboard.

When he finished H. Roger Swain closed his manila folder as though he were closing his Bible at the end of a wedding ceremony and smiled at all assembled. "That certainly seems to cover it," said Bramer. DeSousa said something about Roger having done his homework and hoping that copies would be available for Ray. And himself, too. ("Of course, of course, they're right here.") Ziza said her duties as youth minister didn't seem to be covered.

"Oh, but they were," H. Roger Swain said. "Perhaps your mind was wandering. I know it was pretty heavy stuff, but I believe it was under Point Eighteen. You report directly to the Pastoral Committee, Dale, Ray, and myself."

"We've been calling them the Holy Trinity," said Bramer.

"And that's all?" Ziza asked.

"We're keeping things fluid for now," said H. Roger Swain. "No need setting anything in stone prematurely."

"Where's my office?"

"You have a whole *house* over at St. Hubert's."

"I'd rather be more 'on-line,' as they say in the computer business. I want to be where the kids are."

"Ziza has a point there," DeSousa said.

"Maybe Ray can find some room at Mt. Zion," said Swain.

"That's assuming . . . ," Bramer began.

"Time for lunch," H. Roger Swain said.

Lunch—tuna sandwiches, courtesy of Mrs. Swain—wasn't leisurely. H. Roger had his appointment with the Morlands, and he was sure Ziza had things to do to settle in. ("Been in town only two days, my goodness.") They worked out an arrangement for Ziza to appear briefly at each of the churches' services the next morning so she could be introduced. And Mrs. Swain suggested that Ziza stop by at the five o'clock hymn sing to say hello.

"It's an institution," Bramer said. "The first Sunday of every month, all the sinners in town who like to sing hymns but don't like to go to church turn out. Great fun."

"Actually," DeSousa said, "most of them are churchgoers, but it's the only regular interchurch event in town. People come down from Hastings and Dobbs Ferry. Make a party out of it. Drinks somewhere first. Then the hymn-sing. Then dinner."

Ziza said she wouldn't miss it and asked where the Studio was. Adele Baraclough Bloodhorn's Studio? She'd been asked there for tea.

"Aladdin Baraclough's studio," Bramer said. "She's only the great-granddaughter, who got all the loot."

"You sure you've been here only two days?" asked DeSousa.

"Watch your step," Swain said. "I'm serious."

"What do you mean?"

"She's a woman—how can I phrase this?—with an agenda. She doesn't have people drop by idly."

"I've never been there," Bramer said, "except for the annual fund-raiser. Then it's ten bucks a pop."

"I've never even met Mrs. Bloodhorn," said DeSousa, who told Ziza how to find the Studio by taking Fulton downhill from the Star. "Last house on the left before the river. Looks like a museum."

"It *is* a museum," said Bramer.

"Don't altogether trust her," said Swain.

"I suppose I could always call the police if things get out of hand," Ziza said.

"That's right, I forgot. You have a friend at Village Hall."

"That twerp," said Bob Bramer.

   🙚 🙚 🙚

It was five minutes after four when Ziza turned into the driveway of Aladdin Baraclough's old studio. She immediately encountered the twerp himself. He was heading away from the house, walking alone. Two men, walking side by side, followed him at a distance they might have thought was out of earshot.

"Hello, Mr. Monteagle," she said.

"Monty," he said automatically without glancing up, and then, as though suddenly remembering someone had spoken, looked back at her and said, "Oh, hello," as though he meant it. "How did it go with the Morlands, rough?"

"No, no, it was fine. They were fine. They want to see Dennis." She noticed that when Monty stopped walking, the other two stopped as well. They did not want to catch up with him.

"It's all arranged," Monty said. "The police chief's back in town and everything's going by the book." He gestured toward the house. "You've been summoned by her nibs?" And without waiting for an answer, he added, "Good luck."

He continued on his way. The men behind him seemed to count to five and then resumed walking. Ziza nodded to them. The small, well-dressed one nodded back. The taller one kept looking straight ahead.

Adele Baraclough Bloodhorn was waiting at the front door, her silver hair catching the light as though it were molded chrome. "Politics," she said, motioning toward the men leaving her driveway. "You can't live with it. You can't live without it. Come on in, we'll have some nice girl talk." She flashed a smile that was more chilling than inviting.

Don't take candy from strangers, Ziza thought.

"It's Ziza, isn't it?" She said, rhyming it with "pizza."

"Zi—long 'i'—za. Rhymes with Liza."

"I'm sure it does. You'll call me Adele. Now come in for that tea you were promised." She led the way through the simple, sparsely furnished cottage into the soaring octagonal studio. Ziza reacted with all the surprise expected.

She grasped no details, just a mass of impressions. Dark paintings everywhere in huge, old frames. The heavy, circular iron staircase winding up to a balcony. Light pouring in through tall windows. Layers of Persian carpets. A clutter of papers and charts in front of the fireplace, piles of thick ring binders, maps, pasted-up architects' drawings on rickety easels that looked like folding music stands.

"Can't stand another minute in the same room with all that

paperwork," Adele said. "If you want the Grand Tour come back next Saturday. It's the annual fund-raiser for the Village Arts Club. The place'll be overrun with bright-eyed volunteers eager to bore you stiff with all kinds of facts and dates." Behind the iron staircase, another spiral, this one of contemporary steel and oak curving toward the floor below. Ziza followed Adele down into a kitchen that must have been described by its designer as "state of the art."

"It doesn't have to be tea," Adele said. "It could be coffee. Could be something stronger. Assuming your holy vows permit that sort of thing."

Ziza's first reaction was to stick with tea, but then she remembered H. Roger's warnings and thought, what the hell. "Scotch would be wonderful."

"Scotch it is. I'll go to your church anytime."

They sat at a thick oak slab that still kept the contour of the original tree. Scattered around its center was a jumble of wrought-iron candlesticks and glazed tiles covered with brightly colored—and somewhat fanciful—animals: howling foxes, crows, frogs, dancing iguanas, a pelican whose breast was being ripped open by its young.

"Aladdin Baraclough's work?" Ziza asked.

"Iron, yes. Tiles, no. I only wish he'd had that much fun in him. He collected them, though. They were done by an Englishman, a friend of William Morris's, William de Morgan, maybe the only painter in history who supported himself— very successfully—by writing novels. Worth a fortune."

"De Morgan?"

"The tiles."

Ziza raised her glass to take her first taste.

"A toast," Adele said. "To Ziza's adventures in Quarryville." She took a healthy swallow. Ziza took a wary sip.

"Adventures?"

"You know what you're getting into with those preachers? Of course you probably don't."

"I smell a power struggle of some kind."

"Good girl. Between?"

"H. Roger Swain and, I suppose, Ray Rickert."

"A-plus. H. Roger is a horse's ass. Some dotty schoolgirl once called him Heavenly Roger, and he still tells people about it. Ray—I used to go out with him, you know—is an interesting case. On matters of religion he's hopeless, as fundamentalist as Billy Graham, more so. But he runs the food distribution program for the homeless. He set up a counseling service for pregnant girls. He's against abortion, but its not one of those fake clinics that tricks them into having their babies. He gives real information on real options."

"An unusual combination."

"Birth-control pills and the Bible as the true and literal Word of God, that's our Ray. All in one package. The kids love him, of course. Looks like some slightly overage movie star."

"You used to go out with him?"

"You know, Ziza, how your mother would ask you about some friend, 'Does she date?' Well, dear girl, I date. The plumber, the fire chief, Ray, the mayor . . ."

"Monty?"

"Oh, Monty, yes. It's hard to keep remembering he's mayor and not still some kid outside the A&P trying to get you to sign some petition. Him, too, but I was thinking of the last mayor. I have friends in the police, as they say. Others. You've probably heard about me."

"Not yet."

"Nice way of putting it."

"H. Roger warned me that you don't have people over to tea idly."

"He's more observant than I thought. I'm trying to woo you. I have plans for this town. Those two men you saw skulking behind our friend Monty are my advisers. And we're going to set this place right by cleaning up the waterfront,

pull some of those old buildings down. There'll be a Baraclough art center to knock your socks off. But that's just the
centerpiece."

"You have to woo *me* about all this?"

"There's opposition. Friend Monty seems to think we're
up to something that's not quite kosher, and he just got
elected as a 'Can-Do Guy,' 'A Breath of Fresh Air,' 'Mr.
Reform.' "

"And he's your opposition?"

"He wants to make a name for himself, wants low-cost
housing. A haven for the homeless and the elderly. Streets
paved with gold, for all I know. He thinks I'm an elitist."

"And him?"

"A puppy, housebroken, I suppose, but not much more.
What he is really is the son of some two-bit local lawyer,
dead now, the guy who wrote the wills and did the house
closings for people who didn't want a lawyer from the city.
Monty seemed all set to follow his father's footsteps. Went
to some one-horse college upstate, Schenectady or some-
place, some one-horse law school up there, too. Was all set
for the wills and the closings, and then he found causes. Any
cause, you name it. The Ralph Nader of the lower Hudson
Valley. Finds industrial waste and PCBs under every rock.
Never seen a tree or a frog he didn't want protected. Probably
has Pete Seeger already signed up to sing at his funeral."

"You're predicting an early grave?"

"He's going to be the death of us all. I'm predicting trouble,
nitpicking trouble, and it's already begun."

"So you're wooing me? Doesn't figure."

Adele topped off her own glass for a second time, made a
pass at Ziza's and was waved away. She put another dollop
in her own. "You're about to become a community leader,
dear girl. I'm just filling you in, playing the part of Miss
Welcome Wagon. Next thing you know I'll be handing you

a pamphlet from the League of Women Voters telling you to register for the school board election."

"And maybe while you're at it, you're checking me out, too, seeing if I've never met a tree I didn't like."

"Could be."

The subject switched to where Ziza was living, St. Hubert's, the church without a congregation. It had been built in the twenties, Adele said, by one of the riverfront mill owners, and for a while it was the showplace it was designed to be. There were articles in architectural magazines, a congregation of sorts, the pulpit filled with one semiretired clergyman after another. In the Episcopal diocese it had been designated as a chapel rather than a full-fledged church, and, in time, thanks to local indifference, the Depression, and the death of the mill owner, it even lost that.

"So they're letting you camp out without furniture?"

"There's a bed, a chest of drawers, a kitchen table, a couple of chairs. Bob Bramer said there was going to be more by next weekend. I think people are going through their attics."

"You need a picture. Come on."

Adele finished off her drink and went over to what looked like a door into a walk-in refrigerator. She turned a few handles, swung it wide and switched on the lights. Inside was a long narrow hallway of a room lined on both sides with tall metal racks filled with artwork, oil paintings, framed and unframed, watercolors, drawings, fat rolls of what seemed to be wallpaper or architectural plans. The air was cool and filled with the steady hum of temperature-control equipment.

"Swing the gate behind you," Adele said. "We can't let all this expensively maintained air get away. Now, what you'll want is down at the far end, catalogued under Late Work."

Ziza closed the door and followed along.

"Here," Adele said, "one of these," and started flipping through a selection of what at first looked like identical reproductions of the same scene in different sizes: a bend in the river, the sun setting over the cliffs on the left, more gentle hills on the right sloping down to the water.

"This is how my great-grandfather finished out his life— long after he had given up doing those silly Aztec ruins— painting this scene over and over again, gradually leaving out people or boats or buildings, even details of the water and rocks, until finally, at the very end, there was almost nothing but horizontal bands of color. Those very last pictures are going to be the great surprise when the riverfront museum opens. Aladdin Baraclough: Pioneer Abstract Impressionist. Take this one."

Adele blew invisible dust from a framed watercolor, about twelve inches by eighteen.

"It's beautiful. I couldn't."

"Yes, you could. It's not one of the *very* late ones. See, there are boats. Even a few buildings. You'll be signed out for it in the card catalogue. The Baraclough Archive stamp and number are on the back. So, if you try to sell it I can have you arrested without much trouble. Take it. There are six more like it still in the racks."

Ziza paused, wondered if she was about to make a very stupid mistake, and then reached out for the picture. Instead of handing it to her, Adele carried it to the door and slipped it into a large Jiffy bag.

"Another drink?" Adele asked when they were back in the kitchen, asked in a way that Ziza knew was a clear signal to say that no, thank you, she had to be going.

"No, thanks, this has been a wonderful welcome to Quarryville."

"Better than a dead boy, at least," Adele said.

Her offhandedness stunned Ziza. "Dennis Morland," she said, as though saying his name helped in some way.

"One of your flock? There aren't that many that you can afford to lose them."

"It's a very sad thing."

"Of course. But, then, they say the good die young."

"His parents . . ."

"Heartbroken, I'm sure. How did they react to that button he was wearing?

"Button?"

"One of Monty's campaign buttons. I heard the boy was wearing one."

"Hadn't heard that. Someone told me about the body but I never saw it."

"Hear any speculation about the killer?"

"The River Rats've been mentioned."

She snorted, then added, "Better them than me." They had climbed to the top of the spiral staircase and were heading across the studio. "I'd heard you got stuck telling the parents."

"Just the messenger," Ziza said.

"All part of the job, I suppose. Routine for you."

"Not really," Ziza said, "no."

At the front door Adele handed her the Jiffy bag. "Don't drop it," she said.

"What's the title?"

"Don't know that it really has one, but you can call it 'Point No-Point.' That's what it's a picture of."

"Here in Quarryville?"

"No, upriver about twenty miles or so. You can see it from down on the waterfront, way off in the distance. That's how it got its name. You can see it for miles heading toward it and for miles after you pass. But when you're right on top of it, you can't see it at all. Good afternoon, Ziza."

"Good afternoon, Adele." She turned and headed back down the driveway, hearing the gravel crunch under her feet, feeling that she had been warned about something but not really knowing what.

5

Adele Baraclough Bloodhorn regretted wearing her white linen slacks. Before she left the house she had remembered to change into her running shoes, and she put on a sensibly lightweight designer sweatshirt (a decidedly inaccurate facsimile of the Whitney family racing silks), but she came to regret wearing trousers that would never lose the kind of dirt she was bound to pick up on the waterfront.

Her decision to walk over to the Baraclough foundry was made on the spur of the moment. Lord knows she had been spending most of her time hearing about the old place. It occurred to her it was high time she took a good look inside, on her own, without someone telling her what to think. She took the heavy key ring from behind the door in the studio and had no trouble picking out the key to the padlock on the gate. It was the newest, brightest one of the bunch. She expected there would be more of a problem finding the key to the building's front door.

But when she got there she found the lock missing and made a note—literally made a note in her pocket notebook—to have Fogle have Whooten get right on that. Fogle hated it when she approached Whooten directly. Then she drew a large *X* through Fogle's name. She'd damn well approach Whooten any time she damn well pleased.

She pushed open the ancient, heavy doors that her great-grandfather had taken—bought, her father said, for a pretty penny—from a suitably picturesque fishermen's church in Brittany. The bright sunlight fell across the sooty stone floor, and that's when she regretted her white slacks. The room was smaller than she remembered, more crowded with the filthy machinery Fogle claimed still worked. Piles of ashes were heaped around the old hearth. Fresh ashes. Adele could smell stale smoke. Nearby, a cardboard box was half-filled with empty cans whose lids had been opened with the jagged sawtooth cuts of beer can church keys: spaghetti, pork and beans, Vienna sausages, that sort of thing. Either someone had made a stab at cleaning up, Adele thought, or the person cooking there had some latent tendencies toward good housekeeping.

Adele could only vaguely remember seeing the foundry in operation. She must have been very young and the business must have been in its last days, but she could recall a huge, dark room and the leaping flames. She remembered the bright, burning ribbon of molten iron and the warnings, over and over again, that she must never, never touch anything. Anything. Surely her father had been with her, but she didn't remember him. What she did remember were the workers shouting back and forth in a language she couldn't understand. She thought they were mad at each other.

Now that huge dark room had shrunk and become a sooty junkyard. Fogle's idea of reopening the foundry was absurd. However the official zoning read, Lillian Meservey would never allow a working ironworks to operate. There would be legal loopholes—laws against smoke or open flames or something—that the village manager could use to keep the place shut down. And rightly so, Adele thought. They should stick to her original plan for the museum, with Whooten's underground galleries.

Stacked along the walls were the crated-up molds Fogle

had mentioned. She went over to look at them and wished she'd brought along a flashlight. Titles had been stenciled on most of the wooden boxes: CONDOR IN ANDES, WASH CROSS DEL RIV, CACTUS FENCE, HEN HUDS AT STRM KNG MT, VIRGINS. The last was broken open completely to reveal the negative and positive molds for the back of a heavy park bench decorated with the Seven Wise Virgins holding their lamps. Bits and pieces of other crates had been pulled off in a hit-or-miss fashion.

It was too dark, Adele thought. Whooten was going to have to cut some new windows into the old building. The light that came down from above simply wasn't adequate. She was squinting up at the decorated iron cross ties when she saw him standing there, not ten feet away. He was so motionless that at first she thought it was another mold, a full-sized figure like they had behind the altar at First Presbyterian. Then she saw the black sleeveless sweater, the corduroy pants, and the Hush Puppies. He was standing there motionless but he was breathing.

"Took you awhile," he said.

"You're trespassing."

"Forgive those who," he said. "I've been standing here since you walked through that door, right here in plain sight, and it took you, I'd say, a good five and a half minutes to focus in on me. If I had a watch I'd be more exact. I'm sure you have one."

She covered her left wrist with her right hand. "You stole the lock from the front door, and I'll have the police on you for that."

"Actually the lock was there until a week ago. Useless, but there. Since then there's been a lot of coming and going. But I'd guess you're well up on that."

"Breaking, entering, vandalism, vagrancy. This is a registered historical landmark."

"You want to see the blood stains? There isn't actually

much to see, but the light's good over there, next to the door. But I'm sure you know all about that, too."

He took a step toward her and gestured at the door. He could have been almost any age but he wasn't young or healthy. If he tried to lay a hand on her, Adele knew she could flatten him without having to make a fist.

"See," he said, smiling, "it's right over there."

She refused to look where he was pointing. There was nothing about this man to like, but what she liked least was that he smirked like a headwaiter with a secret.

"I'm walking out that door and through that gate and over to that pay phone and dialing 911."

"911 in Westchester just gets you the telephone company. You'd be better off knowing the number of your local police department." He smiled again. He obviously hadn't seen a dentist in years. "You have keys. That make you the boss lady around here?"

"You said it."

"Then I think we can come to an understanding."

"I've come to all the understanding I need, thank you." She headed toward the doorway, but paused, ever so slightly, she thought, to see if she could see blood stains.

"They're there," he said. "If you take the time to really look you'll see that." He followed along behind her, not rushing in the least to catch up. "That's where the body was for almost two days."

"The boy?"

"I saw him. I saw a lot more. To put a fine point on it, I saw it all. As you know all too well, people don't see me but I see them. Need I say more?"

"You certainly do."

"I like the way you said, 'You said it,' a minute ago. Means you're a take-charge kind of gal. I think we can talk as professionals. I've seen what I've seen. I've seen a killing, and I've seen some hanky-panky with a dead body. As boss lady, that's just the sort of information you'd probably like to put your own spin on. I think, for a limited cash outlay, you can contract for the exclusive use of my information."

"Why should I pay blackmail to you?"

"It's hardly blackmail—is it?—if you're not the guilty party."

"I'll stake you to a one-way ticket to Grand Central. Take it or leave it."

"Take it or leave it, boss lady? A five-dollar train ticket? Six-fifty during rush hour? No trouble leaving that. No trouble at all. Now . . ." He looked as though he were laughing but made no sound. "Now it's your turn to make a counter-offer."

"You're quite the little shit-faced weasel," she said, walking out into the bright sunshine. "You'll be out of here before lunch."

"Lunch?" he said, remaining in the dark building. "If that's a warning, I suggest you give it a second thought. And think about the fact that there's others in this auction. People who offer more than train tickets."

"I'm using that phone."

"I'll be here for one more day. One. Just drop in anytime. The name's Dave. Don't bother asking for me."

As promised, Adele walked out the gate and up to the pay phone.

"Damndest thing," she said after she dialed a longer number than 911.

"What?"

"Someone says he saw that boy killed in my foundry. Worse, says he saw who moved the body."

"Impossible."

"I just talked to him and he wants a payoff."

"Don't write a check."

"He's camped out down here on the river, a tramp of some kind, and says he'll sell what he knows to the highest bidder."

"Don't worry about it."

"I'm not worried. I want something done."

"Don't worry about it."

She dialed another number and then hung up, quickly.

The man who said his name was Dave watched her walk away from the pay phone without checking to see if she got her quarter back. She walked over to the gate, swung it shut, and padlocked it. She stood a moment, staring toward the foundry. He knew she couldn't see him in the darkness, but just to piss her off, he pushed at the huge door as hard as he could and it slammed shut with a bang she had to hear.

Then he started counting, and when he reached a hundred he slowly pulled back the door a few inches and looked out. She was gone. He headed for the hole in the fence. He wanted to check the phone to see if she'd left a quarter in the coin return. If so, he had a call to make.

6

"There are some things we must never talk about," Whooten said.

"That," said Fogle, "goes without saying."

They were sitting in Whooten's BMW. It was almost three o'clock on Sunday afternoon, and they were the only car in the vast Quarryville train station parking lot. They were waiting for Lillian Meservey.

"Some rendezvous," Fogle said. "Some secret meeting. I suppose we could have been more obvious about it. Like standing under the stoplights in the middle of the Star."

"This is not a rendezvous," Whooten said, "and we're not even trying to be secretive. We're here because it's handy for all concerned."

"Tell me about it."

"She's late, though."

"It goes with the territory."

"Meaning?"

"She's a southern lady. It's ladylike to be late."

A northbound train came around the bend, slowed down, and stopped at the platform. They could hear the doors rattle open. A metallic monotone that sounded prerecorded announced, "Quarryville-Next-Stop-Hastings." The doors rattled shut. The train coughed and then with a long, straining squeak it slowly began moving again. No one had gotten on or off.

Whooten remained silent until the train was out of earshot, much as he would have waited for a hovering waiter to leave his table in a crowded restaurant. "Now that they've found the boy's body, now what?"

"That," Fogle said, "is one of those things . . ."

". . . best left unsaid, I know. But they *have* found him. And something's bound to happen. What?"

"What? I'll tell you what. Pissing and moaning. A couple of bleeding-heart editorials. Maybe they'll name something after him. Ever since Kennedy they've been big on naming things after the latest dead person."

"And then?"

"Then nothing. Another newspaper comes out, another body turns up and everyone forgets."

"Not in Quarryville, not another body."

"Then the high school principal buys his wife a fur coat with tax money. A cheerleader gets raped. The A&P burns down. There's always something."

"I just wish, Fogle, that I could always look on the bright side the way you do."

A Jeep Cherokee pulled up in front of the train station, paused a moment and then turned into the parking lot. It didn't drive directly to Whooten's BMW but slowly circled the outside perimeter of the lot and then, having taken the lay of the land, swooped up to the passenger side. Fogle had to look up to see Lillian Meservey sitting behind the wheel. She did not look at him but kept her eyes straight ahead.

"Follow me," she said, not moving her lips. She threw the car into gear and cut diagonally across the lot toward the exit.

"Follow her," Fogle ordered, and Whooten followed, although he kept to the lanes and the One Way–Exit Only arrows painted on the blacktop. "Offhand," Fogle said, "not putting too fine a point on it, I'd say there is indeed an element of secrecy at play here."

"You said it yourself, she's a southerner. They appreciate a certain sense of drama. This is to be, in point of fact, a very ordinary business meeting . . ."

"In a parking lot on a Sunday afternoon . . ."

"With an unusually busy village official, yes."

The Cherokee crossed the narrow bridge over the railroad tracks and headed north on the old River Road, skillfully maneuvering a slalom run of the potholes and broken pavement. Whooten kept a discreet distance behind and followed every swerve at half the speed. They caught up to Lillian Meservey when she pulled up to a chain-link gate just before the road dead-ended at an oil company tank farm.

"Be a dear and pull the gate to," she called to Fogle. "It only looks locked." He got out and stepped into a mud puddle. "And then close it after us. We don't want the livestock to get loose, do we?" Fogle followed her instructions slowly enough to show that he wasn't happy about it.

"Wipe your feet," Whooten said when he returned to the car. "I don't want you tracking things up."

"Buy a Dustbuster," Fogle said, hopping right in. "What was that livestock shit?"

"Humor."

"Fuck that."

Lillian Meservey drove on to a tall aluminum-covered building next to the river and was unlocking a double padlock when they arrived. No one bothered saying hello. "No roof, but a lock on the door," she said. The place smelled like a wet dog. "Come on up, I want to show you something. This is the show-and-tell hour." She started up the stairs two at a time. "Just ignore the smell. It's rotting books, thousands of cases of them totally rain-soaked. They probably weigh enough to pull this whole place down, Lord knows why they haven't. Some publisher went bankrupt years back, skipped town, and left these all here to molder."

Fogle kept up with Lillian Meservey as they rounded the landing of the third floor. Whooten, with his short legs, lagged behind. When he finally caught up with them, they were at a bank of glassless windows on the top floor looking out at the river.

"I just inquired of Mr. Fogle—"

"Just Fogle, please."

"—what he saw when he looked out there. He has yet to respond. Feel free to add your two cents' worth, Mr. Whooten."

"Just Whooten, please." He almost added, "Ma'am."

The sun played across the rocky face of the Palisades, bringing out every fissure and crevasse with surrealistic clarity. From where they stood, four stories above the river, perspective was all but destroyed. The Hudson—a muddy brown below them, oil-slick blue at midstream, gray on the far shore—seemed to be churning past at an unnatural speed for something so huge and so silent. As far as they could see to the south, as flat as the painted backdrop for an expensive electric train layout, were the towers of Manhattan. Upriver, the Palisades petered away to the dim line of the Tappan Zee Bridge and beyond that, looking close enough to walk to, a point of land reached out into the river.

"The lordly Hudson," Fogle said. "Although, as you might not know, Hudson didn't really discover it."

Whooten tried to pick out the old Baraclough Foundry a couple of hundred yards to the south. There were other buildings in the way but he could make out the top of the peaked roof and of course the campanile-style smokestack. He chose not to add his two cents' worth.

"Boys," Lillian Meservey said, "I'm afraid you are a pair of hopeless romantics. When I look out there, I see money."

"Well, of course—" Fogle began.

She cut him off. "I set up this meeting because I wanted to talk about your meeting yesterday with Monty Monteagle. No"—she raised her hand as though she were stopping traffic—"don't tell me. I know without hearing that it was a fiasco. He probably wore a Greenpeace T-shirt with a SAVE THE WHALES button and did nothing but talk EPA and environmental-impact statements. He wants to sic every outfit in the state government with three or more initials on you."

"Feds, too," Whooten said.

"Feds, too, I believe it," she said. "Now, we have to do something about all that. Quarryville deserves better. If I remember Sunday school correctly, Satan took Jesus up to a high place and tempted him with all kinds of goodies. And Jesus, being Jesus, of course, declined all offers. Well, here *we* are at a high place. I'm here to tempt. And since I don't see our friend the mayor, I'd guess we're short of Jesuses."

"Tempt away," said Fogle.

"I've seen your plans, Whooten, and they are works of art, simply beautiful. All that grass, those skeletons of old buildings . . ."

"Ghost memories," Whooten said.

"A very poetic turn of phrase. Architecture drawn with a perfumed pen. Beautiful indeed. But—and here, I think, Fogle is the man I should be addressing—I'm afraid you boys are in serious danger of fucking up and fucking up good. Your choice of Adele Baraclough was inspired. A chicken prime for plucking. The money's there, no doubt about that. But look what she wants. Greenswards. Herbaceous borders. Family piety. Underground art galleries and ghost memories . . ."

"Those last two were my ideas," Whooten said.

"You'll be rewarded in heaven, I'm sure," Lillian Meservey said. "But you know what's under all that rubble down there?" They all looked toward the foundry as though there were something to see. "There's trouble down there just waiting to happen, that's what. Once those EPA creeps start drilling their test holes and sniffing their fingers, it's all going to start. Lord knows what chemicals have been dumped here over the years. It may look like Snow White's wedding chapel but that place was a foundry, flushing Lord knows what down the drain."

"I know someone who can write environmental-impact statements that read like Sierra Club ads," Fogle said.

"Dream on, sweet prince," Lillian Meservey said. "You haven't heard the worst of it. There's no sign of it now, and the dear souls at the Historical Society don't seem to know exactly where it was, but somewhere down there on the south end there was a little munitions factory back at the time of the Civil War. You don't even want to try imagining what they buried."

Fogle did not act the least surprised. "I've been working on an alternate plan," he said, "that would reopen the place as a working foundry."

"Since when?" Whooten asked.

Fogle seemed not to hear him. "Since it's zoned for that, it may be a way around a lot of problems. If I've read the statutes correctly."

"Don't count on it," she said.

The two men were still looking south toward the Baraclough chimney. Lillian Meservey took them both by the arms and moved them around so they looked toward the river.

"What do you see?" she asked. "Want a hint? Think view. Think loft space. Think big bucks per square foot. Think renovation."

"You're saying we should turn our attention to these buildings and forget about the foundry?" Fogle asked.

"Exactly," she said. "Nothing to knock down. Major sewer lines in place. Nothing for the EPA to come sniffing up. And if no one down the line"—she paused, nodding back toward the foundry—"is causing trouble by doing handstands and throwing in monkey wrenches, this is where the future is. Think big, boys. Think apartments. Think condos. Think what this view is worth per square foot. Think"—she turned to Whooten and smiled—"design concepts."

"We can't abandon the foundry plans," Whooten said. "It's the heart of the waterfront."

"Make it into a jim-dandy dollhouse," Lillian Meservey said. "Plant grass. You'll never go wrong with a flowering bush or two. Put a nice foolproof fence around it and leave it alone. Let that sleeping dog lie. I don't mean to butt into your and Adele's plans in any way, but some Baraclough Trust money sunk into options on this property will pay off handsomely and painlessly. As an investment in the arts, of course."

"And Mayor Monty?" Fogle asked.

"Monty is a child. Just Ask Monty. Children can be trained. Or sent to their rooms."

"This is something we should discuss with Adele," Whooten said.

"Maybe if we call it Baraclough Park City she'd eat it up," Fogle said.

"I think," Lillian Meservey said, "that discussion with Adele may *not* be the way to proceed. But I'm sure, Fogle, you can appreciate that there's more than one way to skin a cat."

Whooten was afraid of what he might hear next. His plans were in danger, and he could see that Fogle was moving into his wheeling-and-dealing phase. Fogle gallantly brushed away the last shards of broken glass, and he and Lillian Meservey sat down on the wide window ledge. They began talking numbers, tolerances, zoning limits.

She leaned forward toward Fogle, nodding in agreement, offering encouragement and minor corrections to the nearest whole numbers. Whooten couldn't bring himself to watch. He could hear her citing local ordinances by paragraph and subparagraph. She knew the footnotes where the variances were hidden away, and she knew, she said with a laugh that made Whooten sick, how to count votes on the Zoning Board. To his disgust he heard Fogle say they could go a long way with that.

Now and then Whooten heard his name mentioned in terms of whipping up a rough sketch or working out a schematic of some kind. But they ignored him, and he wandered away from the windows, back into the reeking maze of waterlogged book cartons. Above them, whole sections of the corrugated roof were missing, blown away in some storm. The book cartons had been soaked and dried so many times they were as fragile as charred paper.

He stuck his fingers through cardboard, touching bloated, rain-soaked books that felt like the damp, chilly skin of someone who had just fainted. He tore away a box and found dozens of copies of the *Insider's Outside Guide to Spelunking.* He soon discovered *Insider's Outside Guides* to volleyball (defensive), volleyball (offensive), polo, water polo, bobsledding, luge. Then came the cartons of the *All the People in . . .* series: Dickens, Proust, Jack London, Jack Kerouac, Mickey Spillane, Barbara Cartland (the '60s & '70s).

When he reached *All the People in Upton Sinclair* he was about as far away from the riverside windows as he could get, but thanks to the holes in the roof there was still enough light to read titles by.

Just below the Upton Sinclair cartons, a bright patch of sunlight fell on a foot—a human foot, male, no shoe, dirty white sock with red and blue bands around the top. The sunlight illuminated it with all the intense sharpness of the rocks on the Palisades, so clearly in focus that it seemed perfectly natural, perfectly ordinary.

Whooten's first worry was that it was only a foot, something severed from a body, something that would prove to be messy. But it wasn't. It was all very tidy. The foot led to an ankle, then to a leg in filthy corduroy (Whooten found himself

whistling, "Them bones, them bones, them dry bones . . ."),
a filthy blue shirt, an absurdly flimsy black sleeveless sweater
with a line of moth holes across the chest. He was all there,
a complete man, a white man. His shoes, oily Hush Puppies,
were lined up neatly next to him. He was in his forties maybe,
maybe thirties, or fifties; with a vagrant like this it was hard
to tell. He was dead, of course, the way his mouth and eyes
hung open left no doubt of that. He was on his right side.
One leg was drawn up to his chest.

Something was in one of the shoes. Whooten bent closer,
closer than he really wanted to get, and saw that it was a disc
camera. He picked it up, put it in his pocket, and turned
back toward the window, following the path of torn cartons
as though it were a blazed trail.

Fogle and Lillian Meservey looked annoyed when Whooten interrupted them. They were still at the window, although
Fogel was now standing up and writing in his pocket
notebook.

"Fogle, you called it right," Whooten said. "Another body
has turned up."

He assumed their silence meant "Where?" so he told them.

Fogle dashed back but returned so soon Whooten knew
he could not have had a good look. "Any sign of violence,
blood, anything?"

"I think, as the old saying goes, he went peacefully in his
sleep. A vagrant. No one is going to be missing him."

"We're leaving this instant," Lillian Meservey said and
headed for the stairs.

Fogle followed her, calling out to Whooten, "Check to
make sure we've left nothing behind."

Whooten checked, found nothing but the broken glass they
had brushed away from the window ledge. When he got back
outside he found Fogle behind the wheel of the Cherokee
with Lillian Meservey at his side.

"Fix everything up, here, lock it tight," Fogle said, "and

I'll see you back in the city. Ms. Meservey is too upset to make it home alone."

"So I see," Whooten said.

After they pulled away (Lillian Meservey waved good-bye in the broken windshield-wiper style of the British royal family), he went back inside, went up the stairs—slowly, this time, at his own pace—and followed the blazed trail of cartons back to the body. He paused a minute, making up his mind, and then took a picture with the disc camera. There was only one exposure remaining on the film, and he thought he fit the whole body into the shot. Before he left he took something else out of his pocket, a small campaign button, JUST ASK MONTY, and pinned it on the sleeveless sweater.

He said out loud, "For you, Fogle, just for you."

7

❧

Three church services before lunch must be some sort of a record, Ziza thought.

It was all part of her formal introduction to the congregations that made up the Quarryville Community Pulpit, and in fact there weren't three complete services before lunch but bits and pieces of three services. She began at First Presbyterian, processing down the flagstone center aisle side by side with H. Roger Swain, then off to Trinity Baptist for the Scripture lessons and finally to Mt. Zion Methodist for the benediction. When Bob Bramer told her the schedule, he seemed especially proud of setting things up so that she was in no church for the sermon.

But by noon she was wondering what on earth she had gotten herself into.

If there were such a thing as high-church Presbyterian, First Pres. was it. The nave was long and dark, and along one side were two shadowy niches that in Europe would have been crowded with family tombs. Here they were used to store folding chairs. The opposite wall was filled with a sprawling stained-glass window the size of a billboard that suggested the darkness before dawn on Easter morning. The central figure, though, was not biblical but an elaborately outfitted knight who would have delighted any Pre-Raphaelite Victorian. He held a mighty shining sword in one hand and in the other was a flowing scarlet banner that read "Put on the whole armour of God. Eph. 6:11."

A giant Celtic cross flanked by two dwarfed candles stood on the altar and behind it in the gloom lurked four life-sized wooden statues: men in robes—Matthew, Mark, Luke, and John, probably. The phrase "graven images" crossed Ziza's mind. She had, after all, grown up in a Presbyterian church plain as a Quaker meeting house.

"Full house," H. Roger Swain whispered to her. They were crowded with the choir into the narthex, waiting for the organist to finish an endlessly convoluted fanfare so they could start down the aisle. "Between you and Dennis Morland we've drawn an Easter-sized turnout." The organist, who was hidden away in the balcony above them, wound through yet another variation an octave higher. "Although, of course, the turnout here is never shabby."

The organ suddenly stopped and the word "shabby" drifted through the church. "This," H. Roger called out in his most joyful voice, "is a day that the Lord hath made! Let us rejoice and be glad in it!" The organ exploded again into thundering chords. The choir began to sing: "Guide me, O Thou great Jehovah . . ." H. Roger tappped her arm and they moved forward singing, "Pilgrim, through this barren land." As they started down the aisle—he was right, all the pews were full —she could see members of the congregation look up from their hymnals to watch her as she walked by. In the gloom she couldn't tell whether they were singing or not. She certainly couldn't hear them. The organist had pulled out all the stops, drowning out even the choir behind her. The entire building shook. "I am weak but Thou art mighty,/ Hold me with Thy powerful hand."

"You'll probably find," Bob Bramer said a few minutes later as they waited for the lights to change so they could cross the Star, "that Trinity is going to be a lot less crowded."

Ziza was wearing her black robe, the one she bought for her ordination and had rarely worn since, and it blew out behind her like a great cape (Batgirl, she thought) as they crossed the street. "It's smaller to begin with. Westchester really isn't Baptist country . . ."

H. Roger Swain had handled her introduction better than she expected. Or feared. His tone was conversational. He made no great claims for her and attempted no jokes. He simply welcomed her to the Quarryville family, asked the congregation to stand to show their support, and said they would all join her in meeting their new challenge with the young people. He mentioned that she would be at the five o'clock hymn sing in the Undercroft, and then moved on to what he called the "Great Tragedy" that had befallen them and their community.

To Ziza's surprise, the Morlands were actually there, sitting down toward the front. Mrs. Morland kept her head bowed, but Mr. Morland—she could swear—nodded to her during H. Roger's introduction. She nodded back. A new hymn was announced. The organ roared into life, and Bob Bramer led her away.

Trinity was also singing when they arrived. It was nothing she was familiar with ("Bane and blessing, pain and pleasure/ By the cross are sanctified") but she could hear every word ("Peace is there that knows no measure/Joys that through all time abide"). The place was about half the size of First Pres. and about half as crowded. It was a standard turn-of-the-century Protestant church, dark walnut wainscoting and stucco walls, floral stained-glass windows that let in a good deal of light. There was no choir, just a quartet of two men and two women, and instead of an organ there was a piano.

When the Reverend Dale DeSousa saw her come through the back door, he called out "Welcome," gestured for the singing to continue, and came down the center aisle to greet her. They walked back toward the altar together. The polished wooden floorboards moved slightly under their feet in a way that reminded Ziza of small-town Woolworth five-and-dimes. He took her arm, father-of-the-bride style. "Let us, Saviour," the congregation sang, "take Thy cross and follow Thee."

There were few people in the congregation under forty, and what kids there were were not sitting with their parents but hanging out together in the back pews. Sitting right down front, by himself, was Monty Monteagle, all dressed up in a dark suit, dazzling white shirt, and a dark bow tie (clip-on) that made him look like an unnaturally pale Black Muslim bodyguard. All during Dale DeSousa's introduction—he said just about the same things as H. Roger—Monty kept making elaborately surreptitious gestures pointing toward Ziza and then himself, as though he were afraid she had somehow missed noticing him.

"And now perhaps Ziza would like to say a few words," said Dale DeSousa.

She hadn't been warned about that but she was ready and said all the properly appreciative things about how eager she was to get to know each of the Quarryville young people personally. She threw in words like *challenge, potential, dynamic, a program that will make a difference* and—finally, for the fun of it—*fun*.

"Let us bow our heads in prayer," the Reverend DeSousa said.

"If you'll pardon me," Monty said, standing up. "I promised Bob Bramer I'd get Miss Todd over to Mt. Zion without a hitch. So, if we aren't going to be late . . ."

The minister sighed and reluctantly agreed. "Go in peace until we meet again," he said and then, as an afterthought, added, "I know we don't applaud in church as a rule, but let's make an exception and send Ziza off with a nice show of hands."

And applaud they did, some of the kids in the back taking

advantage of the situation to whistle as well. Ziza waved as she went up the aisle, and the mayor, right behind her, alternately clapped and waved until they were out the front door.

"Dale's a great-enough guy," he said as they darted through traffic to the next church, "but once he starts praying, time stands still. You owe me one." To her surprise he took her hand and pulled her along as though she were a reluctant kindergartener.

"Maybe I needed that prayer."

"Don't kid yourself. You haven't missed a thing. I grew up in that church, and I promise you they're back there praying away for you right this minute." They paused beneath the classic Palladian portico of Mt. Zion Methodist. "You know Ray Rickert, the minister here?"

"No more than what you learn at a job interview."

"Prepare yourself for something different. I'll be around after." He opened the door and patted her on the back, a coach sending in a late replacement.

Ziza's first thought as she walked into the church was that Monty, for all his good intentions, had taken her to the wrong place. This great, bare barn of a room was surely a gym and all these people were fans. Where were the pews? The altar? Where was all the everyday *stuff* of Christian worship? Then she looked again and thought, Good Lord, they've taken all they had and given it to the poor, just as the Bible said.

The room—jammed with people in folding chairs that might have been in orderly rows once but were now a formless jumble with no defined aisles—was probably about the same size as Trinity. But because the walls had been stripped to bare brick, it looked larger. There was a slightly raised platform in the front, but no pulpit. A plain pine table held the largest Bible Ziza had ever seen, and looming over it was a tall, rough cross made from the branches of a freshly cut tree. It still had its bark and the ends of the crossbar were not neatly sawed off but crudely splintered. Ropes hung down from it as though a body had just been removed, and a hand-lettered sign tacked to the top read HE IS RISEN.

In fact, hand-lettered signs and banners were the only decorations in Mt. Zion. JESUS IS THE ONE, LOVE LIFTED ME, JOHN 3:16, TAKE UP THY CROSS, WASHED IN THE BLOOD, DO IT UNTO THE LEAST, and perhaps most oddly, LITTER HURTS. The banners hung haphazardly on the walls; the placards were arranged in clusters of flag stands throughout the room. Like state signs at a political convention, Ziza thought, or the captured standards of Roman legions.

Whatever had been happening in the service stopped the moment Ziza walked into the room. Ray Rickert—not in ecclesiastical robes but all in black, a black sweatshirt, black chinos—came forward to greet her, threading his way effortlessly through the folding chairs. He seemed to be in his thirties, with a hawklike face and black hair, almost but not quite too long, that was artfully turning gray at the temples, the way the hair of baby-faced politicians turns gray when they begin to have aspirations for higher office. He had a Hans Holbein–Tudor face, and Ziza was reminded of a college drama club Hamlet in an experimental and underfunded production.

"Ziza," he called out, "welcome to this old room we all love so much." And then he threw his arms around her, giving her a kiss on the cheek. When he stepped back, everyone else moved in. Ziza could hear folding chairs being knocked over as the congregation moved toward her, arms outstretched. There were hugs and kisses from everyone.

Ziza was never formally introduced. After the commotion died down (it was a young congregation, Ziza noticed, but it had far more old-timers than Trinity had kids), Ray Rickert simply announced, "It's time to say, 'God be with you.'"

They all clapped their hands once. "YES!" they shouted,

and then they sang, "Jesus loves me. YES, Jesus loves me."
It was the ending of an old Sunday school song Ziza remembered from childhood. "YES, Jesus loves me. The Bible tells
me so."

"Don't forget," Ray Rickert called out as people began
folding their chairs and carrying them to racks in the corner.
"The Moonlight Rounds for the homeless will be an hour
early on Tuesday night. Same time as usual on Thursday."

He turned to Ziza and smiled a smile so dazzling it would
have had to be phony if it hadn't seemed so heartfelt. She
was overwhelmed. What do you do after being gang-hugged,
shake hands? She offered her hand. "You're going to love
working with this bunch," he said and gave her another quick
kiss on the cheek. "There's hardly a shirker in the lot. Well,
maybe a couple. Come by tomorrow morning and we'll find
you an office. Heavenly Roger told me we'd be putting you
up here. We've lots of room for those who pull their weight.
And you should plan on doing a Moonlight Rounds once this
week. Why not make it Tuesday, the early night? Be here
by nine-thirty to make sandwiches." His smile slowly drained
into a look of honest concern. "Hope all's well over at St.
Hubert's. You'll need some mod. cons., I suspect. We'll talk
about that tomorrow. Dreadful thing about that boy, Morland. Spent the sermon on him, death, youth, whatnot, so
you were a needed change of pace. I'd like to be able to invite
you over for lunch—"

"No need," Monty interrupted. "I'm taking Ziza down to
the Economy for a true introduction to Quarryville." He had
walked up behind Rickert and hadn't been noticed.

"Monteagle," the minister said. "Mayor Monty Monteagle." He said it like a picture caption. His smile was completely gone.

"Thanks for the welcome," Ziza said. She extended her
hand again. "It certainly wasn't what I expected."

She got another kiss. "It's our way." The smile was back. "And watch out for this guy," he said, nodding toward Monty without looking at him. "He's a dangerous character."

It was the second time she had been warned about someone in Quarryville.

The Economy turned out to be the local diner, not a classic railway car diner but a plain brick shoebox with a neon sign out front that read !!ECONOMY!! IT PAYS TO EAT WELL. Monty seemed to think the place was pretty special. He used the phrase "the real Quarryville" several times and pointed with pride to the surly boredom of the waitresses in their starched salmon-colored uniforms. "No name tags," he said. "They don't wear name tags saying 'Wendy' or 'Colleen' or anything like that. It's a sign of class. The owner's a Greek who's never been known to speak to a customer. He just sits at the end of the counter near the kitchen and drinks coffee. The cashiers are always his daughters. They read paperbacks and never even *look* at customers. See that waitress over there?" He pointed to a sweet little old lady right out of a Mother's Day ad. "That's Polly. She swipes the other girls' tips if they aren't looking. They hate her. Avoid her tables. She doesn't refill coffee cups."

They were sitting at a side booth, facing each other across a milk-glass jar containing two plastic lily-of-the-valley stalks. Ziza had removed her robe as soon as they left Mt. Zion, and Monty had shed his jacket, unclipped his bow tie, rolled up his sleeves, and ("My public expects it") pinned on a JUST ASK ME button.

"Don't order anything that sounds Greek," Monty warned. "If you're interested in soup, ask me. I know which one is fresh each day. They have a regular schedule, and you don't really want the day-old stuff. Some place, right? When they went looking for America, they should've come here."

To Ziza, it looked like every Formica-era coffee shop

she'd ever visited, but Monty was clearly a connoisseur.

"Notice anything funny about this table?" He couldn't wait for an answer. "No paper napkin dispensers. The kids come after school for plates of French fries and gravy (not bad, actually), and the Greek thought they were using up too many napkins. Now you get one with your order and that's it. This, Ziza, is the *real* Quarryville."

Ziza ordered a western omelette. Monty asked for a hamburger special ("That means you get fries but not as many as when you ask for them on the side") and the waitress, who treated the mayor as though she had never seen him before, said "Hamburger *royale*" as she wrote it down.

"V. frosty, notice that?" Monty said after the waitress left. "Name's Louisa. She was in my high school class and worked part-time as a meter maid until they let her go when I took office. Chief Malfadi's doing, not mine. Actually probably Lillian Meservey's doing. Prudent fiscal belt-tightening blah-blah-blah. But I get the blame." He reached across the table as though he were going to take her hand and said, "It's lonely at the top, Ziza. When are we going running together?"

"Are you really trying to come on to me?"

"You mean you gotta ask?"

"I wonder," Ziza said, changing the subject, "if Louisa was working last Monday, the day Dennis Morland disappeared. He might have come by for fries and gravy?"

"No kid," Monty said, "would be caught dead in here *alone.*"

"That was a joke?" Ziza asked, and getting a blank stare added, "Caught dead?"

"Oh, sure," Monty said and remembered to laugh, "a joke." He thought a minute and said, "If I had taken holy orders and dressed up like a freaking hippie undertaker I suppose I could get away with giving you a welcoming kiss. *'It's our way.'*"

Ziza smiled. "Reverend Ray's quite a piece of work, isn't he?"

" *'Watch out for this guy, Ziza. He's a dangerous character.'* Give me a break, for cryin' out loud."

"I'm beginning to see," Ziza said, "that the situation here isn't quite what I thought at first. There was supposed to be an organizational meeting yesterday of the three ministers, and Rickert didn't show up. The others were trying to talk over my head about that, and I took it to mean they were afraid Mt. Zion was pulling out of the deal."

"Wrong."

"Now, I think the big threat to them is that the Methodists are going to take over the whole show."

"Getting warmer."

"That Ray Rickert's going to *be* the whole show."

"Bull's-eye."

"And I'll be walking a tightrope."

"Word is, you know, that you weren't the first choice for the job. Ray, so the story goes, was pushing some Bible school tub-thumper and Heavenly Roger was all for somebody-or-other's niece who wore a nice set of pearls to the interview. Back and forth on that for several meetings, so they say, until everyone got bored and poor old Dale DeSousa asked, *'What's wrong with the red-haired social worker with freckles and the funny name?'* So you got the nod."

"A ringing endorsement if I ever heard one."

"Don't knock it. They could have made you mayor."

It was, he said, an office no one really wanted. "In the old days, the mill owners picked someone for the job. For years after World War II, the runner-up in the election for chief of the volunteer fire department was named mayor as a consolation prize. Nowadays, Hillside people think they're above local politics. (Special protest committees, yes; mayor, no.) Riverside people know it's too much work for too low a payoff, reportable or otherwise."

Louisa came around with a coffee pot. "Hot up your cup?" she asked Ziza and refilled Monty's without saying a word to him.

"So," Monty said, "the time was obviously ripe for a reform candidate. Me, the local gadfly who's always bothering people with petitions to sign. I got a lot of school kids involved, and they turned out to be mostly the same bunch who had been attracted to Ray Rickert's youth fellowship. Ray still thinks I'm trying to corrupt them or something, as though the choice were between me and Jesus."

"Or you and him."

"Same thing, isn't it? Anyway, I ran against the guy who loses the school board election every year (you know him, Bob Bramer), and he protected his record by losing one more time. *Voilà!* Mayor Monty."

Their coffee cups were empty again. It was time to go. After paying the book-reading cashier and passing up the saucer of complimentary breath mints, they went out into the cool, bright sunlight.

"One more church service to go," Ziza said.

"The hymn sing? You've got hours," Monty said. "Come on, I'll show you the part of town that interests me most."

It was the old factory area on the waterfront, and they got there in Monty's black Honda CRX with Day-Glo JUST ASK ME bumper stickers fore and aft. He parked outside the gate leading to the old Baraclough foundry. Upriver, far off in the distance, Ziza saw a familiar sight. By ignoring factory smokestacks, power lines, and the squat towers and roadways of the distant Tappan Zee Bridge, she could see the same scene that was in the watercolor Adele had loaned her.

"Incredible building," she said, nodding toward the foundry as they walked down to the riverbank.

"Incredibly ugly."

"Where's your soul, Monty? It looks like a church designed by mad blacksmiths."

"I rest my case."

"Well, if you have no soul, where's your sense of humor?"

"I don't think your new buddy Mrs. Bloodhorn would see anything funny about it. And for once she and I agree."

Ziza noticed that he seemed to go out of his way to call Adele "Mrs. Bloodhorn." They stood on the water's edge. Monty picked up a stone and threw it as far out as he could. Then he chose a flat stone and skipped it six times across the water. He chose another one and handed it to Ziza.

"Contest?"

"Give it a try."

She threw.

They both counted the splashes as it hopped along. They counted together until they reached four. Then Monty stopped and Ziza kept counting. At seven he stopped her.

"Cheater," he said.

"You just have bad eyesight. It's still going. Skipping all the way to New Jersey."

Then he told her his plan for the waterfront. He had something for everyone: a park, a marina, trees, grass, a row of expensive town houses, low-cost mixed-income apartments down here on the south end, group housing for old folks.

"Senior citizens," Ziza corrected.

"Old farts' pearly-gates no-downpayment condos, is that any better?"

"And the Baraclough building?"

"You've hit upon my stroke of genius. At your tea party with Adele I'm sure she bored you stiff about her museum. The ghost building that dwarf of hers designed. The underground art galleries. All that elitist shit?

"Well, we encourage her all we can. And at the same time alert every environmental watchdog organization in the book about the project. They've been making stuff down here since the Civil War. Every disgusting thing you can think of's probably been spilled on this ground. Dig a hole. You're bound to find something the EPA thinks will make you sick. That maybe in fact really *will* make you sick."

They had been walking north and came to a rusty wire fence Monty pulled apart so they could slip through.

"Who'll pay to clean it up so we can build our waterfront for all the people?" he asked. "Easy. Who wants a museum and has millions of bucks to spend? And who—after months and months of negotiations—will be allowed to keep her ugly art museum if she does the right thing for Aladdin Baraclough's beloved village? It's as simple as that. Maybe some of it's even tax deductible. And it all begins when Adele starts writing checks."

"You really think it *is* that simple?"

"Swear to God."

They had just come around the corner of a World War II Quonset hut that had been knocked off its cement block foundation when they heard a car's engine start up. It was ahead of them and close enough for them to hear the gravel fly when the wheels spun to make a fast getaway.

"Someone's in a rush," Ziza said.

"Odds-on it's a couple of your teenage parishioners," he said, slipping into a hick sheriff's accent, "bein' where they hadn't oughta bin. Did you catch a sight of the car?"

"Couldn't."

"But you can see a stone skip from here to Jersey?"

Another engine started up and Monty sprinted up the factory street toward the sound. No pebbles flew this time. Buildings were in the way, but Ziza could hear what seemed to be a car go a few hundred yards and stop. There was a squeak and a clang of metal. Ziza started running and caught up with Monty in time to see someone getting into a gray BMW on the other side of the gate. Before he pulled away he seemed to look back toward them.

They were standing next to what looked like the tallest

building on the waterfront. "Damndest thing," Monty said. "Adele's dwarf architect . . ."

"He isn't a—"

"He came right out of this building, locked it up as cool as you please, and then drove down there and closed the gate behind him before he left."

"I think he saw us."

"Actually, he wasn't really as cool as you please. I think he was too mad about something to see much of anything."

Monty walked over and tugged on the lock. It was secure. "At least he's a good citizen who locks up after himself. But why here?"

By the time they got back to Monty's CRX, it was almost time for the five o'clock hymn sing at First Pres. "It's in what H. Roger called the Undercroft," Ziza said.

"That's just the cellar," Monty said. "Lots of columns and brick arches. It would make a great pizza parlor if they just put in some booths with red-checkered tablecloths, but they use it for a meeting room. Boy Scouts. Church suppers. Last time I was there was the League of Women Voters' Candidates' Night. Myself, Bob Bramer, a madam chairperson, Bramer's wife, and the ladies from the refreshments committee. That was our first clue that turnout on election day was going to be piss-poor."

When they got to the other side of the bridge over the train tracks they saw the gray BMW waiting. It let them pass and then, after a pause long enough for the driver to count to fifteen, it pulled in behind them.

"Don't look back at him," Monty said.

Ziza looked into the side mirror. Written across the bottom was the warning OBJECTS IN MIRROR ARE CLOSER THAN THEY APPEAR. The gray object behind them appeared close enough for her to see the long, weather-beaten face peering over the dashboard. Young Abe Lincoln at the wheel, she thought.

When Monty slowed down in anticipation of the traffic lights at the Star, the BMW slowed down even more and fell farther behind. A police car, flashing its lights but not using the siren, cut around both cars, sped toward the Star in the wrong lane, growled a couple of times to get through the red light safely, and headed up into Hillside. In the distance they could hear another siren heading in the same direction.

"Out of these clothes," Monty said, "and into the clothes of *Supermayor.*" Blowing his horn rapidly at regular intervals, he followed the path of the police car.

Ziza held on tight. "Maybe you should get one of those removable bubble lights you could put on your roof the way plainclothes cops do on TV." The prudent BMW didn't follow, but cars all around them began slamming on their brakes to let Monty pass. "Or maybe those flashing lights that the volunteer firemen have."

"Never tried this before," Monty said, "but it's amazing the way other cars get out of the way when I act as though I really have to get though. Maybe they think you're pregnant or something."

Ziza slumped lower in the seat as they cut in front of a sixteen-wheeler, horn blaring, and turned into a side street that led steeply uphill. Once beyond the Star, the problem was no longer other traffic but people walking in the streets.

"Something's going on," Monty said. The streets were not crowded. Traffic was not being stopped, but everywhere they looked groups of two or three people were walking along, not rushing, just walking, slower, if anything, than usual.

"They're all kids," Ziza said.

"All headed in the same direction. There can't be any school event this time on a Sunday afternoon."

Some of them, Ziza noticed, were carrying flowers. "Where was that place they found Dennis Morland?"

"The Meadow. Good thinking. They're all headed for the

Meadow. Someone must've spread the word. Mind skipping your hymn sing?"

"No one needs four church services in one day. Anyway, I was hired for the kids, not their parents."

They drove—no need for horn-blowing now—to the grade school parking lot, where they left the CRX. Off through the trees, on the wide trail to the Meadow, they could see the flashing light of a police car.

If the kids they passed drifting slowly up the trail were talking among themselves, they stopped when they saw Ziza and Monty. The result was a curious, shuffling silence. Off in the distance ahead of them Ziza could hear what sounded like random chords being struck on a guitar—guitars, maybe—and closer by were the squawks of police radios.

Two police cars were pulled up where the trail entered the Meadow, and an officer was leaning on the rear fender of the second car watching the kids walk by.

"You gotta see this," he said to Monty. "Danny Minihan's inside keeping an eye on things."

"Why don't you turn off those flashers," Monty said. "This isn't a highway accident." Wasco made a great show of rolling his eyes and then reached through the open window and flicked a switch. The lights went dark.

"Has Chief Malfadi checked in?" Monty asked.

"He went to a PBA communion breakfast in the city this morning, and I don't think he's back. All quiet, though. Just dopey kids."

"Dopey?" Ziza asked.

"As in dumb," Wasco said and then added "ma'am." He had seen her yesterday in front of the church, but they hadn't actually been introduced. "Not druggy. At least no more than usual."

They left Wasco and walked into the clearing. At first glance Ziza was reminded of one of those double-spread illustrations in nature books that show every imaginable kind of bird and animal standing around a watering hole, each displayed as though in splendid isolation, oblivious of what is around. The Meadow was crowded with teenagers, but it seemed to be a collection of ill-at-ease loners. Ziza had seen her share of newspaper photographs taken at funerals of high school kids—suicides, traffic deaths, athletes who collapsed in the midst of a game—and they always showed lots of sobbing and hugging, always lots of hugging. There was none of that here, just stunned incomprehension.

Two boys with guitars were sitting on top of a boulder with RIVER RAT painted sloppily across the front, but they each seemed to be searching for different tunes. Off behind the rock, next to some deep, fresh tire tracks—the ambulance must have gotten stuck in the soft ground—was a small pile of fresh flowers that seemed to be guarded by two younger boys, younger than most of the other kids, self-conscious in their Boy Scout uniforms. Girls, it was always girls who brought flowers, added them to the pile and then had nothing more to do.

The mourners, if that's what they were, seemed to look around for those they knew and stood with them, but there was little talking. One of the guitar players began singing something about how nobody knows what it's like to be a bad one, a sad one, but no one joined in or even seemed to notice, and he went back to playing chords.

"The Who," a voice next to her said. She turned. It was the miniature Abe Lincoln. He had followed them after all. "That song. Recorded by The Who rock group. A golden oldie for this bunch."

Monty had left her and was walking through the crowd, solemnly shaking hands every now and then as he would have with adults outside a funeral home. He didn't try to talk with anyone. Eye contact. A nod. A handshake. We're all grown-ups here. She sensed that the kids somehow appreciated that.

Some of them reached out and touched the campaign button he was still wearing.

The architect said no more but he stayed next to Ziza's side. What, she wondered, did he want?

And what should *she* be doing? She had been trained to deal with occasions like this. She had read the books, taken the seminars. She had dealt with ugly, ordinary death before, with widows and mourners, grieving parents, even with people who had caused death. But this muted demonstration baffled her. She had not felt more of an outsider since her arrival in Quarryville.

Yet she actually recognized more people than she at first realized. From the party on Friday night, from the church services that morning, there were dozens of familiar faces. She followed Monty's example. Not shaking hands, but nodding to those she thought she recognized. I'm here, she wanted the nods to say, I'm with you. They nodded back. Many smiled. No one wanted to talk.

The second guitar player launched into something more upbeat. It seemed to be a particular favorite of the crowd and there were a few who tried to say the words along with the music, but it wasn't a song made for group singing. Much of it was a litany, a repetition of variations on the line "He got . . .": hair down below his knees, muddy water, walking fingers, Coca-Cola, early warning. When it got to the line about one and one and one are three, just about everyone sang and then the song petered out.

"Beatles," the voice said. "Cut one, side two, 'Abbey Road.' "

Her first reaction was to scream, "I *know!*" Instead, she said. "I don't think we've actually met. My name's Ziza Todd."

"I know," he said, but didn't offer his name. "I've got to talk to you about something."

"I'll be at Mt. Zion Methodist tomorrow morning. I have an office there. Or will."

"No," he said.

She waited for more of an answer than that.

"Now," he said.

"Here?"

"If you combine the words 'now' and 'here' you get 'no-where.' A friend of mine who collects stuff like that told me that once. More than once, actually. It's the sort of thing that people who like that sort of thing will tell you a lot."

Ziza did not like the sound of this. "I think regular office hours would be the best way to handle it," she said. "I guarantee the office will have a door we can shut."

"Now's better, a walk down the road to your house?"

"Tomorrow at ten. You'll be my first customer."

"If I must," he said, and, before disappearing into a group of teenagers who towered over him, added, "I trust you keep secrets of the confessional inviolate."

8

A yellow Post-it note on her front door had been waiting for Ziza when she got home from the Meadow. It said, "You were missed, sorely. In profound disappointment, H.R.S." For once, she thought, the installers' strike that kept her telephone from being hooked up was a blessing. She didn't have to hear how profoundly disappointed Heavenly Roger was that she had missed the hymn sing. At least not that evening. Unfortunately, there was a P.S.: "Call me at First Pres. Earliest A.M. tomorrow."

Now it was Earliest A.M. tomorrow, eight-thirty to be exact, and Ziza had turned up at Mt. Zion to claim her office and use the phone.

She half expected to find no one around. But the door to the Sunday school wing was unlocked. Lights were on. She could hear the sound of typing and followed it to the church office. Inside a blue-haired little old lady with harlequin glasses leaned nearsightedly over the keyboard. Her pearl-gray pants suit had just the hint of a chalk-line stripe. Ziza bet her feet, hidden under the desk, were enclosed in pristine tennis shoes.

"The Reverend's not in," she said without looking up. "Monday's the Reverend's day off, day off for clergy and hairdressers." She looked up ready to share a laugh. What caught Ziza's eye was the huge crucifix she was wearing, not a bare Protestant cross but an honest-to-God Catholic crucifix with a writhing Jesus nailed to it.

"Where's my manners?" the woman said with a directness that made Ziza expect she wanted an answer. "You're Miss Todd, recognize your picture. Reverend Rickert said you'd be by to see your room. I'm Marge Benecosta, church secretary, jack of all trades." Ziza extended her hand. "And to set things straight right at 'go' you should know that I'm a parishioner across the way at Sacred Heart. The Reverend doesn't believe members should be church secretaries, too much room for gossip and whatnot. When he took over ten years ago he interviewed me and a woman named Rosenthal. We both could type but I knew how to change the typewriter ribbon so I got the nod. She's now receptionist for a dentist on Main Street, nice Jewish fellow. I recommend him if you need a checkup. Call me Marge."

"Ziza."

"I'll show you your office. Two windows. Rug. Everything you need."

By ten o'clock, when she expected her visitor, Ziza felt indeed that she had an office of her own. It was about the size of the worn nine-by-twelve carpet that had obviously just been put down. The creases where it had been folded for years in some attic stuck up like furrows.

Ziza thought of calling Heavenly Roger, but put it off.

The floor space was crowded with a battered wooden desk bearing a surprising number of cigarette burns around the edges, an eight-shelf bookcase holding stacks of papers and an incomplete set of *The Interpreter's Bible* (about half the volumes shelved upside down), and an oversized leather chair that looked too seductively comfortable for Ziza to dare trying out.

As she had promised her mysterious friend the night before, there was a door that could be closed. Right now it was open as Marge came and went with fresh supplies. The last thing she dragged in was a huge cork bulletin board, brand-new and still showing its orange Caldor special sale price tag. "You'll find this handy," she said. "The Reverend is very big on keeping schedules posted. He left a message that you be sure to come along on tomorrow night's food distribution."

"Fine."

"I'd write it down if I were you." She handed her a box of felt-tipped pens.

"I was expecting someone to come by at ten," Ziza said.

"An appointment?"

"Sure."

"You'll find that half the people who make appointments to church offices never turn up. I think it's a matter of cold feet."

By eleven-thirty he had still not arrived, and Ziza began to wonder if she had made a mistake in not talking with him last night, creepy as he was. What she interpreted as annoying insistence may have been serious desperation. She made her call to Heavenly Roger, but his secretary said that although he had been in, briefly, *much* earlier, he was never, as a rule, in his study on Mondays. Ziza left her name and the secretary said she was certainly sorry to have missed seeing her last evening at the hymn sing. "It was a nice turnout," she said. "A lot of people were disappointed that you didn't attend."

Ziza noted that she said "didn't" rather than "couldn't" and that she pronounced "disappointed" just the way her boss would have. Ziza said something apologetic about going to the Meadow and immediately regretted it. The woman's response was simply "Those kids . . ."

After she hung up, Ziza found that she was waiting for Marge's next appearance. She had been coming in all morning long with more supplies, boxes of stationery, a shiny new set of keys, even a flashlight ("We blow fuses on a regular basis"), and each time she stayed to talk.

At first she reminded Ziza of a certain kind of mother she had begun to recognize and distrust as a teenager, mothers of her friends who seemed especially chatty and interested but always ended up asking a lot of personal questions. Amid Marge's gush and gossip she asked her share. Ziza answered them as honestly and as simply as she could: no fiancé, no steady boyfriend, no boyfriend period, hadn't worked in a church in years, never worked with kids who weren't "problems," didn't know Reverend Rickert well at all.

Marge headed for her own office, then stuck her head back into the doorway. Her grandson, she said, was picking up some takeout at the Economy for her. Did Ziza want anything for lunch? Tuna on toasted rye and a Diet Coke would be great, Ziza said.

"The Reverend," Marge said, "has been discouraging people from eating tuna. Something about tuna fishermen killing off the dolphins. He won't even let the homeless have any."

"It's Monday," Ziza said. "Reverend's day off."

"It'll be our secret, dear."

Ziza went through the motions of reading the files the committee had left for her to review, but found herself thinking more and more of the kids last night at the Meadow, of the little man who had followed them from the waterfront, the little man who wanted so desperately to talk with her, of the Morlands in their living room hearing her tell them their son was found dead in the Meadow ("What a stupid place to be," Mr. Morland said), of her walk back alone to St. Hubert's when she asked herself what she could really be doing for these grieving people, of that prissy little yellow note attached to her front door.

She heard a man's voice at the end of the hall and Marge speaking quickly and excitedly. Lunchtime, she thought and reached for her wallet. When she looked up there was a policeman standing in front of her desk. He was holding a brown paper bag.

"Leonard says you already know each other," Marge said, coming through the door. "My daughter's oldest boy, Leonard."

"Officer Wasco?" Ziza said.

"Ma'am." He handed her the bag. The check was stapled to the top.

"Quarryville is full of surprising services," Ziza said. She glanced at the bill and handed him some money.

"As long as you don't tip, everything's kosher," he said. Ziza took the money back and carefully counted out change.

"Leonard comes by once or twice a week. He doesn't forget his old granny. Usually we have a nice lunch together but today he says he can't stay. More dead bodies, or something."

"Wouldn't you know," he said. "Another stiff and we're short-handed again."

"Doesn't rain but it pours," Marge said.

"Chief Malfadi left this morning for an FBI refresher course at Quantico, and someone calls in an anonymous tip. This body's down in one of the warehouses. I'm supposed to report there as backup."

"Where?" Ziza, thinking of the little man who hadn't shown up.

"The old Transformer Building, the tallest place down there. Two bodies in a week, that's something for the record books."

"Can I come with you?" Ziza asked.

"It's against department policy to provide rides for civilians."

"I might know something about this."

"Really?" he said, with more doubt than curiosity.

"Really . . . cross my heart. I was on the waterfront yesterday and maybe saw something."

Both Wasco and Ziza looked at Marge for a judgment.

"So what's the harm?" she asked.

Wasco flicked on the siren and the flashing lights as soon as he turned the key in the ignition, but as they straddled center line all the way to the bridge across the train tracks, he did not say a word. She kept waiting for him to ask what she might know about a dead body on the waterfront. When they turned north on the rutted River Road, Ziza, thinking that she had to say something, said that he had quite a grandmother. "Full of beans," he said.

They drove through the gate she heard the little man close the day before. "You a good buddy of Monty's?" he asked as he parked next to the other police cars.

"Just met him, why?"

"Always curious who his good buddies really are, that's all."

They went through the door the little man had padlocked and up the stairs. Would she find him dead? she wondered. Is that why he never made his appointment? Had he come back here when she wouldn't talk to him and killed himself? Or would she instead find someone he had killed here yesterday, someone he had wanted to tell her about last night?

At the top of the stairs Ziza glanced toward the bank of windows. She had been in town long enough not to look twice at the river. The place stank, a rotten smell like raw sewage. Light filtered down through the holes in the roof, but there were shadows everywhere. She followed Wasco down a long, dark aisle of torn cartons to a far corner of the building where they found a circle of men in uniforms. At the center, bathed in the light of several flashlights, was the stretched-out body of an old man in filthy clothes. Not her little man.

Whatever had been going on around the body stopped when they arrived. The sudden silence was a question.

"Miss Todd," Wasco said to the group. "She thinks she might know something about this."

She didn't know who she was supposed to be talking to.

In the gray light, it was hard to even see who was there, so she continued to look at the body.

"He wasn't murdered," she said in relief, more to herself than to them.

"Someone make a note of that," a voice said, sarcastically.

"No, I mean he looks dead but not murdered, with his shoes lined up like that as though he had just gone to sleep."

"Is that what you know about all this?"

"No. Yesterday I was down here walking around . . ."

"This entire area is off-limits," someone said. "Restricted. Authorized personnel only. That's why the fence. You saw the fence?" The tone was patronizing, provocative.

"I'm new in town and just wanted to get close to the river."

"And you saw something," Wasco suggested, almost as through he was trying to be helpful.

"I saw a car drive away from this building."

One of the flashlights moved, and she saw the JUST ASK MONTY button on the man's moth-eaten sweater. She was glad she had not mentioned Monty's name.

"What kind of car?" The tone had changed. She had their attention.

"I'm not sure." Why, she asked herself, was she lying? "It was foreign." She had the strange intuition that by not telling these men she might find out more on her own. "Expensive."

"You're up on car makes? What about a license number?"

One of the flashlight beams moved to her face.

"I'm pretty sure it was gray."

"License?"

"We were pretty far away."

" 'We'?" Wasco asked.

"Me. I."

"Sure sounded like 'We,' " another man said.

"What I meant was 'I.' "

"You just saw the car?" Wasco asked after a long pause. "No driver?"

"No one I could make out. Nothing I could swear to."

"You were both pretty far away."

"I was pretty far away."

"But you saw a car?"

"Gray."

"But not a driver?"

"Boys, boys," a woman's voice said. It was a light, almost teasing voice, a kindly Den Mother quieting her unruly Cub Scouts.

She must have just arrived, Ziza thought. She was sure she had not been there before. The shadows were not that dark.

"Miss Todd—it is Miss Todd, isn't it?—has stepped forward as a helpful citizen only to be harassed and given some kind of rude interrogation. You have your information now. Useful information, I'm sure. And I think you should thank her kindly."

The woman had a southern accent. The flashlights drifted off in a different direction, away from the body, away from Ziza, away from the newcomer. There were some mutters that could have been thank-yous.

"My name's Lillian Meservey," the woman said, "and I'd hoped to catch you at one service or another yesterday but I was just overbooked." She led Ziza toward the wall of windows. "I'm village manager, which means I dabble in everything from potholes to tax assessments to keeping our new mayor on the straight and narrow." Ziza could hear someone following along behind them, a policeman judging from the jingling his equipment made. She hoped it was Wasco, who seemed to be the closest thing she had to a friend around there. "And I hope this community Sunday school scheme of yours works out just beautifully." They headed down the filthy stairs. Ziza stole a quick glance behind her. It was Wasco. "The young people of a town are its bright future. I heard you were up with the children at the Meadow last night—you and Monty, wasn't it?—and I really appreciate that. They needed help and support with their grief. That Dennis Morland was a lovely boy, I'm sure of it. The whole town appreciates how you've stepped right in to do your part."

She climbed behind the wheel of a Cherokee that was parked next to Wasco's cruiser. "And now the problem of the homeless is coming right here to Quarryville. That poor, sad soul inside, drifting off in his sleep. I fear that this is just the beginning. Come by my office in the Village Hall some time soon and we'll have a real nice chat. Hear?" She threw the Jeep into gear and sped off. Ziza realized that she had not said a word to her.

"I'll take you back to the church," Wasco said. "I think you have a tuna on rye waiting."

This time the ride was in complete silence. No talk, but no siren either. She could feel his presence next to her and waited for a question. When a red light stopped them at the Star, Ziza asked to be dropped off at St. Hubert's instead of Mt. Zion. She had skipped running that morning, and she felt a need to make it up. "You know," Wasco finally said, pulling up to the curb. "About yesterday, I know you were with Monty. Lillian Meservey knows. Half the kids in town know. Hell, even the waitresses at the Economy knows. What was all that crap about being alone down on the waterfront?"

She slid out the door, thought a minute and said, "Beats me. Maybe I'm too protective for my own good."

He made a snorting noise and with a quick U-turn was gone.

She had her key out before she reached the door. Her first objective was the bathroom, and she was halfway up the stairs before she saw the man standing in her empty living room. He was holding the Baraclough watercolor.

"You missed our appointment," Ziza said.

"I was having second thoughts. Qualms."

"But not enough to keep you out of here. How did you get in?"

"The kitchen door was unlocked, an unwise practice for a household not without its art treasures." He waved the picture at her.

He was a young, miniature Abe Lincoln dressed for the racetrack, a tattersall shirt, a paisley tie, a beautifully cut houndstooth suit, and a pair of expertly polished boots that if they weren't the most expensive Ziza had ever seen, at least they looked it.

"Why don't we start over," Ziza said. "There are two chairs next to the kitchen table. Let's go there. We can sit down. Have a cup of coffee. And maybe you'll even tell me your name."

He handed her a card with quite a number of names printed on it. "Call me Whooten," he said. He carefully placed the watercolor back on the chrome mantlepiece and looked at it as though he were studying it for the first time. "Just on the brink of Aladdin Baraclough's late period. Mint condition. Worth an easy couple of grand, a bit more if the market is up today on late period Hudson River School. And she let you walk right out the door with it?"

"On loan. Registered in the files. She insisted. Mrs. Bloodhorn is a very generous woman."

"Indeed she is. I'm sure she only wants what's best for us all." He stepped closer and examined the signature and date on the lower-right-hand corner. "She has these by the gross, of course, and if she tried to sell them all at once there'd be no market value worth mentioning. Like DeBeers selling off its warehouses of diamonds. Still, it's a nice one. Don't lose it."

"She warned me."

He laughed. "I can just hear her."

"Tea?" Ziza said, hoping to get to the point. "Coffee? Talk about last night?"

"This is a wonderful house, you know," he said as he polished away a smudge on the chrome with his handkerchief. "Maybe the most original private house in town. Which I know isn't saying much. You might be interested in hearing that it had a woman as its architect."

"So they say."

"Alice McDowell, her only known building." He corrected himself. "Buildings. This and the church, of course. She must have studied in Germany, don't you think? Look at the way the banister turns around that glass brick wall. I'd love to know what argument she used with the factory to get that curve fabricated so superbly."

"Kitchen?"

"A fine-enough room, but I'd say the least imaginative space in the house. I suspect Alice didn't spend much time in kitchens."

"Shall we *go* to the kitchen and have our talk? That's where the chairs are."

"So you said. I prefer instant coffee to tea."

"All the coffee I have is espresso. I own my own machine, believe it or not. My secret passion."

"I hate the taste of coffee, which is why I love instant. I could live on instant, especially when it's mixed so there are little flakes floating around. With nondairy powdered creamer."

"Sorry."

"Make it tea, then. Lipton bags, preferred."

"Only Twining's. Prince of Wales label."

"It'll have to do, I suppose."

She put a kettle on the stove. "Well, now . . . ," she said.

"Are you up on coincidences?" he asked. "My partner, Fogle, you saw him when you passed us walking up Adele's driveway. Fogle is a writer and he specializes in proving that most of the so-called facts of history are wrong. Newton didn't watch an apple fall. Galileo never even went up into the Leaning Tower of Pisa, let alone dropped anything off it, Christians weren't thrown to lions in the Colosseum, that sort of thing.

"Now he's interested in branching out into coincidences and I've been on the lookout. Thomas Wolfe—*You Can't Go Home Again* Thomas Wolfe, not *Bonfire* Tom Wolfe—and James Joyce were once on the same tour of the Waterloo battlefield, Hart Crane and Ernest Hemingway were born on the same day of the same year and both killed themselves, the bodies of F. Scott Fitzgerald and Nathanael West were both at the same Los Angeles funeral home at the same time."

If you can't beat them, Ziza thought, you might as well go along for the ride. "How about Thomas Jefferson and John Adams dying on the same Fourth of July?"

"Everyone knows that one. And anyway, it's the sort of thing Fogle likes to disprove. Maybe he already has, for all I know."

She put the steaming mugs on the table, a black tea bag tab sticking out of each one. "Now we *will* talk about what you wanted to tell me last night," she said.

"Very well," he said. "That boy, Dennis Knowland . . ."

"Morland."

"Whatever his name, that was my work."

She wasn't surprised, but of all the things she thought he might say, this was the one she most hoped he wouldn't. "Dear God," she said. "Where?"

"Down at the Baraclough foundry."

"And you hit him with something?"

"Heavens, no. I found him there, lying right inside the door, his head all—"

"Found him?"

"Dead. Dead a day, maybe. Probably less."

"And you moved him?"

"Not right away. I locked the place up tight and began to think. A dead body down there wasn't going to do anyone any good. Especially a nice young kid like that."

"Not like that vagrant who died in his sleep."

He seemed honestly surprised. "They found *him?* Already?"

"Just a couple of hours ago."

"Police?"

"The whole circus. Even Lillian Meservey."

"That witch." For the first time he looked directly into Ziza's eyes. "They know you saw me there yesterday?"

"I told them I saw a foreign car, gray. I don't know what Monty will tell them. Let's get back to Dennis."

He stirred the cup with his finger without removing the tea bag and then licked his finger dry. "You called the business with the old bum a circus. Imagine how much worse it would have been if the body had been a murdered teenager. There are enough stumbling blocks ahead for our waterfront project without that. All those ecological and environmental inspections are going on. I couldn't have one of those people find the boy. The big charity open house at the Studio is this weekend. We don't want that ruined. I'm going to have my model of the new underground museum at the foundry on display for the first time. So . . ."

"It was better for all concerned."

"My thoughts exactly," he said, happily accepting the phrase, "better for all concerned. After giving it a lot of thought and a good night's sleep, I went back, bundled the kid up and took him to the Meadow. I knew they'd find him right away there. No harm was done."

"None?"

"None."

"Who did you talk with while making up your mind?"

He paused a second too long before answering. "My idea. My actions."

"You must have talked with Fogle about it. Adele, too?"

"My actions. Mine alone. It's best for everyone concerned."

"Including the killer," Ziza said. "Lord knows what evidence you destroyed moving him around. You may well have made a solution hopeless."

"No, no, it was probably one of those River Rats. The cops'll have the whole thing worked out, once those forensic lab people get involved. They're smart cookies. Maybe that vagrant, the dead one in that book warehouse, maybe he did it and died of a guilty conscience, a pounding heart attack."

Neither cup of tea had been touched.

"The boy *was* dead when you found him?

"Stiff, yes. The blood wasn't even sticky."

"Tuesday morning?"

"Wednesday, actually."

"Then you spent a night thinking it over, which brings us to Thursday. The body wasn't found until Saturday morning."

"He was in the trunk of my car. Once I got him in there all wrapped up, I felt uneasy about unwrapping him again."

"Unwrapping?"

"The weather had been on the chilly side, but by Friday night it had all gone on too long. I had always planned on using the Meadow, but for an out-of-the-way place it's amazingly busy. I dropped him off at sunup on Saturday. Too late for the party animals, too early for the bird watchers."

"And then, less than a week after you found Dennis, you find the vagrant? Two unexplained corpses in town and you're connected to both of them. That's a nice coincidence for your friend Fogle to think about."

Whooten laughed. It was almost a merry laugh, a laugh of genuine relief. "You don't know how good this makes me feel, talking this all out with you."

"There's a difference between 'talking it all out' and 'talking.' I'd say we've just been talking."

"A load off my mind."

"Now you have to call the police and tell them."

"Whoa, there. None of that's on the menu. And you"—he laughed again—"your lips are sealed. I've seen all those priest movies."

Ziza leaned across the table and joined in the laughter. "The joke," she said, "is that you've got the wrong church. I'm bound by no seal of the confessional."

He stopped laughing.

"Oh, it would be unethical and improper for me to say anything," she said. "I can think of no occasion when a truly honorable person would tell, but if I were, in fact, a truly terrible person, I suppose I could just pick up a phone and call down to Village Hall."

"You're just teasing."

"That's something for you to think about. You'd feel better if you made the call yourself."

He leaned toward her and smiled. Surely it was the way young Abe Lincoln had once smiled at Ann Rutledge. "But you won't," he said. "You would never do it. We'll talk about this some more. You'll try to convince me to do the right thing and tell the police myself. I can see hours and hours ahead of rich discussion. But you won't tell." The smile grew even more loving. "This is our bond. Our pledge. Our troth."

He bowed down and kissed her hand.

9

When H. Roger Swain asked Ziza to help out at the Annual Arts Club Open House Tour—Mrs. Swain was on the committee—Ziza's first reaction had been "Good God, no!" but she didn't say a word and let him talk on and on about all the good works the Arts Club provided for the village, the free concerts in the schools, the classic film program, the scholarships, the art classes, the . . . And, as usual, she thought, What the hell, and said, "Sure, what time, where?"

There were always two houses on the Arts Club Open House Tour: Aladdin Baraclough's studio (which brought in the out-of-towners, since it was the only time during the year the place was open to anyone with ten tax-deductible dollars) and an additional house in town the committee hoped was inaccessible or mysterious enough to draw the locals. This year the extra house was the van Runk Homestead, a grand old frame house set on ten pristine acres of what had once been farmland, high on a bluff above the river on the north end of town. Passersby on Main Street could catch just a glimpse of the front porch down a long gravel driveway. Every spring, a week or so before Memorial Day, the ancient lilac bushes that lined the drive would be so heavy with blossoms the branches would bend down to the ground.

But just about no one had ever been inside. Professor van

Runk—retired from the Columbia English department, a widower—spent most of the year somewhere else (California, some said, or maybe Colorado). But even when his wife was alive, the van Runks, who were childless and escaped all the activities associated with having children, had never taken an active role in village life. He had turned down so many invitations by the Friends of the Library to speak on his specialty, Washington Irving, that they had long ago stopped asking.

The house had stood furnished but largely unlived-in for years, the grounds maintained in a halfhearted way—like a died-out family's "in perpetual care" cemetery plot—by a local lawn service. A caretaker came in once a week, or so his contract said, to check things out. The real caretaker was Lillian Meservey, who rented the old hired man's cottage beyond the barn.

The committee gave Manager Meservey—as they called her in the souvenir program—full credit for getting Professor van Runk's permission to show off the house (first floor only) and grounds. Among themselves they thought having the place would probably at least double local ticket sales. What they hadn't expected was the professor's insistence that he himself be there, in person, standing on the porch next to the front door, greeting every visitor personally and having each one sign a dust-stained guest book that had last been used on May 21, 1959, for a dinner party.

When Ziza said, "Sure, what time, where?" H. Roger replied, "First shift at the Homestead," in such a casual way that it might have been his homestead. "Two hours on duty. That'll give you time to take the tour when you're through and then get over to Aladdin Baraclough's and have a good look around before closing. You'll be at the end of the drive taking tickets, which makes you exempt from the docents' seminar on the house itself. You don't have to know anything about the place."

"That's a relief."

"Just sell tickets or punch ones already purchased at the Studio and pass out programs. You'll have a protective guardian as well."

"Is that something I wear?"

"It's a large-sized high school football player for your personal safety, since you'll be handling money. And, oh, yes" —he seemed about to say something indelicate—"being a volunteer does *not* exempt you from buying a ticket. After you establish your ticket-taking station I suggest you be your own first customer."

"And my protective guardian? Do I sell him one, too?"

"Student service personnel will be granted scholarship passes. They're red and numbered. He'll have it with him. You should probably ask to see it."

"In case he's a ringer?"

H. Roger sighed. "We're all going through difficult times, Ziza."

"I know," she said.

Dennis Morland's funeral had been on Tuesday afternoon at First Presbyterian. On Tuesday morning Ziza received a call at her office from Mr. Morland asking if she would take part. It was all very businesslike. "We're burying Dennis today," is how he began. He knew it was short notice, but they wanted her to do the Old Testament reading. Something of her own choice. Something about the outdoors if possible. "We'll see you at two," he said. "I'm sorry you never knew him."

Something about the river, was her first thought. "I do not know much about gods; but I think that the river/is a strong brown god—sullen, untamed and intractable . . ." But that was T. S. Eliot, not the Bible. Among the jumble of books Marge Benecosta had put on Ziza's bookshelves was a Bible concordance. Under "River" she found references in the Psalms to a "river of thy pleasures" and a river "whereof shall

make glad the city of God." Ezekiel went on and on about a
flooding river "upon the bank thereof" where trees "whose
leaf shall not fade, neither shall the fruit thereof be con-
sumed," while Isaiah spoke of a time when a man—the Mes-
siah probably—"shall be . . . as rivers of water in a dry place."

A dry place indeed. None of that was right, but how could
she expect a desert people whose notion of a river was the
trickling stream of the Jordan to describe a body of water as
overpowering as the Hudson? The other great natural presence in Quarryville was the familiar sight of the high wall of
the Palisades towering over the far shore of the river. And
Ziza ended up choosing an old standby from the Psalms.

"I will lift up mine eyes unto the hills," she read that afternoon, "from whence cometh my help. My help cometh from
the Lord which made heaven and earth." The church was full.
The high school had excused any of Dennis's classmates who
wanted to attend and either out of grief or simply to get away,
they were all there. Some of them had even dressed up for
it. Their stillness made Ziza believe their grief was real. "The
Lord is thy keeper," she read. Almost half the people there
were adults. Monty Monteagle, Dale DeSousa and his wife.
Ray Rickert alone. The Bramers. Wasco and his grandmother
in a back pew (he had come in late from directing traffic out
front). Many other familiar faces. Miss Gatewood, wearing
her dark glasses and sitting as close to the door as she could
get. Sitting next to Mrs. Morland, holding her arm as though
she were afraid she might try to flee, was Lillian Meservey.
A relative perhaps, although it seemed unlikely. Mr. Morland
sat next to his wife on the other side as though he were alone.

"The Lord shall preserve thee from all evil: he shall preserve thy soul. The Lord shall preserve thy going out and thy
coming in . . ."

Ziza had not gone along on the food delivery for the homeless that night even though Ray Rickert had made a point of
insisting. She had shown up at the church to help make and

wrap sandwiches, baloney and government-surplus American cheese on day-old white bread with mustard. She met the other volunteers and told them she would be sure to go into the city with them next week. It was a jolly group that laughed easily and enthusiastically and was quick to defer all decisions to Reverend Ray, as they all called him. After the Reverend Ray heard that Ziza was not coming along, his mood turned decidedly cool ("I suppose we all have our priorities"), as though she had proved to be a great disappointment.

She told him that she had to be at the high school first thing the next morning to help with individual grief counseling. She had promised the school psychologist and the head of the guidance department, and she didn't want to turn up half asleep after getting home at three A.M. from a night of good works at Grand Central. For the rest of the week, as she spent her mornings at school and her afternoons at Mt. Zion, Reverend Ray maintained his sense of injured propriety.

What she heard from the kids, over and over, was not quite what she had anticipated. They were upset about Dennis, but they were more upset about his body being found in the Meadow. That was their refuge from the adult world, and now it had been violated. It was no longer a safe haven.

"He wasn't killed there," she told them. They knew that, of course. It didn't make any difference. He was dumped there. Most of them used the word "dumped." It echoed through her thoughts all week long.

                         ♨   ♨   ♨

The Arts Club had lucked out. It was a sunny Saturday afternoon, one of those still, warm, early October days before the leaves seriously begin to change color. Not a cloud in the sky. Ziza established her "ticket-taking station," as H. Roger had instructed, at the end of the van Runk driveway. The station was actually a white wire-mesh patio table with a sun-faded flowered umbrella. Also as instructed, she sold herself a ticket (paid by check since she was low on cash) and in the first hour sold or punched well over a hundred more. Her protective guardian (accepted on faith without checking his red card) sat under a nearby copper beech and read *Tortilla Flat*. He'd asked permission. She said she'd let him know if someone was about to rob her.

"Great," he said. "I have a five-page paper due on Monday. On the second level of meaning."

"Meaning of what?"

"Anything. In American lit. *Tortilla Flat*'s short and my sister at Oberlin said it's really all about King Arthur and the Round Table, but I can't see it anywhere and I've already gone through seventy-five pages, seventy-seven, actually."

"I went to Oberlin."

"*Great.* You must have heard about this King Arthur stuff."

"No, but I learned that Peter Pan is a ghost story and that Peter and all those boys who never grow up are really dead. Can you use that?"

"Is it American?" He sounded interested.

"No, sorry."

"Anyway, I'm into this seventy-seven pages and counting. If all else fails I can always call up my sister for help."

His name was Rich. He might, Ziza thought, have been the boy she overheard in the bedroom at that party on her first weekend in Quarryville, but she wouldn't bet on it. Contrary to what H. Roger said, he wasn't on the football team. He was a soccer player, and like the rest of his teammates he had stayed away from Ziza's grief counseling. After the past week, she found it a relief talking to a teenager without having to discuss the body in the Meadow. But it was on both their minds, she thought. It was certainly on hers: ghosts of boys who never grow up, indeed.

Visitors to the Homestead did not arrive in a steady stream but in waves. During the lulls she could hear the reedy voice of Professor van Runk on the front porch, as he repeated over and over again his greeting. Although she had yet to meet him, she guessed he was deaf. Speaking too loud may have been a classroom mannerism, but he also used a deaf man's quick cadence, pausing in the middle of sentences and never at the end, never allowing his listeners to get in a question.

His words came down the long driveway in gusts, like the wind. "Welcome . . . built on seventeenth-century foundations . . . nineteenth-century wings . . . twentieth-century roof . . . cherry wood banister . . . brought directly by steamship from Savannah . . . unloaded right at the Quarryville dock . . . on the very eve of the Civil War . . . local marble fireplaces . . . portrait of me . . . painted by Joseph Hirsch . . . on the occasion of my retirement . . . like to think the house was built on land once owned by Washington Irving . . . and his brother Ebenezer . . . been in the van Runk family for six generations . . . make yourself at home . . . smarter guides than me inside . . . tell you more . . . don't cross any of the velvet ropes . . . guest book on the way out . . . lemonade being served in the backyard . . ."

"He isn't really a van Runk, you know."

Ziza jumped. She hadn't realized that someone was standing behind her. "Miss Gatewood," she said.

"I said we'd meet again. Remember?" She was bundled up in a loden coat with a pointed hood. If it hadn't been for the sunglasses her deeply wrinkled face could have been a monk's. "His wife was the van Runk and when he married her in the front parlor of that place he took her name. He had one of those names that is either Welsh or Jewish. Evans, Davis, Abrahams, something like that. Never used it again, of course."

Ziza was aware that they were being watched. Rich had put aside his book. Lillian Meservey, coming down the driveway from the Homestead, had stopped in her tracks. People in line with tickets to be punched leaned forward to hear what was being said. No one bothered pretending not to stare.

"I wanted to thank you for telling me about finding the boy," Ziza said. "I saw his parents. They appreciated what you did and hoped it wasn't too upsetting for you."

Miss Gatewood's answer was a sound that was somewhere between a snort and a sniff.

"I suppose," Ziza went on, "the police have talked with you about what you saw that morning."

"About the car? No."

"The car—?"

"If you ever want to get the professor's goat," the old woman interrupted, "just ask him about his name."

Questions about the car would have to wait. "You want to buy a ticket?" Ziza asked.

Miss Gatewood looked appalled. "Are you out of your mind?" And with that she turned away and walked on toward the center of town.

Ziza punched four tickets and sold two more. The last person in line was Lillian Meservey.

"I couldn't help but notice that you're on speaking terms with the Walker," she said.

"Miss Gatewood, yes."

"A dear, sweet person, I'm sure, but not one generally recognized as a conversationalist."

"Events, I suppose, just threw us together."

"Do you mind if I call you Zora?"

"I'd prefer Ziza."

"But of course. I also just wanted to tell you how meaningful your Bible reading was at poor Dennis's funeral. The Ninety-first Psalm has always been a great comfort."

"I read the Hundred and Twenty-first."

"Surely not."

" 'I lift up mine eyes . . .' "

"That's it exactly. It was appreciated, deeply appreciated. What did she say?"

"She?"

"I know it's inexcusable nebbiness, but I am dying to know what the Walker says when she has something to say."

"A point of local history."

"Yes?"

"Nothing important."

"I am a trustee of the Quarryville Historical Society and nothing local is unimportant, believe me."

"I think it was something about the van Runk genealogy. It didn't really make much sense."

"The poor dear's mind is probably a hopeless muddle."

"Not at all."

"Really?"

"Really." There was a pause while Ziza punched a few more tickets. "I noticed you were with Mrs. Morland at the funeral," she said. "You're family?"

"No, no, but you might say comforting is my hobby. My granny, bless her soul, used to say, 'When you see grief, fly, fly to comfort it.' It might have been a quotation. But I took it to heart. I'm in a tough business, Zora, small-town governance is not for the faint of heart or the weak of spirit. It's a man's world—garbage*men*, fire*men*, police*men*, council*men*, sales*men*—and there are times when you simply must bust balls. And I do that quite nicely, thank-you-very-much. But I also like to nurture my gentler side and when I see grief —especially a widow's broken heart—or hear of a mother's heartsick cry I do make it a point, schedule permitting, to fly, fly to comfort it."

"I didn't ask you if you wanted to buy a ticket," Ziza said.

"Heavens, I *live* here. In point of fact I'm your replacement, here to take over your station while you go off to see the sights."

"You live in the Homestead?"

"Lord, no. I rent the dinky little hired-man's cottage, off there in the back. Actually it's just the right size for a busy working girl and whoever did it up back in the thirties did a lovely job. It looks more like the old family homestead than the big house does. You'll have to come by one day. Tea, perhaps. I've heard that you get invited places for tea."

"You'd be the second."

"Adele, they say, serves a lovely cup of tea. I just might be embarrassed trying to match her gracious hospitality. Which reminds me." She dropped her voice so that Rich, who was ignoring them, wouldn't hear. "You know to stay on at the Baraclough studio after closing, don't you? It's the Arts Club's annual little party for special volunteers and people who contribute more than the minimum dues. On a lovely day like this, when drinks'll be served on the lawn rather than in that gloomy house, the event's actually worth attending." Her voice dropped even lower. "But for future reference: avoid it when it rains."

Ziza began to introduce Rich as the protective guardian, but Lillian Meservey interrupted, speaking loudly so the boy under the tree would be sure to hear. "I know the young man very well indeed, he's one of our soccer stalwarts. The whole bunch of them play as though their mothers warned them not to get their uniforms dirty. What's it so far this season? Zero for four?"

"One for four," he said, not bothering to take his eyes off his book.

"Is the loss of Morland going to make much of a difference?" Lillian Meservey asked.

Rich looked up, stunned, perhaps because she called Dennis by his last name—no one had done that since he died—perhaps because she asked a question no one bothered asking before.

"I don't . . . ," he said, pausing as though it might have been a trick question. "I don't suppose it will."

"You could always dedicate the rest of the games to his memory and then beat the pants off everyone in sight," she said.

"That sounds pretty lame to me," Rich said.

"Works on TV."

"That's what I said," said Rich.

Ziza headed up the driveway toward the Homestead. The professor was going through his routine one more time and got a friendly laugh with his line about the guides inside knowing more about the place than he did. She was surprised when she finally saw him. Not by the way he looked. As his voice suggested, he was one of those tall, wiry, beak-faced old men.

What surprised her was was his costume. At least she assumed it was a costume. An orange awning-striped linen blazer over a gondolier's blue-striped T-shirt, gray duck pants, spotless white buck shoes, and on his head a straw boater with a broad, badly faded red-white-and-blue ribbon. To emphasize his points, he waved a spindly silver-topped cane, a souvenir—she was to learn—of the 1909 Hudson-Fulton Celebration.

The professor was opening the screen door for his guests to enter the house as Ziza reached the porch. When he saw her he called out, "Our new priest-*ess*," the stress on the second syllable, which, of course, got everyone to stop, turn, and look. "Too busy now, but later at Adele's we must have a little talk. Move on, please. Be sure not to miss seeing Mr. Irving's inkwell in the study and then pause for lemonade under the trees." He waved her on and closed the door with exaggerated care as a new group of ticket holders came up the drive.

The house was dark and uncomfortably cool. There was a wide center hallway leading past a grand staircase to the back door and a sunny lawn. On the left a doorway led to a formal living room with a dimly lit dining room barely in sight through an archway beyond. Doors to the right led to two connected rooms lined with crowded bookshelves and filled with writing desks and heavy leather furniture. If it hadn't been for the huge gray television set plunked down in front of an ornately carved marble fireplace, they could have been reading rooms in a London men's club.

In front of each doorway was a guide with a clipboard full of dates and data who plodded on about hand-blocked wallpaper, export china, and Palladian over-mantles. Ziza liked the television set best and was tempted to ask the guide for its date.

Since coming to Quarryville, Ziza had been exposed to a lot of architecture and interior decoration, and she suddenly realized how she distrusted these little stage settings. So much of it seemed to be a simple matter of intimidation. What she liked best about Ray Rickert, she thought, was that on the Sunday she was introduced at Mt. Zion he simply referred to his church, stripped bare as it was, as "this old room we all love" and let it go at that.

She walked toward the door at the end of the hallway over a sheet of clear plastic that had been put down over the carpet ("This especially fine Persian runner was purchased by the late Mrs. van Runk's parents in Beirut and may date to the early nineteenth century"). After being stopped by one of the guides to sign the guest book ("Name *and* complete address, please"), she was allowed to go outside.

Leaving the house was like stepping back into summer. A table with a huge bowl of lemonade surrounded by leaning towers of paper cups had been set up under some maple trees. People served themselves and then—drawn by the river they knew was there but couldn't quite see—strolled across the rough stubble of the freshly mowed field.

"You spent more time in there than I would've expected.

I, for one, am getting thoroughly bored with the whole production."

It was Professor van Runk, his bamboo cane tucked under his arm like a swagger stick, his straw hat pushed to the back of his head. He was waiting at the bottom of the steps for her.

"What you see before you is an optical illusion," he said, swinging his cane at the view. "Just out of sight, straight ahead, is an oil tank farm and the train tracks. To the right behind the hired-man's house and those trees are more condominiums than you want to know about. Behind the trees to the left are the traffic jams of downtown Quarryville. But what you see is a nice little world, isn't it?" He was still using his classroom voice, and people in the field stopped to listen.

"You'd never think," Ziza said, "that we were just a few minutes away from the city."

"Most people say that you'd never think you were just a few minutes away from New York City."

He was either even deafer than Ziza guessed or he was putting her on. "I'd offer you a drink," he said, "but all they've got here is watered-down lemon juice. Let's go over to Adele's. We can probably get them to open a bottle early. Professional courtesy."

Since it did not occur to him that Ziza might say no, he headed around the side of the house without looking back. "I'll give you a ride."

What the hell, Ziza thought, and followed along.

The car, a beautifully preserved Volkswagen beetle convertible, bright yellow, was parked, top down, in the shade beside the porch. "You don't see many of these," he said. "Don't slam the door. It plays hob with the glass. Buckle up. It's the law. I had to pay good money to get them installed in this buggy."

With the concentration of a jet pilot preparing for takeoff, he placed the key in the ignition, turned it, listened to the engine turn over and catch, checked all the dashboard dials, adjusted the rearview mirror, tapped the gas gauge, eased off the hand brake, and carefully slid the floor shift into first. She could see his left knee rise with the clutch, and they moved down the drive with a stateliness that, for Ziza, seemed majestic. Who would have thought you could go so slowly without stalling? Several people leaving the house on foot passed them and waved.

"That Lillian Meservey," he said, nodding toward the end of the driveway where the village manager watched them move ever so patiently toward her, "tears up and down this stretch like a banshee in that Jeep of hers. Scatters gravel all over the lawn. It's a scandal."

"Quitting time?" she asked, as they pulled up next to her table. If he heard her, Professor van Runk was too intent on studying the passing traffic to answer.

Ziza had a sudden inspiration. "Rich," she called out. "Hop in. We're going to a party."

It was hard to tell who was more startled, Lillian Meservey or Rich. Then they both began shaking their heads, no.

He waved the book. "Ninety-three more pages to go and still no sign of King Arthur," he said. "I gotta be calling Ohio on this one."

"It's *not* an open-door occasion!" shouted Lillian Meservey.

"Next time, then," Ziza said.

The professor saw his opening—no oncoming traffic for a good two hundred yards—and eased the car onto Main Street.

"I really should be civil with that woman," Professor van Runk said. "Star tenant, government official, and all that. She's the one that's got me into this, you know. Says the time's right to make myself known again in this town. Says there's some 'dip stick' of a new mayor—I believe that was the term, no need to point out I'm quoting—floundering around with all kinds of pie-in-the-sky plans at a time when the town's going to be changing. Adele Baraclough, she says, has some sort of plan for the waterfront, with all kinds of fancy-pants advisers. Says my two cents' worth might be worth a good deal more than that."

Ziza wondered if she should attempt a real conversation. She smiled reassuringly.

"Also says that even though you're new in town you're in a good position to throw some weight around."

"Me?"

"You haven't heard any talk about Adele being a murderer, have you?" Without waiting for an answer, he said, "I suppose not." He had made it up to second gear before they were stopped by a red light in the middle of the business district. He watched the light, not trusting himself to speak until it turned green and he got the car moving again.

"You know, of course, Washington Irving's views on this sort of business we're headed for."

"What sort of business?" she shouted.

"Fancy parties. Some dreadful upstarts named Coit—they made their money in Cuban sugar, of all things—tried to make themselves social lions by giving any manner of fancy parties. Their so-called villa was not far from my place. No sign of it these days, of course, nothing but woods. In 1853 Mrs. Coit threw a *fête champêtre* that was a disaster. Irving wrote to his niece that he was sorry the party was such a failure but added"—his voice took on a curiously British accent—"'I am no friend to these attempts to bring city show and extravagance into the country.'

"Typically, when his nephew Pierre published a mixed bag of Irving's letters in 1869 he dropped that line. Not the letter, mind you, just the line. But I've seen the original document, dated July 1, 1853. I make no secret of my opinion that Pierre Irving was nothing but a well-born opportunist. Which, I suppose, is a damn sight better than the low-life opportunists we have these days."

He made the turn onto Fulton Avenue and slowly edged around the wooden sawhorses blocking Adele Baraclough's driveway and bearing NO PARKING, NO VEHICLES BEYOND THIS POINT signs. He parked next to the front porch, being especially careful—as a good citizen, since the last of the house tour people were still leaving—not to block the steps. "Now, young lady"—he patted her knee—"let's see about those drinks. I'm assuming, of course, that you're of age."

Although the caterers were still in the midst of arranging buffet tables on the lawn behind the studio, Ziza and Professor van Runk were far from the first guests to arrive. A young man who had not yet put on his white barman's jacket was busy making drinks and handing them over with exaggerated but good-natured covertness. After a bit of negotiation by gesticulation between him and the Professor (Ziza noticed that van Runk twice handed his drink—Scotch, by the look of it—back for more) she got an almost full plastic cup of gin, tonic, and a single hollow ice cube.

"We're too early for lime slices," the Professor said.

Later, when Ziza tried to fit together pieces of what she could remember of the abbreviated Arts Club party, she came up with a series of images that didn't really fit together:

—The rich, green lawn—dotted with white wrought-iron benches and flowering urns—that seemed to run down right to the river's edge but, like the field at the van Runk Homestead, was only an illusion that hid the train tracks and power lines.

—Adele Baraclough Bloodhorn, acting like an authentic hostess and dressed in a billowing white silk pants suit that was probably supposed to make people think of Pierrot (it made Ziza think of grainy photographs of World War II parachute drops) and decorated only by a Louis Comfort Tiffany art-glass scarab pin ("A twentieth-wedding-anniversary gift of my great-grandfather's to my great-grandmother," she said to those who asked about it, and everyone did).

—Ray Rickert, in his Hamlet getup and wearing dirty white running shoes, snubbing Ziza with a chilly wave but having a long talk at the end of the garden with Adele.

—Only brief glimpses of Whooten as he darted among the guests, reminding them that he would be on the front porch where he had set up his new model of the proposed Aladdin Baraclough gallery and art center.

—H. Roger Swain, browbeaten—perversely, Ziza thought —by Adele into getting down on his knees and crawling under a wrought-iron bench to look at an original Baraclough Ironworks copyright seal.

—Lillian Meservey, no longer dressed as a volunteer ticket taker, arriving in an extravagantly flowered garden party hat—a well-preserved antique, surely—just as a periodic lull had fallen over the crowd.

—The sound of Professor van Runk's well-practiced voice—he had wandered off soon after handing her the gin-and-tonic—repeatedly cutting through the cocktail party babble with the phrase "city show and extravagance."

—Monty Monteagle, tieless, with a modest JUST ASK ME lapel pin on his baby-blue cotton blazer, wandering near the front porch alone, finding no one to talk with.

"I thought a seasoned pol. like you would be working a hot ticket crowd like this," Ziza said to him. "Look at Bob Bramer, he's shaking every hand he can reach."

"Yeah, but remember who's mayor and who isn't," he said. He shook his glass. "I was going for a refill, want one?"

"I'll come along."

This time she got three ice cubes and an oversized lemon slice, which didn't leave much room in the cup for anything to drink.

"So this"—Ziza motioned to the crowded lawn—"is the heart and soul of Quarryville-on-Hudson."

"It's people who think they are telling other people who think they are that they all are."

"Are what?"

"Hot shit."

"Been having a bad day at City Hall?"

"Village Hall. No, not really. I guess I'm just beginning to understand what the job's all about. Lillian Meservey's been giving me good lessons in Local Government 101." They both watched Lillian as she bent over to give Mrs. Swain a better view of the cabbage roses on her hat. Monty drained his glass. "I'd better go up to see what million-dollar wonders that dwarf has on display. Later?"

Before Ziza could reply, he slapped her hand, 1960s-style, and headed toward the front of the house.

Ziza was sure that Adele had been watching them, and once Monty was gone she came over.

"Haven't a moment," she said, as though she hadn't been waiting to catch Ziza alone, "not a moment, now. But please stay after the others leave. It's a silly thing, but I need some advice on something."

"A moral question?" Ziza said. She almost threw in a laugh but sensed that Adele had something serious on her mind.

"I can never keep straight the difference between ethics and morality, but whatever it is, we need to talk."

"I'll be here," Ziza said.

Then, as though to verify something, Adele added, "You were down on the waterfront when they found that dead tramp, weren't you?"

Ziza nodded.

"Whooten said . . . We'll talk later."

As the late afternoon grew later, the crowd around the buffet grew larger than the one around the bar. Ziza decided to skip the line of people waiting with their paper plates and was considering heading back for another drink when she noticed she was standing next to Fogle and introduced herself. He shook her hand but didn't bother giving his name.

"I hear you collect coincidences," she said.

"No secrets in this town," he said, looking over her shoulder for someone else to talk to.

"Oh, I believe there are," she said.

"Name one." He looked at her for the first time.

"Then it wouldn't be a secret, would it?"

"You put a lot of importance in knowing secrets?"

"I wouldn't say that."

"Most secrets are lies," he said. "Don't forget that, Miss . . ."

"Todd," she repeated.

"One 'd' as in *tod,* 'death'?"

"Two, as in 'gladden.' "

He snorted at that. "You see Adele anywhere?"

"Not recently," she said.

He walked away without saying another word.

Ziza changed her mind (hunger won out over thirst) and was waiting at the crowded buffet when she noticed that something was happening at the Baraclough house. People were dropping their plates and rushing up the slight rise leading to the driveway. A police car had arrived. Ziza heard the words "accident," "fall," "broken," "ambulance," and she followed to see what was going on.

In front of the house an empty police car sat abandoned next to Professor van Runk's Volkswagen, its two front doors hanging open. Most of the crowd stopped at the foot of the porch steps, waiting for news about what was going on inside. The word Ziza heard the most now was "Adele." Professor van Runk pushed his way up the steps. "She's in the studio," someone said and Ziza followed behind him through the parlor and dining room and into the huge octagonal room. She stopped with the others in the center. No one wanted to get too close to the tangle of white cloth lying at the foot of the heavy iron staircase.

A collapsed parachute, Ziza thought.

Adele, who had something she wanted to tell her.

A policeman—she saw it was Wasco—was making tentative movements around the body. Another stood as though he were holding off a crowd, but no one had to say, "Stand back and give her air." Someone did say, "I'm a doctor." He crouched over the body for a few minutes and then stood up, shook his head, and walked over to Wasco. By the time the volunteer rescue squad arrived everyone inside the house and out knew Adele Baraclough Bloodhorn was dead.

After talking among themselves, and getting a nod from one of the policemen, the men from the rescue squad carefully rolled Adele over on her back. Ziza made herself look. Adele's eyes were open. Her cheek was bruised. There was no blood but a thin red smudge like smeared lipstick below her nose. Her hair was still perfectly in place, but the impact of the fall had shattered the Tiffany scarab pinned to her white silk blouse. The blouse itself was soiled now from the floor or from striking the stairs on the long way down. She *had* fallen, surely. What else could have explained the way she was lying there?

It looked to Ziza as though there were something in Adele's left hand. From what she could see it looked like a small computer disk. Adele was holding on to it tightly, as though it might have saved her from falling. Beneath the sterling silver pin of the shattered scarab was a JUST ASK MONTY button she hadn't been wearing earlier.

Ziza returned to the front porch. She had been inside for less than five minutes but most of the crowd had gone, fled. When a party is ruined, Ziza thought, everyone is eager to get away. The yellow Volkswagen convertible was gone. The rescue squad van was in its place. More police cars were arriving, and Lillian Meservey was in the driveway showing them where to park. Monty waited at the foot of the steps. So did Ray Rickert and Fogle. Each stood alone, none showing any signs that he knew—or cared—that the others were still there.

10

Marge Benecosta had the word on Adele Baraclough Bloodhorn. Actually, between what she heard after Mass on Sunday and what she picked up at breakfast that morning at the Economy she had several different versions of the word, and she was eager to share them all with Ziza. Ziza, after all, had been there.

"None of this, I assure you, comes by way of Leonard," Marge said as she came into Ziza's office at Mt. Zion. It was still early on Monday morning and the telephone had yet to ring. She carried two takeout coffee containers from the Economy, baby blue, decorated around the rims with a white Greek key design and bearing the words—inscribed like stone lettering on the Parthenon—SERVING YOU IS OUR PLEASURE. She handed one to Ziza. It was so hot Ziza almost dropped it.

"Leonard?" she asked. "You mean Wasco?"

"Of course." Marge sat down in the leather chair. "Leonard is very professional and refuses to say word one about cases under investigation. Others," she said, pausing to blow softly across the steaming cup to cool it, "are not so discreet."

She waited for Ziza to offer a comment, but Ziza kept quiet.

"They say Adele was drunk as a skunk," Marge said, "hardly able to stand up."

"I think not," Ziza said. "I only spoke to her briefly but she seemed sober as a judge."

"Skunks, judges. Six of one . . ."

"I hardly knew the woman, but I'd never seen her in a better mood, smiling, charming, a real hostess."

"There you are." Marge nodded. "She was clearly deep in drink. Adele was not a charming, smiling person. You didn't have to know her to know that. And what about that silly clown's outfit she had on, so baggy she couldn't help tripping over the pant legs, especially in the condition she was in."

"It wasn't a clown's suit," Ziza said. "It looked very good on her, pearly white silk, very fashionable . . ."

"Expensive, you mean."

"Well, yes, I suppose so. But it wasn't a clown's suit, and it fit her very well, very . . ." Ziza paused, wondering if she should use the word with Marge. "Sexy."

"Sexy?"

"In its way, yes. Of course, it was nothing you or I would probably choose to wear."

Marge laughed. "Maybe not you, dear." She let her smile ride a few seconds before dropping it. "But what they're saying is that it was the combination of booze and fancy clothes that made her fall on those stairs of hers and she went right over the edge." She slapped the corner of Ziza's desk.

"Climbing stairs under the influence?"

"That's what they're saying."

"At the Economy?"

"And other places as well."

Marge had sipped very little of her coffee and it looked to Ziza as though she were settling in to hear all the details of the Saturday afternoon party when they heard someone open the outside door. "A customer," Ziza said. Marge groaned and went down the hall to see who it was.

Whoever it was—a man, by the sound of it—was being greeted enthusiastically and a minute later he was at Ziza's door.

"Have a minute?" Wasco asked.

"Sure," Ziza said, motioning toward the leather chair.

Marge followed along behind. "Forgot my coffee," she said, but after Wasco handed it to her she remained at the office door, smiling at the young people.

"Gran," Wasco said, reminding her.

"This is something official?" she asked, backing into the hallway and looking first at her grandson, then Ziza.

"Not really," he said, "but would you mind shutting the door?" She looked as though he'd slapped her. "Please."

Ziza and Wasco watched the door close slowly, very, very slowly. "Not official?" Ziza finally said. One of them had to say something.

"Unofficial, off-the-record, and for all I know as illegal as hell." He took two One-Hour Photo envelopes out of his jacket pocket and put them on her desk. "But"—he looked again at the door to be sure it was indeed closed—"I believe I'm onto something." He paused to let that statement sink in. "Something that requires a few simple answers from you."

He fingered through one of the envelopes, selected a snapshot, and slid it over the desk toward Ziza. She recognized herself immediately. It wasn't a close-up but she was clearly recognizable in her jogging clothes, running past some scruffy trees along the Aqueduct.

"It's me." Then she absentmindedly corrected herself. "It's I."

"Me's good enough for me. Who took it, any idea?"

"None."

"Sure?"

"Want me to say, 'Cross my heart'?"

"You're sure you don't know."

"Positive."

"Okay, look at these. I'll put them in the order they were taken." He carefully arranged fourteen color photographs across the desk. The fifteenth he kept face down.

Most of them were of old warehouse buildings. She didn't recognize any of the interior shots, but she knew the exteriors from the walk she took with Monty along the waterfront. The tenth, eleventh, and twelfth were all so dark she couldn't make out much at all, just a few distant light patches with thick lines cutting across them, maybe skylights and rafters. It was hard to be sure. The thirteenth picture was of her. (That's lucky, she thought.) The fourteenth was oddly familiar: the distant Palisades framed by the shadowy outline of windows.

When he turned over the last picture, she knew where she had seen those windows. They were in the warehouse where the body of the homeless man had been found. The fifteenth was of the man himself, stretched out as though asleep, the shoes neatly arranged next to his head.

"Any of that jog your memory?"

"Not about the photographer. But look, he's not wearing one of Monty's buttons, the way he was when we all saw him."

"Good point," Wasco said and wrote something in his tiny pocket notebook.

"Now look through this bunch." He handed her the stack of pictures from the other envelope. They were all waterfront warehouse pictures like the first nine fanned out across the table.

"Same photographer?" she asked.

"Same camera. There's a scratch or something on the lens. The same little spot is on the lower-left-hand corner of every picture. I discovered that. I noticed the mark on one picture in the first bunch when I had them developed last week. Then I saw they all had it, even used a magnifying glass on them. This morning, when I picked these new ones up, there

was the old spot again. So, I put two and two together." All
the "I"s were said with emphasis.

"And?"

"The ones in your hand are from a photo disc the Morland
kid had in his pocket when we found him. The ones on the
table are from a disc I took out of Adele's hand when we
picked her up."

Ziza remembered the computer disc she thought Adele
was clutching with a death grip.

"You never saw Adele taking your picture?" he asked
again. "You're sure of that?"

"Yes, I'm sure."

He carefully put the snapshots back in their envelopes.
Twenty-three warehouse pictures, a picture of her, a picture
of the Palisades, a picture of a corpse.

"Chief Malfadi took off a few days after that FBI course
for him and the wife to see Williamsburg and Washington,
D.C. He'll be back later this week. I'm just trying to put
some pieces together until he gets here, but I think I've come
up with the big one: murder and suicide."

"You're talking about Adele?"

"She kills the Morland kid, right? Maybe she made a pass
at him or something and he acted up. Whammo, right over
the head. The bum in the warehouse, maybe he saw it happen
and she had to get him, too. Don't know how she worked
that, but maybe forensics will come up with something in its
report. Prelims suggest he was hit on the head, too. Anyway,
she's so proud of that she takes his picture with the camera
she lifted from the kid. Then she gets a guilty conscience.
They say she was really knocking back the drinks at the party
and maybe that sent her over the edge."

"Literally?"

Wasco looked puzzled for a moment, then he smiled.
"Over the edge, right. Off the balcony or the top of the stairs."
He slapped Ziza's desk just as his grandmother had done.

"Have you talked about this with anyone else on the force?"

"I'm playing it close. No one knows anything."

"Not even Monty or Lillian Meservey?"

"I told Monty about the kid's pictures. No one knows about these." He patted the second One-Hour Photo envelope as though it were a trusted pet.

Ziza thought about Whooten telling her of moving Dennis, about the shadowy body laid out among the torn book cartons, about the heap of white silk on the studio floor.

"What about the snapshot of me?" she asked. "What's that all about?"

Wasco shrugged. "That's why I'm here. I thought you might have the answer."

"It makes no sense," she said.

"Makes perfect sense. It all fits together."

"Adele didn't seem . . ."

"The type? You didn't know her the way a lot of guys in this town did. And I mean a lot."

He said that with a confidential smirk that annoyed Ziza.

"It doesn't all fit together," she shot back. "Why is there a picture of me? Why was Dennis moved to the Meadow? How did the man in the book warehouse die? And *where's* the camera?"

"The camera," he said as though he had not thought about it before. "Now that's something to work on."

He stood up and opened the door. Ziza followed him out into the hallway. As soon as she heard their footsteps Marge came out of her office. "I hope you young people had a nice private chat," she said, smiling bravely. "I know how people my age can often be a bother."

"Oh, Gran," Wasco said, leaning over and throwing his arm around her. "I was just trying to sell the Reverend a book of chances for the PBA drawing. She's taking it under advisement."

He waved good-bye to Ziza, without actually looking back at her. She didn't bother returning a wave he wouldn't see. Inside her office, she thought about closing the door, but didn't and called Monty at Village Hall anyway.

"How about lunch at the Economy?" she asked.

"You run yet today?" he asked.

"Nope. Rather do that?"

"I'll meet you in half an hour where the Aqueduct cuts behind St. Hubert's."

"Is this clandestine?" she asked.

"I hope so," he said.

11

ॐ

"What do you suppose Baraclough's greatest contribution to this town has been?" Fogle asked.

He and Whooten were relaxing on the lawn behind the studio. They had avoided the uncomfortable cast-iron benches and brought out emerald-green L. L. Bean deck chairs they found while poking around in the garden shed.

"Adele?"

"Lord, no. The old man. What was his most lasting influence on Quarryville?"

"Some sort of reverence for the representational arts, I suppose. An appreciation for the grandeur of the lordly river? Will I be graded on this?"

"Don't be a pompous ass. It's his name."

"Baraclough?"

"No," Fogle said. "Aladdin. Have you ever noticed how many dogs in this burg answer to the name Aladdin? Probably more dogs are named Aladdin in Quarryville than anywhere else in the world."

"Put it in your column," Whooten said. Then, after a moment's thought, "What about cats?"

"I've never met a cat named Aladdin," Fogle said. It was a definitive answer. "Even here."

"How about cats named Adele?"

"Watch it, the old girl isn't in her grave yet."

"Body's hardly cold, right?"

"I could say something about some people being more familiar with dead bodies than others, but I'll let it pass. I'm not in this for debating points."

"Watch it," Whooten said.

Ideally, Whooten and Fogle would have been sipping gin-and-tonics. But the police had locked up the house and put official seals and crime scene ribbons on all the doors. They had been lucky to be able to retrieve the deck chairs, dusty as they were.

"I don't think those things should read CRIME SCENE," Whooten said. "Although I don't suppose they have separate ones saying POSSIBLE SUICIDE, POSSIBLE ACCIDENT."

"One size fits all," Fogle said.

"I suppose," Whooten said.

They were sitting at just about the spot where the bar had been set up on Saturday. Below them, upriver, were the waterfront warehouses with the Baraclough ironworks smokestack sticking up like a Gothic minaret (a simile Whooten had used more than once). With the river and the hills beyond—and the factories removed—it could have been a Baraclough landscape if only the sun were setting.

"If I asked you which way was north," Fogle said, "I bet you'd point in the wrong direction."

Whooten had been through this before. Without saying a word he pointed well off to the right of the spot where the river touched the horizon.

Fogle ignored him and continued his prepared remarks. "Nine out of ten people in the Hudson Valley, probably in all of the country, think the river flows north to south. In fact, the source is considerably west of the mouth."

"But then," Whooten said in his most bored voice, "how many people know that Reno is farther west than Los Angeles?"

"Exactly. And the only reason you know is—"

"I read it somewhere." He'd be damned if he'd supply footnotes on demand.

Fogle tented his fingers and stared through them at the smokestack. "The thing to do is for me to move up here, establish myself in the house."

"You don't want to rush into—"

"Nothing unseemly. We know what the will says. We all —you, Adele, and I—have talked this through time and again. If anything happened to her, the Baraclough Foundation Trust is to continue with me as its head. All the plans will go apace."

"With a half dozen new lawyers thrown in. How about probate and all that?"

"The Trust agreement's the best money can buy. Adele, bless her, saw to that. The work will continue, but I don't think this house should stand empty. It sends out the wrong message."

"And your lolling around in madam's bedroom—what kind of message does that send out?"

"I'll be in the guest room."

"And that, I assume, will be dutifully reported in *The Weeekly Spy* for all to contemplate?"

"Don't be—"

"But things will go better now, won't they? No more trouble? No more . . . problems?" Whooten asked his questions as though he were trying to extract a promise.

A car door slammed in the driveway. Fogle and Whooten craned their necks to see who was there. A second door slammed. They hadn't heard anyone drive in.

"Boys," a woman's voice called out, "I've come with whatever solace I can provide."

They still could not see her, but Fogle and Whooten said, simultaneously, "Lillian Meservey."

"Down here," Fogle called out.

"Lord, I know that." She came around a twiggy bank of forsythia. "Half the police force can't do a thing this morning but talk about the two of you camped out here in the backyard." She was gingerly carrying a large paper bag with grease spots on it. "The topic of discussion is whether or not your being here constitutes a clue. The dears haven't much experience with crimes that have clues, so they're not always sure that they know one when they see one."

"We're not camped out," Whooten said, as he and Fogle stood up.

"Can you be a dear," she said to no one in particular, "and rustle up two more chairs?" Professor van Runk had come from behind the forsythia but hadn't followed Lillian Meservey across the yard. "The Professor's deaf as a post but insisted on coming when he figured out I was having my coffee break with you boys." She waved back at him, motioning him to come down.

"While he gets here," she said, "you can fill me in on how dear Adele's sad passing affects the riverfront plans. Knocks them into a cocked hat, I suppose."

"Not at all," Fogle said.

"Not a bit," said Whooten.

"Then," Lillian Meservey said, fixing them each with a look they'd be sure to remember, "I hope you're looking into that matter we talked about the other day at the warehouse."

"Looking," Fogle said.

"Not that looking should necessarily be confused with liking," Whooten said.

"But looking," Fogle said.

"Don't let grief deter you," she said as she reached out her hand to the Professor.

Whooten dragged out two more folding chairs from the shed, flicked them open but didn't bother dusting them off. Lillian Meservey passed out steaming blue-and-white Economy coffee containers. "They're all milk, no sugar. And the doughnuts are all plain. Two apiece. We're being naughty but not sinful."

The Professor didn't bother saying hello. He took his coffee, both doughnuts, sat down in what had been Whooten's chair, and announced, "Adele couldn't stand me, never could, seemed to think I was some sort of enemy and even at that luau Saturday she could barely spare me the time of day. That's no reason, of course, to want her dead. Never thought ill of her myself, although news that she's had a hand in the killing of that boy wouldn't have surprised me." Two bites polished off the first doughnut.

"You know, she'd been a student of mine, briefly. My Cooper-Irving-Poe seminar, before she dropped out of Barnard. She was far out of her depth. The poor girl hadn't a thing to offer academically, as I recall, outside of an almost smutty paper on a love affair she seemed to think Irving had with Mary Shelley when he was in London."

Fogle suddenly looked interested. "The creator of Frankenstein in bed with the creator of Rip Van Winkle? Maybe there's an angle there."

"I made short work of that," van Runk continued, ignoring the interruption. "If that woman had an affair with anyone, which I doubt, it was with Irving's friend Payne." He looked around, waiting for a challenge.

Lillian Meservey took advantage of the pause. "There have been some developments in Adele's sad passing that I think you'd want to hear about," she said. The only chair left empty was one of the dusty ones. As a matter of principle Whooten remained standing. "It has to do with snapshots."

Whooten sat down.

"It seems they found an undeveloped roll of film in poor Dennis Morland's pocket. Apparently that hadn't been a secret but I'd heard nothing about it. What *is* being hushed up is that they also found another roll or disc or whatever it is on Adele's person."

Whooten watched Fogle, trying to gauge his reaction.

"Wasco," Lillian Meservey went on. "You know him? He's one of the police officers, not too smart but cute as a button. He thinks the pictures are authentic clues. He's more or less acting deputy chief and won't let anyone see them until Malfadi gets back from vacation in a couple of days. But he's been dropping hints. It sounds as though both sets of pictures came from the selfsame camera."

"What of?" Fogle asked.

"What of what?"

"The pictures, what are they of?"

"That's where you run into your shroud of secrecy," Lillian said with a knowing smile, "but Wasco's hints are getting more detailed by the minute. They say he even went up to the church this morning to show off to his grandmother. I have him booked for a face-to-face, in my office this afternoon, and I figure I'll know the whole story before the sun sets."

"Keep us in the loop," Fogle said.

Lillian smiled again.

Suddenly, with a roar that made them jump, a train, blowing its whistle as it prepared to pass the Quarryville station, rushed by unseen at the bottom of the garden, shaking the ground as it went.

It was enough to get Professor van Runk's attention. " 'Unearthly yells, howls, and screams,' " he intoned, " 'the infernal alarum of the railroad steam trumpet.' I paraphrase only slightly, but those were Washington Irving's words in the summer of 1850. How little some things change in this dear old valley . . ."

Whooten stood up, brushed off the back of his pants and left. He didn't bother saying good-bye. He hadn't, in fact, said a word since Lillian Meservey arrived with her trained seal, and now he couldn't stand another moment with that old bore.

The snapshot business could be bad news, and the fact that the "cute as a button" cop had been up at the church meant that Ziza probably knew all the details. He had to see her as soon as possible.

He headed up Fulton Avenue and took a shortcut along the Aqueduct to an overgrown path that led to the back of St. Hubert's. He had just turned up the path when he saw them running toward him, running easy, matching strides, talking as they ran, heads turned slightly toward each other, not watching where they were heading, assuming the trail was free of any obstacle that might trip them up. Ziza and the mayor. It sounded like the title of a bad sit-com.

To keep out of sight, he followed the path until it almost reached the parsonage. Then he waited. They stopped just below him. There was laughter, laughter used as punctuation, not as a response to anything. Although he couldn't hear what was being said, he could sense that. Then the murmuring voices became more intense. Something serious was being settled. Through the short, flat needles of the hemlocks he could get glimpses of them, Monty in his absurd JUST ASK ME running togs, Ziza in her just-thrown-together mismatched sweatpants and sweatshirt that told the world she ran to run and not to make a fashion statement.

Monty leaned over to kiss her, but she ducked away. Whooten could see that clearly. Monty tried again and this time caught her. It could have been just a social kiss. But Whooten noticed Ziza's right hand. When Monty kissed her she put her hand on his waist, just at the belt line. Was she keeping him at a distance? Or was she being possesive? Whooten would have to think about that right hand. Then she turned and came up the path toward him. He could hear Monty running on, faster than the pace he kept with Ziza. Whooten stepped farther back into the trees and waited. When she reached him he took her arm.

She did not scream but he could feel the outline of tense

muscle in her arm. He could smell her sweat. He hoped it was only hers and not a mixture of hers and Monty's.

"There's more I should have told you the other night," he said. "I've got to tell you about the camera."

She didn't say a word. He wondered if she were afraid to say a word.

"I had it," he said. "I admit that. I found it in the warehouse when Lillian Meservey, Fogle, and I met there. I took it and put it into the glove compartment of my car."

Her breathing was becoming normal now.

"But," he went on, "when I looked again it was gone. Swear to God. Someone took it from my car. It was gone."

"Whooten," she said, "let go of my arm. It's hurting. I don't think you want to hurt me."

He let go but then reached out and put one hand on her waist. She moved back. He moved with her. She didn't try to run but looked him directly in the eyes.

"And I took a picture," he said. He looked directly back at her. He didn't look away. "Only one picture. That's all the film there was."

"Of me?" she asked.

"Oh, no. The dead bum had the camera, and I took a picture of him. When I wound the film to the next exposure, there was none left. There was film for just one picture, and I took it."

"Now it's gone," she said.

"Taken from my car, yes," he said, "another of our secrets."

She stepped back again, and this time he let his hand fall away.

"Who knew about it?"

He almost answered, but he didn't.

"After you took the man's picture you did something else. What was it?"

He could think of nothing. Then: "I gave him one of Monty's buttons."

"Adele wanted to talk to me about something at the party."

"Not about me?"

"She mentioned your name and said she'd talk to me later. But by the time it was later . . . You have any suggestions?"

"Not about Fogle either, I'm sure of that."

She waited for more, then said, "I have to go."

"I can understand that," he said.

"We'll talk again," she said.

"Yes," he said. "Yes, we will."

12

Monty Monteagle didn't stop running until he reached his office door. He had run up the walk to Village Hall (the *AIA Guide to Westchester Architecture* called it "1930s-Palladian," although it looked to him more like "scrambled Howard Johnson"), past the village clerk who watched over the front door with the grim indifference of a Parisian concierge, and up the gently curving staircase. The office on the left was Lillian Meservey's; the one on the right (the bigger one) was his; and the rest of the floor was taken up with a gloomy chapel-like room that doubled as law court and village meeting hall.

He hadn't locked his door when he left. Inside, out of habit, he checked his watch. Normally he kept a record of exactly how long it took him to cover the carefully measured five miles, but today's wasn't a normal run. There had been Ziza to talk to, and there was good news and bad news.

The bad was all that stuff about the pictures and Wasco's theory of murder and suicide. When Chief Malfadi got back he'd put an end to that. And the good news was that there had been Ziza.

He remembered the old day-after-the-date game in high school, the bragging about having made it to first base, second base, third, or a home run. Since it was bragging, most guys claimed to have at least made a triple and there were always more home runs than physically possible. This morning, Monty thought, he got to first base, maybe on a walk, but he was there.

His office faced the river, and if he stood in the right place and looked in the right direction he could avoid seeing the abandoned warehouses. It was a pleasant room, cool under the overhanging eaves but still with a lot of natural light. After living there only a month he felt quite at home.

The heavy leather couch, the kind he imagined they had in private men's clubs, was far more comfortable than the sagging, clanging bed that had come with his furnished room above the A&P. The rich wooden wall paneling was worthy of a Wall Street law office, and in fact had been in one until the firm went bankrupt after the Crash of '29 and everything, including the woodwork, had been sold off at auction. One wall was filled with a marvelously detailed map of Quarryville. Monty could—and did—spend hours studying it. On another wall, lined up with the precision of gravestones in a military cemetery, were portraits of his predecessors in the office, although none of *them*—he was sure of it—ever actually lived there.

The early faces, men handpicked by the mill owners, had the dignity of Supreme Court justices. The more recent ones, men chosen by the fire department, looked uncomfortable in their suits and ties. But a closer look at the photographs suggested that the later ones simply had a good deal less airbrush work than the first. Those early faces, studied at close range late at night, were clearly not the faces of top management. They were office managers at best, men who wouldn't refuse when the boss said he had a job for them to do, men who probably had gone as high as they were going to go on the corporate ladder.

Being mayor of Quarryville had never been a plum job. Late one night just after he had moved into the office, Monty did some long division and figured out he was being paid about $2.50 an hour, which, while a good $2.50 more than he was making before, was less than he could pull in on unemployment. But to collect unemployment you first have to be employed. At the end of the bottom row was the empty place his picture would go, the first "reform" mayor, the choice of all those people in Hillside who liked to form protest committees and write angry letters to *The Weekly Spy* but claimed never to have the time to devote—they always said "devote"—to local government. He was their first success.

Still, he *was* mayor and no one else could make that statement. His huge old wooden desk was piled high with all the paperwork he was refusing to pass over to Lillian Meservey unread. The desktop—which may once have been tooled leather—also held the onyx desk set that had been in his father's old law office and the clear-glass cookie jar filled with JUST ASK MONTY buttons that his campaign workers gave him on election night. The big bottom drawer on the left side held his clean underwear. The dirty stuff went into a plastic bag in the one on the right.

The best perk of all was the private bathroom, complete with a tiled shower the size of a phone booth. The door to it was so carefully hidden away in the paneling that during the first week he had to go across the hall to ask Lillian Meservey to show him again where it was. The bathroom was what made living in the office possible.

He hung his running clothes on the back of the bathroom door and opened the frosty glass door of the shower stall. He stood with water as hot as he could stand it pouring over the back of his neck thinking that he must force himself to think about Adele, thinking of Wasco wanting to think about Adele, thinking of that boy lying behind the Pulpit in the Meadow, thinking of those JUST ASK MONTY buttons, thinking of running along the Aqueduct with Ziza, hearing her talk of death on a day that was so beautiful he just had to kiss her good-bye.

He stepped out of the shower and marveled once again over the organizational skills of people in the movies. No matter who they are or where they were, if they stepped out of a shower there would be fluffy towels within reach, a bathrobe to slip into, slippers to put on. Monty picked up yesterday's towel from the floor (a damp and faded reproduction of a giant Budweiser label), opened the door, and padded barefoot into his office to get a fresh towel and clean clothes.

Ray Rickert was at his desk, reading through one of the piles of paper. He looked up as Monty appeared, showing no surprise, as though it were perfectly ordinary for him to be at another man's desk, reading his papers, and for the wall to open up and an all-but-naked mayor appear dripping water on the floor.

Instead of hello, he said, "Monty, you have one hell of a job. I thought running a church was bad, but how can you stand this stuff? Two hundred and fifty pages of purchasing orders for public works cleaning supplies, for Christ's sake."

Monty played it just as casually. He strolled over to a gunmetal gray filing cabinet, pulled open the top drawer, and plucked out a frayed Batman towel. From the second drawer he chose a blue work shirt, corduroys, and white athletic socks.

"Mind moving your left leg," he asked Rickert and then retrieved his underwear from the bottom desk drawer. "I'll be right back," he said, heading through the opening in the paneling. "If you want to read the hot stuff, look at the job applications for assistant librarian. I think they're under the marble ashtray, hidden from prying eyes."

When he came back, dressed (except for his shoes, which he couldn't find) and his hair almost dry, he found Rickert sitting on the couch and reading nothing at all. He was glad he'd rolled up his sleeping bag that morning and stuffed it somewhere.

"I knew you were up here," Rickert said, as though that explained his presence. "What's-her-name, the clerk downstairs, said you were. You'd be surprised how much noise that shower makes down there. For personnel morale purposes it might be smart to shower only on your own time."

"Thanks for the tip," Monty said. "Us public servants need all the help we can get." He waited for Rickert to say why he was there.

"We've never been particularly close," Rickert finally said.

"Although kids from your youth group were the backbone of my election campaign," Monty added. He knew it was a sore point.

"Yes." There was another long silence. Rickert sat there as though it were his office and Monty should be the one explaining himself.

"You're here to offer your hand in help when our beloved town is going through a time of grievous trouble?" Monty suggested, trying to sound like Heavenly Roger Swain.

"Good God, no. I want to know about all this talk going around about Adele being a killer."

"Adele?"

"Killing two people and then getting rid of herself—it's crap. You knew her . . ."

"Not as well as you."

"Let's grow up and stop playing games. You knew her. Period. She wasn't a killer. Period. She wasn't suicidal."

Monty sat down behind his desk. "She was too vain to kill herself," he said. "She would never allow herself to be found in a dirty heap at the bottom of those stairs. And if she were going to murder someone it wouldn't be a teenage boy or a homeless drifter. She'd go for bigger fish."

Rickert gave that more thought than Monty suspected it deserved and then said, "I prefer 'egotistical' to 'vain' but you're in the ballpark."

"Thank you."

"So, how are you going to put a stop to it?"

"Me?"

"You're mayor, for Christ's sake."

"For a minister you seem to be pretty free with the 'for Christ's sake's.' "

"It's not swearing. It's what theologians call ejaculations, short, sudden prayers. It's a medieval custom that needs reviving. You can look it up in your dictionary. When I say 'for Christ's sake' that's *exactly* what I mean."

"Well," Monty said, leaning back in his chair and swiveling so he faced Rickert, "I guess this is one case when the gossip's true. I'd heard you were a great one for ejaculation."

"Monty, you're so fucking predictable."

"Another ejaculation?"

"No, it's a colorful example of Reverend Ray's famous street smarts. How are you going to go after those vicious lies about Adele?"

"If Reverend Ray were really street smart he'd say 'fuckin,' not 'fucking.' Now, tell me, how did you hear the story about Adele?"

"Mrs. Benecosta called me at home and swore up and down that she had definitely not heard it from her grandson. That means all of Riverside has heard and it's the main topic of conversation this noon at the Economy, replacing the breakfast rumor that Adele was falling-down drunk."

"My source *was* Wasco. I heard it from Ziza Todd, who heard it directly from him."

"You talk to her a lot?"

"Wasco claims to have evidence."

"Why's he whispering police secrets to Ziza Todd? And why, for Christ's sake, is she slipping them on to you? What's with her? Can't anyone in this town keep his mouth shut?"

"And why are *we* talking?"

Rickert clasped his fingers behind his head and stretched back on the couch. His plain black sweatshirt, Monty thought, must have really been quite expensive. Sweats that well made, with no writing on them, didn't come cheap.

"Saturday was awful," Rickert said. "You and me and that toady of Adele's, Fogle, just standing at the bottom of the porch stairs after the others had left, waiting for the body to be brought out. That awful midget architect, crying over his broken dollhouses . . ." He became silent, staring up at the ceiling as though he were searching for flaws in the plasterwork.

"Whooten," Monty finally said to fill the silence. "He was up here in the office on Friday doing a song and dance about his latest version of the riverfront art center. No dollhouses, just watercolors. He's actually a pretty convincing salesman. Even though the project's all wrong for what this town needs."

"Why didn't any of us say anything?" Rickert asked. "Why didn't we even go inside to see her? Just that strange silence with Whooten sniffling away and Ziza Todd being where she didn't belong. I should've taken charge." He sat up straight. "Or you should've, Mayor Monteagle."

"I'll get on Wasco, find out what the hell's going on, and shut him up. Once Chief Malfadi gets back things'll become more routine." Monty stood up, the way he remembered his college adviser standing when it was time to leave his office. It worked. Rickert got up from the couch and the two of them walked toward the door, Monty still in his stocking feet.

"Nothing's routine now," Rickert said. "She either fell—which I can't believe; she was a mountain goat on those stairs—or she was pushed, which means all hell should be breaking loose. And she wasn't drunk. I can swear to that."

"I'll do the right things."

"Just ask Monty?" He didn't say it as snidely as he could have and he flashed a campaign button Monty assumed must have come from the cookie jar on his desk.

He closed the door behind Rickert and went over to the telephone. He put off dialing the police extension and asking for Wasco. Instead he called down to the village clerk to see if anyone had tried to reach him while he was out.

Only one, she said, the FBI, the FBI in area code 202. "You know what that means," she said.

"Afraid not."

"Headquarters," she said. "The J. Edgar Hoover Building. Washington, D.C." She gave him a number and an extension and told him to ask for Special Agent Turnbladt.

"Agent Turnbladt," he repeated.

"Special Agent Turnbladt," she said.

He was in and he would take the call.

"We've been informed that you have a multiple in your precinct," Turnbladt said.

"Multiple?"

"Killings. As a graduate of the Bureau's local chief's program your Chief . . ."—there was the sound of papers being shuffled—". . . Malfadi is given privileged access to one use of the Bureau's psychological profile service for multiple killings and he chose to exercise his option immediately. We suggested that he should wait but he seemed to think the opportunity might not arise again soon. Therefore, in his temporary absence from . . . Quarryville, we are asking for a representative of your force to interface via fax or telephone, your option, with us on the matter of . . . Dennis Morland—John Doe—Adele Baraclough Bloodhorn—and —possible—others—TK."

"TK?"

"To come. Do you have an identity number registered with the National Association of Mayors?"

"I don't think so. I don't know that I even belong."

"Your name and Social Security number will have to suffice. You are personally responsible for having the qualified police liaison contact this office. His or her name, please?"

"Wasco," Monty said. What the hell was his first name? "Leonard."

"Roscoe Leonard. And list rank, please?"

After that was all straightened out and Monty searched through his wallet to find his Social Security number, he hung up.

The appearance of Ray Rickert in his office had been a surprise and he wondered if he should have mentioned the photographs, especially the photograph of Ziza. That was the aspect of the story she told him on the Aqueduct that bothered him most.

On a whim he decided to look up "ejaculation" and see if Rickert had been bullshitting him. On a shelf near the desk was the last mayor's reference library: a dictionary that looked as though it had never been opened, a thesaurus, and a *Bartlett's Familiar Quotations* (both for more colorful speeches?), a special leather-bound edition of the League of Women Voters' *Know Your Quarryville!* pamphlet, published back in 1968, and Fuller and Swanson's *Westchester: A Pictorial History.*

Something was wedged in between the dictionary and the thesaurus. Monty knew it was a camera, a flat little disc camera that no serious photographer would ever think of using. It was not new. The case was battered, and it looked as though someone had scratched an initial on the back.

An "M," he thought, just like the old Fritz Lang movie about a child-killer being hunted down in Berlin. "M" as in Monty or Monteagle or Morland.

13

&

Except for the fact that Ray Rickert arrived with a lightweight black canvas couch, the evening began as though Ziza were going on a date.

"It smells a little like a dog bed," he said, brushing some long white hairs from the couch's arm rest, "but a few good vacuumings should take care of that. You have a vacuum?"

She shook her head, no. Even from where she stood she could see the dog hairs. It must have been a fairly large animal.

"Oh, well," he said. "It's washable and indestructible, and I guarantee the dog wasn't incontinent."

Ray Rickert had insisted on coming over to St. Hubert's parsonage to pick her up. He had called her that afternoon at the church—from his office down the hall—to say that it was Tuesday, the night for food distribution for the homeless.

"I'll be there," she said.

"Why don't I come over to the house to get you?"

"Afraid I'll skip out again?" she said and immediately regretted it. She had promised herself to be careful with Rickert: no sarcasm, no sly jokes, no irony.

But he laughed. "We seem to have been avoiding each other for the past week," he said. "Make some coffee, and maybe we'll have time to talk before our night on the town."

She made the coffee. He dragged in the couch, perhaps

his idea of a peace offering, carefully arranged it in front of the fireplace, and then sat down.

"Black, no sugar," he said.

She brought the coffee in unmatched mugs, and since there was no alternative, she sat down on the couch next to Rickert.

"There," he said, "we've broken it in." He held up his untasted cup to Ziza and they clinked mugs as though they were having champagne.

Ziza patted the cushions and sniffed loudly. "No dog."

"As the dyslexic atheist once said."

It took Ziza a few seconds, long enough for Rickert to repeat the words "dog" and "God" and then she laughed the way she was supposed to. "That's a terrible joke."

"You've been in the business long enough to know that all preachers' jokes are terrible," he said. "It's because most of us are marked with the twin curses of being both humorless and having a terrible need to entertain. Let me tell you about a truly terrible joke . . ."

After a week of ignoring her, Ziza thought, he seemed to be going out of his way to be charming.

"It was back after I first came to Quarryville, ten years ago, and someone gave one of those get-acquainted cocktail parties. That was back in the days when you could ask for a martini and actually get one made any way you liked it. The school principal was there, the service club presidents, town trustees, everyone supposedly worth knowing in Hillside, even a few Riversiders for local color, I suppose. Adele was there and Professor van Runk and his wife, although they hated each other."

"Van Runk and his wife."

"Adele and van Runk. For some reason I could never figure out she always saw him as some sort of arch-rival. Well, we were all standing around sipping drinks and flailing about for things to say when someone mentioned that the Professor was a notable Irving scholar, and I said, showing what a good guy the new preacher was, 'What question has *Washington Irving* for an answer?'

"The old boy, even then van Runk was an old boy, looked puzzled and finally said, bellowed actually, 'Who was the nation's first truly distinguished writer? Of course.'

"To which I shouted back, 'Possibly, but what I had in mind was,' and here I went into my version—I was *much* younger then—of a Yiddish accent, 'Who vas the first President, Izzy?' Silence. Then Adele started laughing louder than anyone with good sense should have. I had to repeat the line two or three more times, dropping the accent completely.

"Van Runk never laughed. The joke failed, he said, on two grounds: good taste and good punctuation. The answer—he refused to go into the good-taste aspect—was not *Washington Irving* but *Washington comma Irving*. Adele kept hooting away, although I suspected she was now laughing *at* me, and the Professor launched into some minilecture on how underrated Irving's biography of George Washington actually was. The crowd scattered, and I ended up talking with Adele. That's how we met."

Ziza suspected they had come to the real reason she was being picked up for their night on the town. "It's a terrible business," she said, leaving him slack to say what he had in mind.

"The stories have started," he said, "the hare-brained theories."

"I've been hearing them."

"So I've been told. Mrs. Benecosta says you've been meeting behind closed doors with her grandson . . ."

"Once."

"Once is enough."

"As the girl said at the home for unwed mothers."

"Another terrible preacher's joke. Worse than mine, but you aren't getting me off this subject." He smiled as though he, too, were only making a joke. "Monty also said—"

"Monty? You've been talking with him about this?" She couldn't believe Monty would repeat what she told him. "Everyone knows you two hardly speak to each other."

"When our beloved town goes through grievous times, love of community makes strange bedfellows."

"I didn't know you did Heavenly Roger imitations."

"I do Monty Monteagle doing Heavenly Roger imitations."

"Okay, so the two of you had a heart-to-heart. Are you coming to me for confirmation or what?" Rickert was sitting next to the arm on one end of the couch, she next to the arm on the other. The space between them seemed perfectly natural.

"Monty spilled no beans, don't worry. Whatever Wasco told you is still a secret to me. I respect that. But we should do all we can to discourage absurd rumors. It's simply not worthy."

"Wasco's case comes down to what he thinks is a double murder, then suicide."

"Evidence?"

So much for respecting secrets. "He has some snapshots he thinks are important."

"You saw them?"

"Ray, please."

He sat low on the couch with his long legs stretched out toward the empty fireplace. He stared straight ahead as though he were looking at blazing logs. She half expected him to start asking about Whooten and his crazy confessions.

"Her funeral's going to be in the city, a top-of-the-line affair. Some society preacher at some society church will come up with the eulogy, God bless him." He seemed to think about that and added, "Somebody once said you can do whatever you like as long as you don't frighten the horses. Adele scared the horses and had a good time doing it. Know what I mean? She liked the idea that other people thought she was outrageous. She could be like a spoiled little girl wanting to be naughty. It was an attitude as out of date as the word 'naughty.'"

Ziza offered more coffee, but he ignored her and kept talking to the fireplace. "She was a collector. She had her Aladdin Baraclough collection, her collection of old buildings, her oddballs and freaks, and her men. Something of everything, like the nursery rhyme: Rich man, poor man, beggar man, thief. Doctor, lawyer, Indian chief. Or are we saying *merchant* chief these days? Fireman, preacherman, carpenter, cop." His voice trailed off. "Rabble-rouser, advertiser, conniving fop. But she wasn't a murderer, believe me, or a suicide.

"You met her," he added almost as an accusation, as though he suddenly remembered she was there. "That picture . . ." He gestured vaguely in the direction of the Point No-Point watercolor leaning against the wall on the chrome mantelpiece. "It must have come from her."

"A loan."

"Ahh, the grand gesture." He had turned toward her and parodied a smile without quite looking at her. He'd lost his road-company Hamlet look, Ziza thought. Smiling made him look . . . not exactly tired and old, but older and sadder. "I can just see Adele doing it. She probably took you into that climate-controlled closet off the kitchen and casually plucked the picture out of nowhere, 'Take this one, and if you lose it, I'll have every cop in the county after you.'"

"Very close," Ziza said.

"Of course she probably spent most of the night before deciding—over a couple of drinks—which one you'd get. Presumably after passing some sort of mysterious test you never knew you were taking."

"Perhaps we should . . . ," Ziza began.

"You're right." He looked at his watch and jumped up. Hamlet had returned. "And what did the Lord say?" An antic, teasing Hamlet instructing the players. " 'Feed my sheep.'"

Then he sang in a surprisingly deep voice, "Listen to the la-ambs, all a-cryin'. . . ." He stopped as suddenly as he began. "Don't forget to take a jacket, Ziza. Round about three A.M. it gets pretty chilly."

"One more thing," Ziza said. "Adele, just before she died, told me she had something she wanted to talk to me about. Some ethical problem, something bothering her. It might have involved the John Doe in the book warehouse. Any idea?"

"Adele wasn't the sort of person who had ethical problems."

"Sure about that?"

"Positive. Let's go."

As they headed down the walk past the overgrown St. Hubert's Church he asked her if she had ever looked inside and Ziza said she didn't have a key.

"It was on the Arts Club tour a few years ago," he said. "All very out-of-date modern like the house. The oddest thing is that over the door there's a deer's head, like someone's hunting trophy, and right in the middle of the antlers is a crucifix. A real deer shot by the guy that paid for the church."

"St. Hubert's the patron saint of hunters," Ziza said.

"I'm not much interested in saints. There are no saints in the Bible, just plain old Peter and Paul and John and so on. 'There was a man sent from God, whose name was John.' That's what the Scriptures say. Not St. John, and that's good enough for me."

"That little poem you came up with before, that variation on 'Rich man, poor man . . . ,' did you make that up on the spot or was that something you've been carrying around with you?"

"Trying to see if I have any future as a rap musician?"

She let the question hang there.

"Oh," he finally said, as they came up the steps of Mt.

Zion, "I guess it's something that's passed through my mind before."

There were a half dozen or so people waiting for them inside. Rich, her protector from the house tour, was there with Anne Bramer, Bob's daughter. Ziza wondered if the food run also doubled as an excuse for staying out late on a school night. There were a few people Ziza had met the week before when she helped make sandwiches, but the big surprise was seeing Bob Bramer himself. He hadn't struck her as someone whose notion of good works extended beyond attending committee meetings. He was decked out in the kind of crisp safari khakis television reporters like to wear when covering Third World uprisings.

"Welcome aboard!" he shouted out to her, as though he were an old hand. In fact, this was his first trip, too. "We've been letting Anne go once a month," he said, "and I guess my curiosity finally got the better of me."

Ziza suspected there was more to his being there than that.

Rich and Anne were laughing together about something, and Ziza caught in their voices a nervous edge she herself felt, a feeling that they were about to have an adventure, that something vaguely dangerous was about to happen.

"She used to beg for permission to go to rock concerts at the Garden," Bob Bramer said. "Now it's Reverend Ray and feeding the homeless." He laughed. "Who knows what's up with these kids today?"

"Maybe Rich has something to do with it."

"Tell me about it." She half expected him to nudge her in the ribs with his elbow. "Class president, soccer team captain, a lock-on for early admission to Dartmouth. Is this one hell of a cheap date or what?"

If there was a sense of excitement in the room, there was also a feeling of businesslike routine. Ray Rickert had a clipboard and was going down a checklist. Fifty paper bag lunches (cheese sandwich, apple, small box of raisins, a heat-sealed pack of condoms) stowed into each of the four large hampers (actually they were square plastic garbage bins). "Check." A fresh supply of toothbrushes, paste, disposable razors, soap, combs, et cetera for the hygiene locker. "Check." Shoe supply restocked. No "Check" on that one. No decent shoes had been donated in the past week.

"No one," Rickert said to Ziza, "ever wants to give away men's shoes until they are unwearable. But then, we make up for that by having more high heels than we know what to do with."

Extra coats and jackets. "Check." Sweaters. "Check." Shirts. "Check." Small-waist pants. "Check." Large-waist pants. "Check." General outerwear. "Check." General underwear. "Check." Miscellaneous female. "Check."

"Miscellaneous female?" Ziza asked.

"Just about all of our clients are men," Rickert said, "so we put all the women's stuff in one place. Also a few kids' things." He checked his watch. "Okay," he shouted to the whole group, "let's saddle up. Ziza, you sit up front with me and ride shotgun."

The van's sliding doors were pulled back, Rickert got behind the wheel, and everyone else piled in. Someone had ingeniously rebuilt the interior to install permanent slots for the food and clothing containers in the back with three rows of seats in front. There was room in the first row for three people, and Bob Bramer hopped in beside Ziza. There was room for three, but they were close enough for Ziza to feel Bob Bramer's thigh jiggling against hers, and every time Ray Rickert shifted gears with the floor gearshift his hand brushed her leg.

He said "Sorry" the first time. After that he didn't bother.

The roar of the van's engine was loud enough to drown out any conversation in the back seats, and from time to time, Ziza noticed, Bob Bramer glanced back to take a quick look at his daughter. As they drove down the Saw Mill Parkway to the Henry Hudson to the West Side Highway in Manhattan, Ray Rickert reviewed for her what they'd be doing that evening.

"They're expecting us," he said, "don't worry about that. Someone—one of the homeless—gave us the name Moonlight Rounds." The way he said it showed he was proud of that, Ziza thought, as though it had given them—him—some special acceptance.

The first stop would be at a subway entrance near Carnegie Hall. Rickert said he didn't especially like going there, so he got it out of the way first. It was more druggie than the other places, sometimes more raucous. Once or twice things got a bit out of hand. But the regulars expected them. Next they'd go to a small park across from the UN (a lot of older men), then a street corner near Grand Central. After that was another street corner farther downtown on the Lower East Side, near Seward Park, then back to the West Side, a vacant lot near the piers (maybe a few transvestites there, anyway a generally younger bunch than the other stops), then back home, two hundred sandwiches later.

"Get ready for your baptism of fire, Ziza." They pulled up near the subway entrance on Fifty-seventh Street and Rickert asked Ziza to go down into the station. "Let them know Moonlight Rounds has arrived."

"Let them know?"

"There'll be some homeless types hanging around at the bottom of the stairs. Tell one or two and come back up. Word gets around fast."

By the time they all got out of the van, a few men were already standing there. The Quarryville people said hello, speaking a bit too loudly, the way nurses talk to the bedridden, and worked hard to smile. The men stood back and waited in shadows for the plastic bins to be opened.

Ziza went down the stairs to the tiled station. It was now after midnight and the Carnegie Hall crowds had long since passed through. She had no trouble finding the homeless. In the center of a cardboard nest sat a bearded man wearing a clear plastic poncho over a filthy blue plush running suit. "Moonlight Rounds is here," she said to him. He looked as though he might argue with her but decided against it.

"Is it Tuesday night or Wednesday morning?" he asked.

"Wednesday, just."

"If it's Wednesday, you're late. Westchester is always late. Tomorrow night's—tonight's—New Jersey's, Hudson County's. They'll be here by eleven-fifteen tops."

Two men hunkered down against a wall got up and walked toward her. "Moonlight Rounds," she said, and they nodded as though she had given the right answer. She looked to tell others but saw she didn't have to. A dozen or so men were moving toward the exit stairs.

By the time she got back to the street, the van was surrounded. Some of the men took their paper bags and left immediately, others hung around seeing what else there was to offer, maybe looking for some conversation.

"Anybody need soap or anything?" Rich called out. "Anybody cold and need a sweater?"

Ray, she noticed, simply walked around and talked to the men. He could have been the host of a cocktail party. He seemed to know a lot of them by name and brought a loose-jointed man in torn jeans who could have been thirty or fifty over and introduced him to Ziza. "Andy has a job interview tomorrow," he said. "Fix him up so he'll knock their socks off." And the two of them, she and Andy, rummaged through the clothes until they came up with a shirt, a sweater and a pair of pants that seemed to do the job. Actually, Ziza wouldn't have minded having the chain-stitch sweater herself.

Ray came by and looked over the selection. "You need a belt," he said.

"No belts," Ziza said.

"None," said Andy. "Suspenders either."

"Take mine," Ray said, whipping it off his pants as though he were drawing a sword.

"You sure?" asked Andy.

"A loan," Ray said. "When you get your own you can give it back."

"You really sure?" asked Andy.

"It's a deal," said Ray.

The little park across from the UN was a lot darker than Fifty-seventh Street. The shadowy men got up from their dark benches, shuffled over to the van, and fell into line without being asked. Forming lines was something they did well. They took their sandwich bags, but when soap and razors were offered few accepted. Some of them tried on jackets and debated, in silence, whether to take them. Most did. One man refused because there were buttons missing. Ziza wished there was more independence like that.

While Rich and some of the others were putting things away, Bob Bramer led Ziza to one side.

"How *are* things going?" he asked. It was clearly intended to be a meaningful question.

"Tonight?" she answered, evasively.

"In Quarryville. The youth program."

"I think it's all coming together," she said.

"Frankly, some of us—Reverend Swain, myself, one or two others—are getting a bit concerned about your proximity to Ray Rickert."

"Proximity?"

"Your office is right there in his church. You must see him a couple of times a day. Lord knows how much time you have to spend with that secretary of his."

"Marge Benecosta's a delight."

"A prized employee, a jewel, but the impression given out is that your ties to Mt. Zion are getting stronger than those to First Pres. and Trinity. When was the last time you had a good talk with Roger Swain or even Dale DeSousa, for that matter?"

"I haven't been sure that Heavenly Roger was all that interested in having a good talk."

"See, that's the sort of impression that the wrong sort of proximity can induce. I'm really tempted to go forward with my suggestion that you arrange to spend a proportion of each week at each church office." Everyone else was back in the van, and Ray blew the horn to get their attention. "You know, just a little call now and then to the right person might do wonders to improve intra-Community Pulpit relations."

As they got back in the van, Ziza noticed that not only was the name "Mt. Zion Methodist Church, Quarryville, New York," painted on front door but also—in much smaller letters—were the words "Moonlight Rounds" traced out in script.

A small crowd was waiting for them on the street corner opposite the Lexington Avenue side of Grand Central. The Quarryville people went through their paces quickly. More sandwich bags were passed out, more coats and jackets taken away. There were a few women at this stop, and one of them, dressed in a hooded sweatshirt with TAFT printed across the chest and a rather country-clubby pair of tartan slacks, asked Ziza where Quarryville was. Just about a half hour north of the city, she said, and then the woman wondered if Ziza had met someone there by the name of Dave Spencer.

"Dave Spencer? I don't think so. How long's he lived there?"

"I suppose you can say he lives here," the woman said. "He has a spot down in one of the steam tunnels under the station. But you people made him curious about Quarryville, the quality of the clothes you hand out. Everything I have on came from there. So he went up to look around."

"Casing the joint?" Ziza joked.

"I don't believe so," the woman said, just a bit frostily. "But it was a week or so since he left—he'd seen the place listed as one of the Metro North stops on the train—and no one's heard a word from him since. He wasn't the sort to leave for good without a word to the wise. For starters at least, he would've sold his spot in the tunnel to someone. It's prime and now he's lost it."

Ziza thought for a moment and then asked, "Can you be back here Thursday night? I'd like to show you a picture of someone."

"Oh, I never miss the Moonlight Rounds," she said.

"My name's Ziza."

"That's a pretty name. I'm Barbi, with an 'i.' "

Down on the edge of Seward Park and at the vacant lot near the piers, it was more of the same. Ziza took charge of the clothes bins. With the cooler fall nights there had been a rush on sweaters and jackets. Besides Barbi, there had been no women to speak of. Not even any transvestites. The faces blended together. Ziza wouldn't have been surprised if someone had told her the same group met them at every stop.

That was what depressed her about the evening, how unremarkable it all was. Homelessness in New York had become a routine. There were whole neighborhoods of homelessness. Places to be. Times to be there. The right things to say. The expected things to happen. The absence of wiseguys was remarkable. This was New York City, but where were the jokers? What delighted Ziza about the community work she'd done in the Rochester ghettos were the con men, the tricksters, the men and women who were trying to beat the system, to cadge the extra portion of food, the extra pair of socks, the free ride. They were the ones that gave her hope.

By two-thirty the van was on the West Side Highway heading north to Quarryville. The food bins were empty, the warm clothes almost gone. The volunteers in the back seats were all asleep, or at least every time Bob Bramer looked back at them, Anne and Rich gave a good imitation of being asleep.

"So, Ziza, what did you think of it?" Ray Rickert asked.

"I think I'll be back on Thursday."

"Twice in one week?" asked Bob Bramer. "Don't you think that's kinda overloading the system? Moonlight Rounds isn't on your job description. There's lots to do in the village besides this sort of thing."

"I don't know," she said. "I think for the first time out it's worthwhile comparing two days of the same week. Just for curiosity's sake."

They had passed though the bridge toll gate and were crossing over the Harlem River into the Bronx. "Three cheers for Ziza," Ray Rickert said. "Three cheers for curiosity. Now, could you look around back there and see if you can find my Levi jacket? The cold's beginning to get to me."

As soon as he said it, Ziza knew what had happened, but she looked anyway. The jacket, of course, wasn't there.

"A Levi jacket." she repeated, "blue, well-washed."

"Yes."

She bit the bullet. "I gave it away."

"What?"

"At Seward Park. People were trying on jackets, taking them off and just dumping them on the floor of the van. The Levi jacket was there, and I just assumed it was up for grabs like the rest."

"It was mine," he said. Then he repeated it slower. "It. Was. *Mine.*" He had pulled the van onto the tarmac of an abandoned gas station just before the Saw Mill Parkway toll booth.

"I'm sorry," Ziza said.

"You gave away *my* coat!" He was shouting, now, waking the people in the back of the van.

"It was a mistake," she said.

"We're going back," he said. "We're going to find the man and you're going to get it back."

"She said she was sorry," Bob Bramer said. "You'll never find that jacket again. Don't be silly."

"She'll find it because she gave it away." He hadn't shouted that. It was almost a whisper.

"I'm sorry," she said. "I'll buy you a new one."

"Giving away your own belt didn't bother you much," Bob Bramer said, trying to sound reasonable. "Think of this the same way."

"The belt was mine to give, and that jacket wasn't hers." They sat in front of the empty stone gas station, where the gas pumps had been before they were taken away. Ziza could sense that everyone in the back of the van was awake, watching to see what would happen next.

"I'll buy you a new one," she said softly.

He was still gripping the steering wheel, and she reached out and put her hand on his wrist. His skin was deadly cold and clammy. Her fingers felt moist where they touched him, but as she held her hand there she could feel his skin slowly warming beneath hers. She could hear him begin to breathe more normally. She let go.

He laughed. It was an all-in-good-fun laugh. He started up the car and headed for the toll booth. "Well," he said, "I guess I'll just have to hold you to that."

Ziza could hear the people behind her settling back in their seats, as though they might be able to fall asleep again before reaching Quarryville. Bob Bramer's knee pressed against hers and retreated. Meaningfully, she thought.

She kept her eyes on Ray Rickert as they passed through the bright lights of the toll gate, waiting for him to glance over toward her. He never did.

14

✒

Ziza promised herself she'd wait a day before she did anything about what Barbi had told her on that windy street corner across from Grand Central. It would give her time to have practical, sensible second thoughts about what she intended to do. But the day passed and nothing happened to make her think the plan—which came to her as Barbi chatted on about the quality of Quarryville's handouts and the curious way Dave Spencer dropped out of sight—wouldn't work.

Ray Rickert had been unusually chatty the next morning, dropping by her office with coffee, freshly cut carrots ("Better than doughnuts") and one of those little hand-held vacuum cleaners.

"Does wonders with dog hair," he said. "Says so on the box."

"And why would they lie?" she said.

"Why indeed," he said.

No mention was made of his temper tantrum or of anything else that had happened the night before. Ziza said she wanted to go again on Thursday night.

"You're the first VIP to make that return-visit commitment. Everybody's gone once—Lillian Meservey, Monty, Heavenly Roger, even Adele—but you're the first to re-up.

Maybe," he said, leaving the open Ziploc bag of carrots on her desk next to the Dust-Buster, "it'll become a habit."

"Maybe," Ziza said, silently committing herself to her plan.

On Thursday morning, before going to the church, she made her first visit to Village Hall and asked the clerk how to get to the police department.

"Entrance's around back, off of the parking lot," she said without looking up.

"Can I get there through here?"

The clerk looked up, considered Ziza for a moment, and said, "Straight ahead. You can turn right before the stairs and go through the door that doesn't say either 'Men' or 'Women.' But it's *not* the proper entrance." Ziza sensed that if she took that option she would not get a passing grade, but—what the hell—she did it anyway.

Inside the unmarked door was a short hallway almost completely blocked by a giant copying machine and a water cooler. To the right was a dark frosted-glass office with CHIEF and the silhouette of a policeman's shield painted on the door. To the left was a small, brightly lit room crowded with more gray metal desks than the fire laws probably allowed. The only desk in use was occupied by Wasco and Lillian Meservey, who were studying a thick, accordion-pleated form.

Ziza had not expected to see her. Neither of them expected Ziza.

"We're going to get our man," Lillian Meservey said, as though she were graciously covering up some sort of social *faux pas* on Ziza's part, "Officer Wasco and myself."

"An official FBI form," Wasco said, with obvious pride. "It just arrived by Fed. Ex."

"I personally find it very interesting that our tax-supported government uses a privately owned messenger outfit rather than the Postal Service," said Lillian Meservey. "But once we get all this filled out and back to Washington, they'll come up with a psychological profile that'll get us our mass murderer."

"Mass murderer?" Ziza asked.

"The Morland boy's always been a definite killing," Wasco said, "and Adele is a definite probable (off the record: forensic says it's a sure thing. She was strangled either seconds before she hit the floor, or just after) and now the coroner's office is saying it's official, the John Doe in the warehouse died of a blow to the head. Off the record again . . ." Ziza began to wonder if she looked like a police reporter. "None of these deaths is natural."

"I think there's something most *un*natural about the term 'natural death,' " said Lillian Meservey. There was a pause, a long pause while Wasco ruffled through the pages. The question not being asked was: Why are you here, Ziza? "Don't you think so?"

"No," Ziza said. "Death seems perfectly natural to me."

"But then," Lillian Meservey said, "that's more or less your line of work, isn't it, dear? You have a rather professional interest in the whole business."

"Not the murders."

"Oh, my, no. Nothing that dramatic. Just death in general."

Ziza had to get rid of this woman so she could talk to Wasco. She put on her most innocent expression. "You're filling out the FBI questionnaire for the police? I suppose with Chief Malfadi out of town, the village manager gets involved in all sorts of odds and ends."

Wasco slid the form to his side of the desk and kept his hand on it as though someone might try to get it away from him. "No," he said, just as Lillian Meservey stood up and said, "Good Lord, no. I just happened to run into Officer Wasco as he was signing for the delivery and out of plain-as-dishwater curiosity took a peep to see what sort of things the Federal Bureau asked. I wouldn't think of infringing on the responsibilities of a law-enforcement professional." She edged past the outsized copying machine. "If you have a moment, Ziza, drop by my office before you go. We can have that cup of tea we keep talking about."

When the door closed, Wasco said, "I wish I could have got rid of her that easy. You should've turned up an hour ago."

Ziza sat down in Lillian Meservey's old chair. "So you've dropped the murder-suicide theory?"

Wasco looked around the room to make sure no one had slipped in unnoticed. "You crazy?" he said. "That's my ace in the hole. I'm just not spreading it around until the time's right. No one's seen the pictures either, just us." He had lowered his voice and the "just us" was said with a knowing intimacy.

"What accounts for the bump you said forensic found on the back of Adele's head?"

He chuckled. "That old fox," he said. "It would be just like her to bash herself one before she jumped just to throw everyone off. That's why she didn't leave a suicide note."

"But she had that film in her hands. Maybe that was her way of telling all."

"The FBI's going to show it all makes sense. You'll see." He turned back to the form and started in on the first page.

"Do you have the pictures with you?"

"Of course." He patted the left breast pocket of his uniform, right over the special embroidered patch commemorating the Westchester Tricentennial. "They don't leave my person. Ever."

"And the negatives?"

He patted the same spot again. "A second set of prints is under lock and key, place undisclosed."

"Do you think I could see them again? Adele's set."

The flap button on the heavily starched shirt was hard to undo, but eventually he had the pocket open and fished out the photo packets. Each was in an envelope printed with a color picture of a family at the beach, children, parents, grandparents, dog, all having the time of their lives under a banner that read FUN'S NOT COMPLETE WITHOUT A CAMERA.

Ziza quickly ruffled through the snapshots (they were still warm from his body heat), stole a quick look at the one of herself running along the Aqueduct, was pleased once again to see that she wasn't caught looking red-faced and puffing, and extracted the picture of the John Doe in the book warehouse.

"Could I borrow this?"

"No can do," Wasco said without looking to see which one.

"I think I might be able to find out who this is," she said. "I'd like to show it to someone."

"Bring him in. Her in. Whatever."

"Her. If she has to come here she won't."

"I'm keeping a lid on."

"How about a Xerox?" she said, pointing to the copy machine. "There's probably even an enlarger on that thing." He kept writing, filling in the blanks, getting information from a file on his desk and transferring it laboriously to the FBI form. "I think I can find his name, and a name will impress the Bureau a lot more than a let's-call-this-one-John-Doe." He looked up at her.

When Ziza went upstairs to find Lillian Meservey's office she had two enlarged photocopies of the picture folded away in her handbag.

At the top of the stairs she paused in the corridor between the two doorways and heard Monty call her name. "Perfect timing," he said as he came through the open door of his office. "I was just about to call you at Mt. Zion, but was making up something to say in case Ray or Mrs. Benecosta answered."

"I think you just ask for me or say you'll call back later."

"It's never that simple."

"I suspect it is."

"Well, come on in and see my world. Your first visit to the seat of power."

"The village manager's expecting me," she said, nodding toward the closed door across the hall.

"This is important," he said, taking her hand and drawing her into the room with him. He closed the door. "I'm sure she has enough plotting to do to keep herself busy until you show up."

The wood-paneled office was grander than Ziza expected, the oversized maps and rows of official portraits more intimidating. Even the sleeping bag bunched up at one end of the mammoth leather couch and the cookie jar of campaign buttons didn't make the place seem particularly casual. It was hard for her to imagine Monty working at that desk.

"I wanted to have some evidence before I talked to you about this." He took out an envelope printed with the familiar picture of the relentlessly happy family at the beach. "I just got these back from the developer. Take a look." The color snapshots he handed her didn't seem remarkable: pictures of Village Hall, the library, the traffic light at the corner of Main and Fulton, the Economy.

"So?" she said. From the look on his face she knew she'd missed something.

"The lower-left-hand corner," he said.

There were the same scratches Wasco had showed her on his pictures.

"More of Dennis Morland's work?"

"Mine. I took them yesterday with this." He pulled the camera from its place between the dictionary and the thesaurus. "Someone thoughtfully left this on my bookshelves. I suspected it was Dennis's. There aren't that many discs around and this one has an 'M' scratched on the back. See it? I remembered what you told me about Wasco identifying the marks that appeared on all the pictures. So I checked it out. Bingo!"

"But why would someone stash it here? You were bound to find it."

"Me or someone else, perhaps someone looking in an official capacity."

She ran her fingers along the back of the camera case, feeling the rough gouge of the "M." "You think some sort of frame-up is in the works?"

"That's one answer, and I can't think of any others."

"Who could have planted it?"

"I've compiled a list, and everyone you can think of's been here in the past week. Wasco's always coming in with something. Lillian Meservey brought by Professor van Runk for me to shout at. Whooten did another update of his dog-and-pony show on the art center. Bob Bramer was here making a half-assed speech about how even though he lost the election he wanted to be part of the Quarryville team. It was the same speech he made a month ago. Your guess why he was back. Maybe he wants to be appointed to something. Hell, even Adele was here. Before she died, of course."

"Of course." Ziza sensed that he regretted mentioning Adele as soon as he said her name.

He rushed on. "But the person I caught messing around my desk was Ray Rickert, and that was just before the camera turned up. He claimed he knew I was here and was just waiting for me, but I have my doubts. Watch out for that guy."

"I believe he once said the same about you."

"Yeah, right, covering his tail."

She handed the camera back to him and fished the Xerox copies out of her purse. "Now it's my turn for show-and-tell. I think I'm onto something, and maybe this evening on Ray's food run to the city I'll find out this guy's identity."

"From Ray?"

"Lord, no. He's the last one I want in on this. No, I think one of the homeless at Grand Central might know something."

"I'll come with you. Maybe I can run interference."

"No," she said, "oh, no," already afraid she'd said too much.

She was telling him about Barbi and Dave Spencer when the door opened and Lillian Meservey came into the room. Monty was still holding the camera and the snapshots. Ziza was staring closely at the fuzzy Xeroxed image of the corpse. She suspected they both looked guilty as hell.

"I thought I heard your voice in the hallway and was expecting a knock that never came," said Lillian Meservey.

"I'm afraid I waylaid your guest," Monty said.

"Going through the family photo album?" she asked. "Baby Monty on a bearskin rug, that sort of thing? Well, never mind that now. Come along, Ziza. This is not the right hour for tea, but perhaps I can provide a palatable cup of real home-ground coffee."

She swept Ziza out the door and across the hall into a pale pink room lined with matching oak filing cases and decorated with more chintz than Ziza had ever before seen in one place.

Coffee with Lillian Meservey turned out to be like an old-fashioned job interview, the kind in which neither an actual job nor a salary is ever mentioned. She had been asked about her schooling, her parents, her experiences at Childtown, her expectations of Quarryville.

"You're an accomplished runner, I believe," Lillian Meservey said.

"Well, I go 'to and fro on the earth,' " Ziza said. "Like Job."

"Book of Job," Lillian Meservey said. "But if you'd been raised a Southern Baptist you'd know it was Satan and not Job himself who was doing the 'to and fro.' "

"You're right," she said. Down one point for Ziza. "Bible study wasn't one of my strong points." To save face, she added, "The Revised English Bible translates Satan—in Job —as 'The Adversary.' "

"Southern Baptists," Lillian Meservey said, broadening her accent as she said it, "don't have much truck with these new-fangled versions of the Good Book."

Ziza laughed.

"I wouldn't continue running south of town, though," Lillian Meservey said. "Those ruins down there may look as picturesque as sin, but there've been muggings."

Ziza had lost track of the number of warnings she'd received since she arrived in Quarryville.

Lillian Meservey's office was not what its first impression suggested. There *was* chintz everywhere, chintz draperies, heaps of chintz pillows on a chintz slip-covered couch. But once you got used to it, it all had the worn look of an article in an out-of-date magazine for business and professional women. "Ten Ways to Make Your Power Office Feminine!" The chintz, the desk that wasn't really a desk but a cut-down round oak dining table, the pictures of nineteenth-century New York—elaborately framed—from old *Valentine's Annuals.* And it now looked a bit tired and threadbare. The real clues to what went on in this office, Ziza suspected, were all those filing cabinets, the piles of papers on the floor, the stacks of yellow legal pads filled with notes, the police radio in reach of the telephone. Here was someone who did her homework and kept on top of things.

"Did you see that sleeping bag over there?" Lillian Meservey asked. "In the mayor's office."

Ziza allowed as how she had.

"That just makes me sick. Sometimes he remembers to put it away, but more often than not, not. A week or so back a group of touring small-town Japanese mayors paid a courtesy call, unexpectedly. They were all as cute as a minute. No bigger than that. And each one of them had a little walkie-talkie he listened into to hear the interpreter explain everything. Well of course they met the mayor and saw the sleeping bag lying there and got all excited about the timesaving idea of living in the office. The State Department guide said it was all they wanted to talk about for the rest of the day. They asked every mayor they visited about sleeping arrangements, and of course everyone else had a home to go to. Our Monty was the hit of their trip."

"I hope you told him."

"We've really got to get that boy out of there and into a proper home. I don't suppose you have any influence on that matter?"

"I wouldn't think so," Ziza said.

"Work on it."

The coffee hadn't exactly been hand-ground, as promised, but it was ground on the spot in a screaming electric device that matched Lillian Meservey's miniature espresso machine. She kept them, and the tiny cups, behind a painted paper screen on her low windowsill. "A gift from the Japanese mayors," she said. "They said it depicted a foggy river scene." She ran her finger across the top of its polished wooden frame as though she were checking for dust. "It's not the sort of thing Monty would have much use for."

Ziza took a small sip and decided the coffee smelled a good deal better than it tasted.

"You seem to be taking a great interest in our local trag-edies," Lillian Meservey said.

"Dennis Morland would have been one of my kids."

"And you and Adele did seem to have hit it off nicely, I hear. Come to think of it, you also happened, by pure chance of course, to be with Officer Wasco when he turned up to investigate the John Doe in the book warehouse. I suppose there was no way you could have avoided getting involved in all this. Even if you hadn't wanted to."

Ziza held her coffee cup in front of her lips so she could inhale the aroma, but she kept quiet.

"I do think, though," Lillian Meservey went on, "that we have a cooks-and-broth situation developing. Since Chief Malfadi isn't here to keep an experienced guiding hand on the matter, I think too many people have felt all too free to get involved and help things along."

"I noticed you were giving Wasco a hand downstairs."

"But was not getting involved, not in the least. No, we don't want this broth spoiled, do we?"

The long silence made Ziza realize this was not a rhetorical question. Lillian Meservey wanted an answer.

"I'm sure all the pieces will come together," she finally said, "no matter what."

"No matter what," Lillian Meservey repeated slowly, as though Ziza had said something that was actually quite revealing.

15

The front seat of the Moonlight Rounds van was not nearly as crowded as it had been on the last trip. Lillian Meservey had insisted on sitting in the middle. "Ziza and I are just wee bits of things," she said, "and Ray, well, he has no hips at all."

Her tone, Ziza thought, was definitely flirtatious.

"Buckle up," Ray Rickert said. He seemed to be trying to sound like a stern father taking the family on a Sunday drive, but he was clearly delighted to have the village manager in tow. "There are enough belts for all."

"Seat belts, of course," Lillian Meservey said. "It's the law and you don't want lawbreakers in a church van, do you?" She was definitely flirting.

Maybe, Ziza thought, "delighted" wasn't the right word for Rickert's mood. "Pleased," perhaps, "curious" about why on earth Lillian had turned up at the last minute. Maybe "wary" was the word.

Ziza herself suspected Lillian of listening outside the door when she and Monty were talking in his office that morning.

"Boy, girl, girl," Lillian Meservey said. Two other volunteers, a husband and wife who didn't even live in Quarryville, had the whole back of the van to themselves.

Even though the evening wasn't cool enough to need it, Ray was wearing a brand-new—almost painfully new with the stitching around the torn-off paper labels still visible—Levi jacket. He had found it on his desk that afternoon when he came back from lunch, and neither he nor Ziza made any mention of it. If Lillian Meservey had meant to be vaguely threatening over coffee in her office that morning there was no hint of it now. She was full of good humor, offers of mints and chewing gum to her fellow passengers, and knowledge-able questions about what had been happening with the food program since her last trip almost a year ago.

"Who are you getting for volunteers these days, Ray?" she asked.

"Oh," Ray said, "I have my regulars, mostly a lot of retired couples who don't have to worry about getting to work the next day, a pretty steady supply of high school seniors, some juniors, looking for late nights and adventure. We're getting into mid-terms, now, so there are none of them this evening. And then there are surprises. You tonight, Lillian. We've had Ziza twice in a row. Even Bob Bramer was along on Tuesday."

Lillian Meservey laughed. "Good old Bob, reliable and durable." Ray joined in the laughter, although a bit guardedly, as though he didn't want the people in the back to think he might be making fun of his volunteers. The engine noise was so loud, Ziza was sure they couldn't hear a thing.

"I don't quite get Bob Bramer," she said. "Lillian calls him 'reliable and durable.' He seems the salt of the earth to me, the kind of guy you need to get anything done in a town like Quarryville. Yet he loses all the elections he runs in. Frankly, no offense and all that, how did an oddball like Monty beat him?"

"It wasn't too hard," Lillian said. "Bramer's too Hillside for anyone in Riverside to vote for. Riverside's used to choos-ing its own."

"But surely Hillside could outvote them."

"Only if it were truly motivated," Rickert said. "Demographics indicate—"

"Forget demographics," Lillian Meservey said. "Bramer has committeeman written all over him and that's all. One look tells you that. Besides, there's his wife, pretty as she is, poor thing, and that just about killed the vote."

"Her Christmas caroling," said Ray. "The sure sign of a fashionable disbeliever around here is regular attendance at Heavenly Roger's monthly hymn sings and turning out all teary-eyed with Christmas spirit to go caroling with the Bramers on the night before Christmas Eve."

" 'Disbeliever' is kind of strong," said Ziza.

"No, it isn't," said Ray. "I could've said 'heathen.' Christmas caroling is *the* big December social event in Hillside, and Mrs. Bramer is in charge of it."

"Or so she thinks," Lillian Meservey said. "Everyone else knows it would happen with or without her. Everyone— everyone invited—meets at the Bramers' and the group wanders around Hillside for an hour or so singing for old folks or shut-ins or anyone who leaves a light on. And then there's the party afterwards. Mrs. Bramer makes an elaborate to-do over who gets invited but never seems to notice that most of the people at the party never make the rounds with the carolers anyway.

"Of course, the real joke is that everyone who does carol is laughing themselves silly. Mrs. B. once took singing classes somewhere terribly genteel and does fancy, little descants and trills on all the carols. *Bel Canto* as all get out, while Bob stands to one side, holding a high-powered flashlight on her so everyone can see."

"That's why he loses elections," Ray Rickert said. "Not because his wife's a horse's ass, but because he stands there every year with that flashlight and never realizes she's making a fool of herself."

"Maybe he's in love," Ziza said.

"Realized it enough to strike up a nice little friendship with Adele Baraclough that was," Lillian Meservey said as though she were speaking to no one but herself.

"And that's how Monty became mayor?" Ziza asked.

"That and because no one respectable wanted it," Lillian Meservey said.

"Small-town politics." Ziza sighed.

"Makes a lot of sense to me," Ray said.

They had turned off the West Side Highway and were driving across Fifty-seventh Street to their first stop at the subway station. Ziza went down the stairs as she had on Tuesday, but this time she didn't have to announce herself. As soon as she came into sight, someone shouted, "Moonlight Rounds!" People started heading for the exit, and the man —she almost thought of him as her old friend—in the clear plastic poncho told her they were on time for once. "Westchester should bring you every time, little lady."

The routine was the same. There were lunches in paper bags, soap, warm sweaters, clothes for anyone who needed them. The men got in line and asked for what they wanted. A few late-night tourists stood back and watched. Someone snapped a picture with a flash camera, a souvenir of the Big Apple. Ziza didn't see Andy anywhere, the guy Ray gave his belt to for the job interview, and she asked a few of the men she recognized if they knew where he was. No one knew anything. No one even recognized the name.

Back in the van, on the way to the park opposite the United Nations, Ray spoke with barely contained rage. "Don't *ever* do that again, Ziza, *ever*. I know you're new. I know you don't know. But don't *ever* ask for someone. Don't sound like you're checking up on someone. And, damn it, don't *ever* use a name of someone you're not speaking to directly. Got it?"

"She didn't know," Lillian said. "Don't be too hard on the child."

Ziza didn't think much of that defense.

"It's common sense," Ray said. "We're here to help, not ask questions. We can't be using names and scaring them off."

"Look," Ziza said. "I'll watch it. Sorry."

"Fine," Ray said.

The same old tired bunch was waiting in the shadows of the park. The almost stunned silence of these men as they took their food bags and shuffled back to their benches depressed Ziza even more this time. There were no requests for any extras. No one, even when asked, wanted soap or a fresh razor. Then the Moonlight Rounds headed two blocks back across town to Grand Central. Ziza checked her pocket. The Xerox copies were there, just as they had been when she looked a few minutes before. She prayed that Barbi would remember to show up. She knew, now, that it would be impossible to ask for her.

The small crowd waiting at the corner of Lexington Avenue had an almost party-time informality about it. Ziza realized they were the true *bon vivants* of the circuit, the Midtown sophisticates. They didn't bother forming lines, but a steady stream of men—and even a few women—broke away from the group and ambled over to the van for their lunch bags. They knew what was being offered, and they knew what they wanted.

Ray dealt with men's clothing, while the retired couple took care of the food. Ziza passed out supplies from the hygiene boxes, and Lillian Meservey was on the other side of the van presiding over what she called the Women's Wear Department. Ziza couldn't see her but from time to time she could hear her voice, and it sounded as though for the first time since they arrived in the city she was enjoying herself.

Ziza was kept busy. Word had gone around that they had a fresh supply of washcloths—donated seconds from a North Carolina textile company Ray kept in touch with—which were normally pretty hard to come by. Barbi had not been in the small crowd that was on the corner when the van arrived, but Ziza thought she had seen—briefly—the heavy block lettering of TAFT on a sweatshirt of someone leaning against a building on the other side of the street. When she looked again, the person was gone. She hadn't gotten a good-enough look to tell who was wearing it. She couldn't even have sworn that she saw it at all.

Then she heard Lillian Meservey's voice: "But it *is* a good school. I had a nephew there, and his mother always said that if you couldn't get into the best schools, it was the best school to get into."

"I don't know," the woman's voice said. Barbi's, Ziza was sure of it. "It just doesn't keep me very warm. Last year I had a Brearley sweatshirt, a nice thick one that really did the job. I didn't realize it at first, but this is really pretty skimpy. Just feel the elbow. I'll be through that in no time."

"Oh, my dear, you're right. It is shoddy goods, maybe one of those Italian rip-offs. You know, all over Rome you can buy sweatshirts for just about any American school you can think of. But sad to say they aren't authentic. Did you check the label? The manufacturer's label?"

"Afraid not."

"Let me."

When Ziza came around the side of the van, she saw Lillian Meservey peering down the back of Barbi's neck. "Hi, ya," Barbi said, "the lady, here, thinks I may have counterfeit sportswear."

"Indeed you do," Lillian Meservey said, patting the sweatshirt back into place.

"I got it here."

"Oh, my," said Lillian Meservey.

"Usually," Barbi said, not wanting to hurt any feelings, "the quality of your merchandise is the very best."

"Maybe I can help," Ziza said. "Lillian, why don't you take the soap and washcloths for a while—it'll be a nice change

—and I'll see what I can find for . . ." She almost said her name.

Lillian Meservey looked as though she suspected she was being sent off to do a more unpleasant job, but she said, " '*Ich dien.*' That's what's on the Prince of Wales's coat of arms; 'I serve'." And she went.

"I'm glad you were able to make it, Barbi. I brought a picture for you to look at."

"I really do need a better sweatshirt."

"We'll find one, but I have this picture. Maybe it's that man you asked me about, Dave Spencer."

Barbi continued looking through the pile of women's sweaters, and Ziza unfolded the fuzzy Xerox print. She looked around. No one seemed to be paying any attention. Both Ray and Lillian Meservey were out of sight. She handed it to Barbi.

"He's not sleeping," Barbi said.

"I'm sorry, I should have warned you."

"Why should a picture of a dead stranger shock me?"

"It's not Dave Spencer?"

"Who?"

"The man you said got curious about Quarryville because of the Moonlight Rounds and went up to check the place out?"

"Yes?" She looked at the picture again, but didn't spend much time on it.

"You said his name was Dave Spencer and you asked me if I knew him."

"This is a stranger, and a dead one at that," she said, handing the paper back to Ziza. "I'm going to look through the men's stuff on the other side. Maybe there's a nice sweatshirt there."

It was about time to move on to the next stop. Grand Central's allotment of lunches had been passed out and it seemed as though everyone had what he needed. Just as Ziza had packed away the last of the women's things, Barbi came back around the side of the van, carrying what looked like a German flag.

"Look," she said, "isn't it a beauty?" and held up an extra-large rugby shirt with broad red, yellow and black stripes.

"Won't be any warmer than what you have," Ziza said.

"I'll wear it over what I have. That's how you get your warmth, layering. Warmth without weight. It's very popular." She slipped it over her head. The shirt came down to her knees and the deep neckline revealed the top of the lettering on TAFT, but when she rolled up the sleeves and cocked her head waiting for Ziza's reaction, she looked downright trendy. Ziza realized that Barbi was a lot younger than she seemed.

"Do you have an extra copy of the picture?" she asked.

"I thought he was a stranger?"

"Well, maybe he's a nice stranger."

"Maybe he isn't a stranger at all?"

"Maybe. Can I have it?"

Ziza handed it over. She lowered her voice. The others were getting back into the van. "It is Dave Spencer, isn't it?"

"How can you ever tell what their names really are?" Barbi said. "You think I'm really Barbi?" She laughed and then ducked through the traffic on Lexington, heading back to Grand Central before it closed for the night.

Ziza climbed into the rear of the van. She didn't feel like squeezing into the front with the others.

As they headed downtown toward Seward Park, Ray Rickert asked, "Did I see you giving that woman something, Ziza?"

"The address sheet for the AIDS and birth control clinics," she said.

"You keep a supply of them in your pocket?"

"Sure," she said.

"Good thinking," he said.

She looked up. Two pairs of eyes were looking back at her through the wide rearview mirror.

16

&

"They hate those baseball caps," Whooten said.

"What's wrong with them?" asked Fogle.

"Nothing's *wrong* with them. *Per se.* It's just that's the only thing they wear that says EPA . . ."

"Environmental Protection Agency."

"The FBI has those windbreakers with 'FBI' written on the back in huge letters."

"So they don't shoot each other."

"Whatever. But when there's a big drug bust or something . . ."

"With lots of guns and cameras around."

". . . they wear them and everyone knows immediately they're the FBI. Who reads baseball caps? That's what one of the supervisors asked me. I was standing right in front of him and I could barely read the thing. I told them they should hire a consultant to redesign their logo. At the very least."

"And you gave him your card?"

"Of course not. Field supervisors don't hire consultants. I may write a letter to Washington, however."

They were standing in front of the Baraclough foundry on the riverfront, watching two men wearing plaid Pendleton shirts, wide-wale corduroys, and baseball caps who were watching six people marking out the property in a grid pattern with chalk lines. The workers' baggy white jumpsuits and breathing masks made it difficult to guess their sex for sure, but they moved like women.

On the backs of the dazzling white jumpsuits the words "Terra-Tech" were spelled out in blood-red letters. Two matching red vans marked "Terra-Tech: Making Ecology Work" were parked inside the open gate next to the EPA's gray motor-pool Chevy.

"When I asked you to talk up the eco-nerds," Fogle said, "I wasn't after fashion news."

"I'm simply making a thorough report of our conversation," Whooten said. "They bitched about their cheap hats as an example of misplaced governmental economy. Meanwhile, the agency pays fortunes to subcontractors who wear snazzy uniforms, drive expensive vans, and buy up every trendy safety device they can think of, like those Japanese breathing filters. They replace them every four hours. Eighteen dollars a pop. Your tax dollars at work."

"I think they're *all* women," Fogle said, "those Terra-Tech people."

"You'd be thinking right. The Feds mentioned that women are making the big bucks in the environment game. A growth industry for girls."

"Probably a step up from dog grooming," Fogle said. "It doesn't sound as though you've learned anything useful."

"Just what we know already. They insist that this all is indeed random and that we haven't been targeted."

"But the site was."

"The foundry is on a list of seventy thousand—or maybe it's 700,000—possible problem locations. They can't keep track of them all. Usually—'traditionally' was the word they used—these things go through a chain of command. First the county gets a chance to check the site out, then if there's a problem the state supposedly takes a look, maybe somewhere down the line the Feds get involved."

"And we were just lucky."

"They've started having random, out-of-the-blue Fed investigations of construction requests for sites on the list. It's a way—they swear—of checking up on whether the locals are doing their jobs. Anyway, when we applied for a building permit something went blip on someone's screen and we became one of their random investigations."

The women in white got out their clipboards and little plastic bags, and the men in baseball caps sauntered with exaggerated casualness over to join them, walking across the grid and making no attempt to avoid stepping on chalk lines. There seemed to be a moment of confrontation, after which the EPA men agreed to put on the breathing masks offered by the women.

What followed was laborious. A grid square was chosen and notations were made on the clipboards. Soil samples were taken from the center of the square with a little silver shovel and deposited into two individual, numbered plastic bags, one of which a Terra-Tech employee put in her plastic tray (red), the other placed in a tray (olive drab) carried by the junior EPA man. The shovel was carefully wiped off with a fresh lint-free cloth and the group moved on to another square, where the whole process was repeated.

It could have been an exotic religious ceremony, with its special costumes and paraphernalia, the bobbing heads, the genuflections, the long train of attendants, the silence broken occasionally by mumbled numbers, a litany caught in the river breeze. With repetition, it became familiar, more of a dance, a slow and stately pavane.

Whooten and Fogle watched, entranced.

"This your idea of a day at the beach?" a voice behind them said. Whooten stiffened in terror. For one horrible moment he thought it was Adele. "Watching the girls play with their buckets and shovels?" It was Lillian Meservey, of course. "I warned you boys that you were about to fuck up and fuck up good, and now you've gone and done it." She had parked her Cherokee behind their BMW on River Road and walked over without them seeing her.

"It's a random check," Fogle said, "purely routine."

"My foot," said Lillian Meservey. "You've grabbed on to the dirty end of the stick, and now I'm going to have to deal with it."

"It has nothing to do with you," Fogle said.

"Who do you think solves problems in this town?" she asked. "Not the boy-wonder mayor. Certainly not the people who cause the problems in the first place. If you listened to me, none of this would be happening."

"If we listened to you," Whooten said, "we'd be taking meetings with lawyers for the rest of our lives."

The women in jumpsuits had separated into two groups, each with its own EPA observer in tow. One group took the silver shovel and went inside the foundry building. The other was now getting what looked like an upright vacuum cleaner out of one of the vans.

"I warned you," Lillian Meservey said, "that messing around this foundry was going to raise a stink."

"You told us," Fogle said, "to turn our attention to the buildings on the north end of the waterfront. Buy up options, you said. Make a bundle in real estate for the Baraclough Trust."

"You said to turn my foundry into a fenced-off dollhouse," Whooten said.

"We did some investigating," Fogle said.

"We're not without resources," Whooten said.

"A few discreet inquiries here and there," Fogle said.

"But not too discreet."

"And it became clear," Fogle said, "that you were trying to set us up for a bout with the tar baby."

"Leading us down the garden path," said Whooten.

"Without a paddle," Fogle added.

"I'm afraid I haven't the slightest idea of what you're going on about," Lillian Meservey said.

"The Wittmeir Parcel," Whooten said, pronouncing it as though it were a secret password.

The women at the van were bolting a three-foot-long bit onto the end of what had looked like a vacuum cleaner so that the gadget now resembled a mechanized post-hole driller.

"Sounds like a matter best taken care of by UPS," Lillian Meservey said, "the Wittmeir Parcel."

"I think you know full well what it is," Fogle said.

"Especially since you're the town problem-solver," said Whooten.

"Perhaps you can refresh my memory," she said.

"The Wittmeir Parcel's all the land north of the Baraclough property on the waterfront," Fogle said, "and it's a legal mare's nest."

"Been in the courts for the last twenty-five years," Whooten said.

"The Wittmeir family has more branches than you can shake a stick at," Fogle said, "and each one of them insists it's the sole owner. Then there's the options that various Wittmeir's sold off over the years. Throw them in, and you get enough claims to that property to support half the American Bar Association."

"That's the tar baby you were setting up for us when you lured us to the book warehouse that Sunday morning," Whooten said.

"*Lured?*" Lillian Meservey laughed.

"There's always a Wittmeir somewhere willing to sell an option. They're notorious."

"A bad joke in the upscale real estate community."

"So, if we followed your advice we would've abandoned work on the foundry, got hopelessly in bed with one Wittmeir or another, and nothing would've been done," Fogle said. "What's your game?"

The Terra-Tech women began drilling a hole in the square on the northwest corner of the grid.

"You misconstrue," Lillian Meservey said. She sounded deeply offended. "You misconstrue me utterly. What I was doing in my own, I'm afraid, inept way, was trying to save you from the horrors now unfolding before your very eyes. Perhaps I went about it the wrong way. But I guess if you make a thousand decisions a day one or two of them have to be wrong."

The Terra-Tech women finished drilling and, using something that looked like an extra-long turkey baster, took two soil samples, bagged them, and moved off to the northeast corner, their EPA observer trailing along behind.

"This is just the beginning, you know," Lillian Meservey said. "Right now it's all pretty much a matter of their picking up dust and lint, surface samples, samples three feet down. Next thing you know they'll have the big drills in here, scooping out deeper soil samples and then going down for groundwater. I suppose you could look on the bright side and pray they hit oil, but I warn you, just like I warned you before, and just like I once warned Adele, they're going to hit trouble. And it's trouble you could have avoided."

She bent down so she could look directly into Whooten's eyes and then pulled herself erect to fix Fogle with a long look that seemed intended to cause harm.

"Now it's begun," she said, "the milk's spilt, the cat's out of the bag, the can of worms is . . . ," but instead of finishing the sentence she turned and headed back for her car.

Whooten and Fogle watched her go. She slammed the door of her Cherokee, pulled around their BMW, cutting it dangerously close, and sped down River Road toward Village Hall.

She didn't notice Miss Gatewood coming around the corner on one of her endless walks through town, but Whooten and Fogle saw the old woman as she stopped and watched the Jeep disappear from sight and as she turned to look first at their car and then, across the chalk grid, at them.

17

Ziza tried to ignore Wasco's French fry technique, but she had never seen anything quite like it before. He had asked for a plate of brown gravy with a side order of fries, a request the waitress at the Economy didn't seem to think at all unusual. Then, dealing with them methodically, one at a time, he carefully forked a fry into the middle of the brown puddle, paused a moment, turned it over so both sides were fully soaked, and then popped it into his mouth. After every fry, he patted his lips with a folded paper napkin he kept in his left hand, a social nicety observed—Ziza suspected—because he was with a lady. She stuck with coffee and was on her second cup.

Ziza had been in no rush to report back to Wasco. She was excited about learning who John Doe really was—assuming, of course, that Barbi's cryptic identification was worth taking seriously—but she didn't look forward to hearing more about Adele as a suicidal murderer.

That morning, though, instead of running north along the Aqueduct as she always did, she headed south, as she had done on her first morning in Quarryville, running behind the condos and through the woods to the overgrown and defaced nineteenth-century Roman ruins in Yonkers. Perhaps because she was no longer a stranger in the neighborhood, the run hadn't seemed as sinister this time. The woods did not conjure up thoughts of Little Red Riding Hood's wolf or even of more contemporary muggers. The ruins themselves now seemed to be gimcrack affairs, obviously made of poured concrete. The rusting Dodge Dart crashed into the back of the playhouse-sized temple simply looked like so much misplaced urban litter. The spray-paint River Rats graffiti just seemed tired and familiar.

On the way back toward home she saw something that clicked in her mind. She had just passed behind the high-rise condos and was thinking about rent—do people on the river side of the building pay more than those who overlook the Aqueduct?—and was passing through a scruffy growth of sumac and aspen near the Quarryville line when it happened. She knew, she was sure of it: this was the place the photograph had been taken, the photograph of her on the film Adele had with her when she died. She doubled back, turned and headed north again. It was the spot.

She stopped and pushed her way through the undergrowth on the river side of the path. Beyond the hedgerow was a well-used dirt road running parallel to the Aqueduct. It had the trashed-up look of a road leading to a dump. Why is it, Ziza wondered, that people bothered hauling stuff all the way to a dump and then at the last minute, just before getting there, left it along the road? There were rain-soaked carpets, bald tires, broken cases of empty beer cans, and a doorless refrigerator, the door lying a few yards away.

Someone on that road, either on foot or in a car, had taken her picture. Why?

Before she went home she detoured to a pay phone near the Star, called Wasco, told him she had some information for him and asked to meet at the Economy. And, oh, yes, she asked, could he bring along those pictures he'd developed?

She picked the Economy, the most public spot in town,

because she hoped it would put a crimp in his desire to make all kinds of wild charges about Adele. They sat in the rear booth—Wasco in uniform, Ziza dressed for the office—enjoying a mid-morning break. Now, Ziza wondered how long it would take for Marge to hear about it up at the church. And how long it would take Marge to mention it to Ray Rickert.

Ziza began, without ever using Barbi's name, by telling him what she had learned on the two trips to the city, about the homeless man who had come up to Quarryville and was never seen again, about how her "informant" tentatively identified the Xerox copy of the corpse's snapshot as him.

Wasco pushed aside his plates. The French fries were gone. A good deal of the gravy remained. "You must think I have some manners," he said. "I never offered you one, sorry." Ziza shook her head in a way that meant "think nothing of it." "It's what we'd always have after school in the old days. A bunch of us would order a plate. Try it some time. It's better than the coffee."

"I'll bet it is," she said.

He fished a small pad and a felt-tipped pen out of his left breast pocket. "David Spencer, you said. You suppose that's with a 'c' or an 's'?"

"Got me. I don't suppose anyone's written it down recently. And she called him 'Dave' not 'David.' "

"She?"

"My informant."

"A woman?"

"Of course."

"What kind of a woman would live in Grand Central?"

"A homeless one."

"She was probably sleeping with him."

"I have no idea."

"They all sleep with each other. There was a story about it in the *Daily News*. AIDS all over the place."

"All I know is that she said his name was Dave Spencer and that he came to Quarryville."

"Why?"

"Ray Rickert's Moonlight Run made him curious about the place, she said."

"Probably came up to case us out."

"That's what I said. Joking. She got very indignant."

"Big deal. Name?"

"Like I said, Dave Spencer."

"Hers."

"I can't tell you that."

"Withholding information from an investigating officer is a crime." He said it in the singsong voice he probably used when he read prisoners their rights.

"*I'm* the investigating officer," Ziza said. "Look, if I give you her name, cops will turn up looking for her and no one will ever find her again. Let's just keep this informal and off-the-record. Maybe we'll need her later."

"Well, okay, for now."

"For now."

"You wanted to see his picture again? You asked me to bring the snapshots."

"Actually, I wanted to see my picture again. Number thirteen, I think it was, on the disc you found with Adele."

He fanned through the pack. "You're right."

The aspen trees, the sumac, the steep hillside in the background. She was running north toward Quarryville. The picture was taken where she suspected.

"I've an idea," Ziza said, hoping it sounded as though it had just come to her. "Why don't we use these to find all the places Dennis Morland visited just before he was killed?"

"It's the waterfront. You can tell that by looking at them."

"But by retracing his steps, we might learn something. You know, detective work? You've kept the pictures a secret, right? That may raise some eyebrows, but when you turn them over to Chief . . ." She had forgotten his name.

"Malfadi. He's due back tomorrow."

"Chief Malfadi. When you turn them over to him, it won't do you any harm being able to pinpoint all the locations."

He tapped his teeth with the edge of the snapshots, considered his options and said, "You're on."

They began on the north end of the waterfront. Ziza carried the pictures. Wasco had a stenographer's notebook and was making a rough map, sketching in the buildings as they walked along. He'd already told her, twice, that he was going to redraw it neatly on unlined paper when he got back to headquarters, with the number of each photograph located and circled in red. It would be a real professional job.

"I used to know this place like the back of my hand," he said. "In the old days it was *the* major hangout, next to the Meadow."

Ziza noticed that when Wasco said "old days" he always meant "high school."

"Now, take these first couple of pictures. They were all shot in the same large room. Ceilings as tall as the building. Skylights. The works. I figure it has to be the place we called the Dance Hall."

He led her down the central street and stopped in front of an aluminum-colored building that looked like an abandoned airplane hangar. "Watch your step," he said as he pulled aside the already-broken door so she could get in without any trouble. "*Voilà!* The Dance Hall."

Ziza felt vaguely like a lady tourist being shown the ruins by a high-priced private guide. She didn't have to check the pictures to know that this was the place.

"I think you should draw the floor plan," she said, "put numbers where Dennis was standing when he took the shots and then draw arrows showing which direction the camera was pointed."

"Very professional," Wasco said.

Ziza wished she could have taken Dennis's camera from Monty's office so they could look through the view-finder to see exactly what Dennis saw. But that would have given Wasco too much information to play with. The two of them lined up snapshots with their subjects in the giant, sooty room with its scummy lake-sized rain puddle in the middle of the floor. Then they left the building and moved on down the center road. Luckily, Wasco said, Dennis had not been very adventurous. The buildings he entered and photographed were always obvious choices. Access was always easy. Yet, Ziza thought, being there alone—was he in fact alone?—with, perhaps, night coming on, the old, creepy buildings must have seemed threatening and scary. At least he didn't know death would come before he ran out of film.

"What's with the River Rats?" Ziza asked. Their graffiti was everywhere.

"All I know," Wasco said, "is that I've never seen one face-to-face."

"Like bogeymen?"

"But I *have* seen bogeymen. I arrest a couple of them a month."

Ziza laughed. Wasco told a joke, she thought.

Dennis had taken picture number nine on his second disc, the last one before the three dark ones, just before they came to the Baraclough foundry.

"Logically," Ziza said, facing the high-peaked brick building, "there's our last stop. Pictures ten, eleven and twelve."

The old place was almost crowded. Two red vans were parked along the fence and crews of hooded people in white jumpsuits were scurrying around, dragging about all sorts of curious equipment, writing away on clipboards. At the center of activity, in front of the foundry's open, Gothic door, standing perfectly still, were Fogle and Whooten.

"Now our morning's complete," Fogle said loud enough

for Ziza and Wasco to hear, "a uniformed officer of the law. Who said you could never find a cop when you need one?"

"And the Reverend Todd," Whooten said. "Always a sight for sore eyes."

"Church and State together. Welcome, indeed," Fogle said. "You're here in time to see your federal government at work."

"What's going on?" Wasco asked, in his official voice.

Fogle told him. "Lillian Meservey is fully up to speed on the whole matter," he added.

"That's good," Wasco said.

"We're just looking around," Ziza said.

"Are those photographs you have there?" Whooten asked. "Pictures of anyone we know?" He reached out and turned her hand so he could see what she had. The top picture was number ten, the first of the dark shots. "Not much of a photographer, I'd say. Not enough natural light. Which of you is the shutterbug?"

"Could we look inside?" Ziza asked, ignoring the question. "This looks like about the most interesting building down here. I remember," she said to Whooten, "the model you had at the Open House."

"Before someone trampled it," Whooten said.

"Before the demise," Wasco said, and walked into the dark building without waiting for permission. Ziza followed.

People in white jumpsuits were drilling small holes in the floor and raising tiny whirlpools of dust. Ventilation was poor, and the smell of wood smoke and urine seemed trapped by the dust in the air. Most of the light in the room came slanting down from the round windows high in the metal rafters. It was like being in a desecrated church.

Ziza didn't have to compare what she saw to the pictures she held tightly in her hand. She remembered the circles of light and the lines that cut across them. Here was where Dennis had taken his last three photographs.

They went back outside.

"I guess that's it," Wasco said as they headed back to his police car. "I want you to know I appreciate the way you protected the evidence back there. I couldn't believe it when that midget tried to grab the pictures out of your hand. Nice save."

"Thanks," she said, "but there's still one photo location we haven't positively identified. We have everything on the first disc, the first twelve on the second. We know the last two were shot in the book warehouse. But lucky thirteen? The picture of me?"

"The Aqueduct."

"But where?"

"You run the thing, you must have some idea of where on the Aqueduct you were."

"That's just it, I think I know exactly and want your opinion."

"My input." He seemed to like the idea. "Why not?"

Ziza described the dirt road, and Wasco knew how to get there. It was the way to the old dump, one of the abandoned marble quarries, actually, that the town had managed to fill up with its refuse.

"It has to sit awhile, settle or something," Wasco said. "Some law about old dumps. There's some law for everything nowadays. But after it sits and settles they're going to turn it into a park. Little League's been trying to grab it, but they won't get it. Not enough kids play Little League ball anymore. It's going the way of the Scouts."

They were almost to the Yonkers city line when Wasco made a sharp left, drove easily around a padlocked chain across a dirt road, shifted down to first and headed steeply uphill away from the river. When they got to the level of the Aqueduct, the road made another sharp right, and Wasco slowed down. "From what you said, it should be along here."

"Stop," Ziza said. "I think we're there."

They got out of the car. Ziza examined picture number thirteen and showed it to Wasco without saying anything.

"Yep. I'll mark this one on a town map for the Chief."

"But why?" Ziza asked. "Why would anyone be here waiting for me? It was my first day in town. No one knew I'd be coming along here. Even I didn't know."

They walked farther along, through the scattered trash. The road made another turn toward the river and the dump was in front of them.

"Seems kind of small," Ziza said. The sagging mound of debris formed almost a perfect circle that at first glance looked like a giant pop-art collage from the early sixties, a mass of weathered and rotting packaging broken up with rusted-out barbecue grills, bedsprings, wheelless lawn mowers, antiquated TV sets, an aluminum canoe bent into a horseshoe shape.

"It's deep. You can't tell now that it's up to ground level, but the thing's very deep. We used to bring our twenty-twos down here and plug away at rats." He picked up a bent beer can and threw it out into the center of the heap.

"A peg to second?" she asked.

"More like to the pitcher," he said. "People are still dumping stuff. Most of this crap on top's been left here since the place closed."

"Maybe that's why the photographer was here. Maybe he was dumping something."

"She. Adele. Maybe Adele was dumping something. Maybe she brought the kid's body and then had second thoughts."

"And took a picture of me instead?"

"Something like that." He threw another can. This one might have reached second base.

"Maybe," Ziza said, "he—or she—was throwing something else away. Something of Dennis's, maybe. Couldn't bear to toss the camera. Was messing around with it. Looking at it.

Realized there was film in it. Happened to see me going by
on the Aqueduct and, on a whim, took my picture."

"Awful lot of whim there. A lot of maybes."

Ziza couldn't disagree with him. "Whatever was thrown in
probably wasn't thrown far," she said. "Assuming. Anyway,
since we're here, why don't we just walk around the edge of
the dump and see if anything catches our eye."

"Since we're here." Wasco laughed and started walking in
a clockwise direction around the dump. Ziza fell in step behind him. "Why don't you head the other way?" he said
without looking back. "We'll do it in half the time."

"No," Ziza said, "two heads are better than one."

"My guess is that you're afraid of rats."

"Four eyes are better than two," Ziza said, keeping in step.

They walked along in silence. Ziza was glad to see that
Wasco was not rushing. He was seriously looking.

"In the old days I remember you could find good stuff at
this dump," Wasco said after about ten minutes. "Now it's
all junk."

"Maybe you're just getting old."

"No, it's junk."

Ziza agreed. It all seemed pretty hopeless. The bent canoe
was clearly the best thing the place had to offer. Then she
saw the flash of blue. "Over there," she said.

"The blue," he said.

"Can you reach out and get it?"

"It's closer to you."

"Your arms are longer."

"Admit that you're afraid to step out onto the dump," he
said.

"I'll admit that I don't want to step out onto the dump,"
she said.

"Afraid?"

"I'm not wearing my dump-walking shoes."

"And I am?"

"You're a cop."

"You're a girl."

"Oh, for Christ's sake," Ziza said and stepped out onto the pile. It moved underneath her feet. She tottered and spread her arms like a tightrope walker. Wasco moved past her, grabbed the patch of bright, Gore-Tex blue and hopped back to solid land. Ziza almost lost her balance, but didn't and jumped back without falling.

"Just wanted to see if you'd take the first step," Wasco said.

"I hope you'll put into your report that I did."

He handed her the small blue knapsack. "Finders, keepers," he said. It was heavy with books and had a dark stain on the back.

Ziza unbuckled the straps. Inside were Volume One of Morison and Commager's *The Growth of the American Republic,* a brand-new paperback copy of Ben Franklin's autobiography, a thick physics textbook, and several notebooks.

"Junior year's when you take all those American subjects, isn't it?" she asked.

"I think, maybe," Wasco said.

The first notebook was just a list of dates in U.S. history. Intolerable Acts. Abominable Acts. Era of Good Feeling.

The second notebook had the name "Dennis Morland" written in a thick Magic Marker across the cover.

Wasco picked up the book of dates. "He had a lot better handwriting than me, that's for sure."

18

🍃

H. Roger Swain hung up the telephone. "You're wanted by the police," he said. He didn't look at anyone in particular, but they all knew he was talking to Ziza.

They were sitting in the minister's study at the First Presbyterian Church, just as they had on Ziza's first Saturday in town. Heavenly Roger was behind his desk. She was sitting in the wing chair next to the imitation fireplace. On the couch were Dale DeSousa and—instead of Bob Bramer—a thoroughly bored Ray Rickert. He had looked at his watch when he came through the door, late. Looked at it again when he sat down and had checked it at five-minute intervals ever since.

"I'm afraid that's typical of the problems we seem to be having," H. Roger said.

"I think 'problems' is far too strong a word," said Dale DeSousa.

"Dale," H. Roger said, "they *are* problems. You keep mentioning some sort of 'shakedown period' when 'things fall into place.' Well, I'm talking about problems and a director of religious education who spends more time riding around in police cars with public officials than she does caring for the children she was hired to minister unto."

"She's sitting right here, you know," Ziza said. "Maybe you could address your concerns directly to her."

"That tone is not in the least helpful," H. Roger said. "You know exactly what I'm talking about."

"I know," Ziza said, "that I've been put into a situation in which I'm supposed to spend a month quote 'getting organized' unquote before consolidation of the Sunday schools goes into effect. That means I've been spending these weeks reading reports (which will be very helpful, I'm sure), memorizing Roger's Standard Operating Procedure, and checking to make sure there are going to be enough chairs and tables. My big contribution yesterday was discovering we were almost out of toilet paper."

"Ziza's selling herself short," Dale DeSousa said. "I know for a fact that she's getting to know the young people. She's been active in Ray's food distribution program. She's been very good about dropping by my Sunday school and youth fellowship. I'm sure she's spent time at your church, Roger."

"What's your total kids' enrollment now?" Ray asked, although everyone there knew he knew. "Fifteen, sixteen?"

"In two weeks, when the unified program goes into effect, we'll make our contribution," Dale DeSousa said.

"My worry," H. Roger said, "is that Ziza may not be getting her priorities straight. Every time I see her head-to-head with the mayor . . . there's been talk, you know, about far too much intimacy in that quarter."

"Monty and me?" Ziza said. "That's absurd."

"The very thought of the two of them . . . ," H. Roger began.

"Was that telephone call something for her?" Ziza interrupted. "If it was, I'm sure she'd appreciate hearing more about it."

"Office of the Chief of Police," H. Roger said, as though such things were painful to repeat. "The Chief would appreciate your coming by as soon as possible to discuss something about evidence and Grand Central Station."

"Thank you," Ziza said, "for holding my messages."

"I'll give you a ride," Ray Rickert said.

"Actually," H. Roger said, "I was hoping the three of us could have a little talk after Ziza left."

"I'm due at an AIDS hospice up at Bedford," Ray said. "I'll just drop Ziza on the way."

"You know," H. Roger said, with unconcealed pride, "I don't believe a single member of my congregation has been afflicted with that dread killer."

"Maybe," Ray said, "you just don't know your flock. Let's go, Ziza."

His car, which Ziza was seeing for the first time, was a Jeep Wrangler, which looked like a bargain-basement knockoff of Lillian Meservey's hefty Cherokee.

"Is my job about to go out the window?" she asked.

"You haven't really started yet. My only qualm is getting my church involved in the first place. It's all beginning to feel like an association of losers."

"Come on," she said. "You're going to end up running this whole show and you know it. Isn't it why you thought up this plan? It was you, wasn't it?"

"Ever hear of Gresham's Law? Bad money drives out good. The rotten apple spoils the whole barrel."

"We aren't talking money or apples," Ziza said. "We're talking kids. Between the two of us we should be able to make it work." She surprised herself by saying that and she sensed that she had surprised him, too.

"You know, after almost three weeks," he said, "I still haven't the slightest idea how sound you are."

"Sound?"

"Theologically. We've never really had a good heart-to-heart about the Bible and what it means to you. Personally."

"I don't think we have time for that now," she said as he pulled up in front of Village Hall.

"I'll come by some evening," he said. "Meanwhile," he added, as though he had just remembered why he'd offered her a ride, "what's all this about evidence and Grand Central? Something *was* going on the other night."

There was no point in playing "I've Got a Secret." "I think I found out the name of the unidentified corpse in the warehouse, that's all."

"That's all?"

"Just out of curiosity," she asked as she slid out of the car, "the person you're seeing at the hospice, is it someone from Heavenly Roger's congregation?"

"I promised not to tell." He reached out to catch the door before Ziza closed it. "About those stories of you and Monty, they're all over town." He waited for her to say something. "The first time you visited Mt. Zion I warned you about him. Just remember that."

She ran up the front steps of the Village Hall and thought she had evaded the steely eyes of the clerk when the woman called out, "Chief Malfadi left instructions to send you in immediately if you came this route. However, for your future reference, the proper way to the Police Department is through the parking lot entrance."

"I'm going to have a brief word with the mayor, if he's in." She headed for the stairs to the second floor.

"Chief Malfadi said—"

"I'll be there in less than five minutes."

As she went up the stairs she could hear the telephone in Monty's office begin to ring, and as she walked though his open door he was putting the phone down. "Chief Malfadi . . . ," he began.

"I know," she said. He tried to give her a kiss. She ducked away. "But I wanted . . ." He tried again. ". . . to make a pit stop, first." She heard the phone in Lillian Meservey's office ring twice. Was it paranoia, she wondered, to think her presence in Monty's office was being reported?

He tried one more time.

"Three strikes and you're out, Monty. What's going on here?"

"I have to tell you?"

"I've just been hearing that we're the hot new item in town. How does a story like that get around?"

"I can't believe I have to tell you."

"You been bragging around the boys' locker room that you're getting somewhere with me?"

"It seems to me that things are going pretty well between us."

"I've allowed myself to be seen in public with you. That's about the extent of our relationship."

"I guess I do have to tell you. It's been a lot more than that, Ziza. Think about it."

"You know who always goes after the new girl in town? A loser, that's who, someone desperate to find someone who doesn't know anything about him."

"You sell yourself short, kid. I just know a good thing when I see it. Think about it. Think about the way you really feel about me, not what you've been told by old ladies like Bramer and Swain."

The telephone on Monty's desk rang again. "For what it's worth, Chief Malfadi wants to see me, too."

"About"—she decided to kid him out of this—"the hottest couple in town having dinner alone last night?"

"I hope not. I'd have a sorry tale to tell." His voice took on a pitiable tenor. "Officer, she lured me to her cottage with promises of exotic food . . ."

"Moo Shu pork direct from Westchester Wok."

". . . and with promises of lurid tales of what she'd learned about the terrible Quarryville murders. Then, sir, things got badly out of hand. If only her phone had been working, I'd've called for help."

Monty's telephone kept ringing.

She didn't duck in time, and he planted a kiss on the edge of her mouth. Humoring him was getting nowhere, Ziza thought. "The Chief," she said.

"He just wants to tell me the hallowed FBI psychological profile of our killer has arrived. I'm sure that course he took down at Quantico has given him some jim-dandy techniques for filling me in on it."

"I think he expects me first," Ziza said.

"I'll go down with you and make the introductions." The phone stopped ringing. He reached behind his desk and took the camera from between the books on the reference shelf. "Time's come to play this card."

"You're going to make Wasco's day."

As they passed Lillian Meservey's door they heard her phone again. One ring, answered as the second began.

"Diamond Lil's been in a snit since the EPA hit the waterfront," he said in a whisper, as though the sound of his voice might draw her into the hall. "Have you seen what they've got down there today? Portable rigs that look like the sort of things they drill wells with. She's in terror that Quarryville's going to make some environmental hit list."

"Sounds like a legitimate worry to me."

"Not a worry, an *opportunity* to get in there—maybe even with some fed money—and clean the place up. Quality of life. You heard my campaign speeches."

"Actually, I missed that pleasure."

If he caught her tone, he ignored it. "She worries that they're going to find more trouble that has to be explained away."

The clerk watched them cross the foyer and reached for a telephone.

Wasco was at his desk in the room full of desks, sitting as

though he had been told to keep an eye out for them. "Chief said to go right in," he said, getting up to follow along behind.

Chief Malfadi looked like a figure from an Egyptian tomb painting, dressed up in a black suit and a white shirt, both a size or two too large. His nose was hawklike, his forehead high. He was thin to the point of seeming two-dimensional, and except for his piercing dark eyes the first impression he gave was one of complete languor. He managed to pull himself to his feet, touch—but not exactly shake—Ziza's hand, and fold back into his leather chair again.

The three of them sat like children in a dentist's waiting room on an overshellacked mail-order (some assembly required) early-American pine bench that faced the desk. Ziza noticed the chief's funereal-blue tie was decorated with maroon FBI logos so tiny you could hardly see them. It looked like the sort of thing you received for being first in your training class.

"I don't see Quarryville friends for more than a month," he said, stretching his hands apart and slowly bringing them together, "and now I have an office full of them. Reverend Todd with information. Mr. Monteagle to hear information. Officer Wasco"—he raised one hand gradually as though he were measuring the distance from his desktop—"my fine right hand. Everyone, I gather, wants to stay." He waited a moment for objections. "So we'll begin with the Reverend and what she's learned about our John Doe."

She ran through the story of Barbi and Dave Spencer one more time.

"And, of course, you won't tell us who the woman is?" he asked softly.

"Not for now," she said.

"For now," the Chief said, even more softly, nodding as though that were a very fine decision. "This morning I had Officer Wasco send out searchers to all possible computer and data-bank sources on all possible combinations of the names David and Dave, Spencer with a 'c' or an 's.' We await answers."

Like a television newscaster, he turned over what looked like a blank sheet of paper on his desk. "And you kindly spent your valuable time yesterday helping Officer Wasco trace the final steps of poor Dennis Morland. You have the gratitude of the entire department. Finding the lost knapsack was an important discovery. It's only unfortunate that Officer Wasco has rendered those last photographs useless as evidence in a court of law." He shook his head sadly. "By keeping them secret—and on his person—he destroyed their . . . integrity."

The very gentleness of the reprimand, the very heartbreak it seemed to conceal, made it all the more damning.

"You have been invaluable, Reverend Todd, with matters dealing with the deaths of Dennis Morland and John Doe (as I must still call him). Has your fine mind turned to the case of Adele Baraclough Bloodhorn?"

"Only that I don't agree with Wasco's theory that she murdered the first two, then killed herself."

Chief Malfadi's eyes shifted sharply toward Wasco—Ziza suspected this was the first he had heard of the theory—and then moved back to her. "You have in your possession, I believe, a valuable work of art rightfully belonging to the Baraclough Foundation Trust." He did not phrase it as a question.

"I do. A loan from Adele, a little watercolor river scene. She filled out some sort of index card saying where it was."

"No such card has been found."

"When the Trust wants it back, it's theirs."

"Of course it's theirs. But do they know you have it?"

"You do. They must."

"Perhaps they aren't as inquisitive as I am."

Monty interrupted. "You're not accusing Ziza of taking that picture, are you?"

"Mr. Mayor," he said, his head dipping ever so slightly in recognition of the title, "Reverend Todd, nothing could be farther from my thoughts. It's all just a simple matter of legal housekeeping. A place for everything and everything in its place. That's how they trained us at Quantico: fill in the blanks, one at a time, and when you're done, you've solved the crime."

"I didn't know the Bureau went in for jingles," Monty said.

Chief Malfadi's expression suggested the mayor had said something improper that he was choosing to overlook. He reached into his desk and took out a thick Ziploc plastic bag that changed color when he broke the seal. "The psychological portrait," he said.

"I'll make you a bet," Monty said. "It's going to say the killer's a loner. These things always say the killer's a loner. And a man. They never consider women."

Wasco made a soft snorting sound.

The Chief ignored them both. "I read through this earlier and resealed it, so I don't think there is a need for me to read aloud the entire document. A lot of heavy-duty psychological analyses by recognized leaders in their fields go into these reports. We had hours of lectures at Quantico on how it's all done. And the actuarially proven, statistically adjusted odds of these analyses being dead-on-the-nose accurate is something in the range of ninety-eight point eight percent. Let me, then, just paraphrase the summary.

"We should be looking for a twenty-five- to 35-year-old white, educated"—he gave Monty and Wasco the sort of smile St. Francis must have favored upon lepers—"male loner. Loner, in the sense that he has no permanent sexual partner or close personal friend of either sex. He may, however, be gregarious in his social appearances, by which the report means he is the sort of individual active in political protests, demonstrations, picketing, and petition-signing campaigns. He may even run for public office but because of his doctrinaire frame of mind would probably be unsuccessful. It's highly likely that he sports facial hair, either a beard or mustache or both."

Monty reached up to stroke his scraggly beard, but stopped before his hand reached his chin.

"Since the victims were an adolescent male, a derelict male, and a matron, the killer is seen as sexually inadequate and immature. His father was probably a professional man but unsuccessful in his chosen field (or he may have died early). His mother was the strongest influence on him, but she was a weak, sickly or perhaps alcoholic figure who required constant care and attention.

"He did not attend a highly regarded educational institution. He does not live at a permanent address. He believes he is surrounded by enemies, but they are not of any specific group, such as Jews, blacks, women, etc. The putting of political campaign buttons on the victims may indicate a poorly developed sense of humor or—like killing victim number three at a public event—may be an attempt to make his capture more easy. He may have some obvious physical defect, but more likely he simply regards himself as physically unattractive. As such, he may indulge in some manner of compulsive physical activity, such as weight-lifting or long-distance running. No team sports. No social sports, such as tennis or golf.

"He does not dress well, has poor eating habits, reads paperbacks rather than hardcover books, and joins record clubs for their introductory offers and then never buys any records.

"None of the killings was plotted in advance. The subject does not plan to kill again but will—as he has before—if he believes it's necessary.

"The fact that none of the killings was particularly messy suggests the killer is rather lazy. The fact that victim number one was moved and victim number two's body was arranged (arms crossed, etc.) suggests the subject may have a passive but domineering personality. Probably works—and kills—alone."

Chief Malfadi carefully lined up the edges of the pages, slipped them into the plastic sleeve, and pressed the Ziploc shut. "So who are we looking for?"

Wasco laughed. "Sure sounds like good old Monty to me." To show he didn't mean it he playfully punched the mayor, who was sitting next to him on the bench. Monty, surprised, dropped the camera he thought he'd carefully kept out of sight.

"Oh, my God," said Wasco, when he leaned over to pick it up.

"You going to give that to me now?" Chief Malfadi asked, speaking slowly, never in a hurry. "You've been holding it like an eighth-grader trying to hide a pack of cigarettes ever since you walked in here."

"Someone hid it in Monty's office," Ziza said. "He can provide you a list of all the people who've been in his office, the date he found it, all pertinent information."

"Oh, I'm sure he can and will," the Chief said.

"I wasn't hiding it," Monty said, annoyed about the eighth-grader comment and about Wasco. "I brought it down here to turn in, now that we finally have a proper police chief on the job around here. I felt—"

"In fact," Ziza interrupted, saying something she had never told Monty, "I *know* who had the thing before it turned up in Monty's office. Maybe not immediately before, but—"

At first it didn't sound like an explosion but like distant thunder, the familiar sound of a storm coming over the Palisades from New Jersey. But the sound did not roll to a stop the way thunder would. It kept going on like a long train passing through town without stopping. Then the building shook, ever so slightly. People later claimed that coffee cups fell off shelves, mirrors cracked, and all the bottles toppled off their spice racks. But as Ziza remembered it, the building seemed to only barely shudder. An unfamiliar siren started wailing.

"Air raid," said Wasco. "Duck and cover."

It was the Civil Defense alarm that no one had heard in years.

"Don't be stupid," Monty said.

Chief Malfadi was already out of his office and heading down the hall to the radio room when the village clerk ran in shouting.

"Terrorists!" she screamed. "They've blown up the waterfront!"

19

❧

Whooten had become thoroughly bored with the whole drilling operation. Terra-Tech was still in charge. Even the driver who had backed the truck-sized portable rig into position had been a woman in a spotless company jumpsuit. But the actual drilling was done by men dressed the old-fashioned way, jeans, dirty T-shirts, work boots, bent-out-of-shape baseball caps that said Mets, Yankees, John Deere, Myers Pumps, Bud.

Fogle, in one of his just-one-of-the boys moods, had spent a lot of time chatting with them as they set up and began to work. Whooten thought he was being absurdly pleased with himself over the pointless information he picked up. "Stan, he's the one in the olive-drab shirt with a pocket, says they use a down-hole hammer drill," he told Whooten. "Between seven hundred to a thousand strokes a minute and if all goes well they won't have to halt drilling to put in casing until they hit bedrock or exceptionally hard hardpack."

"Wonderful," said Whooten. He went back to the shade of the Baraclough foundry where he had left the oversized green leather portfolio (Il Bisonte, bought in Florence) that contained his presentation sketches of the waterfront project. Looking through it all once more was as pointless as Fogle's macho workman's lore, but it was something to do. The more these people picked and probed the more he came to believe Lillian Meservey was right: they had fucked up good and proper. The project was doomed.

Fogle had gone back to Stan and his crew. His presence there—and the rather jolly-looking conversation he was getting into—seemed to have emboldened one of the EPA men into joining them. Now it was the Terra-Tech women who appeared to be keeping their distance.

Whooten had a vague childhood memory of the sound of a water well being drilled, a slow, relentless pounding just a little less rapid than a heartbeat, a pounding that went on and on for weeks at a new house being built on the last vacant lot in his suburban neighborhood. As he prowled around that house every night after the workmen went home, seeing the beautifully relentless logic of raw wood being turning into a building, he had his first unformed thoughts about becoming an architect. And every evening a principal topic of his parents' dinner-table conversation, he remembered, was not just how deep the new people were having to go for water, but what that must cost.

The sounds he heard today were different. They were more like muffled bursts of machine-gun fire, those seven hundred to a thousand beats of the down-hole hammer, and every now and then there was a strange scream—the noise an outboard motor makes out of water, the whine of beaters on an old-fashioned Mixmaster lifted from the batter—as the drill hit air pockets in the landfill.

After one shrill screech, there was another familiar sound from his suburban childhood, the sharp, metallic clank of a whirling power-mower blade hitting a rock, followed by a cough and the silence of a stalled motor. What happened next was described by some as "all hell breaking loose." It hadn't seemed that way to Whooten, not at first.

Nothing dramatic happened, none of the exaggerated movement amateurs with video cameras always capture during catastrophes, none of the arty slow-motion effects so popular with Hollywood directors. Whooten later described it as like standing on Sixth Avenue when the D train roared through the subway tunnel underneath you. You knew something had passed by. You had felt the vibrations. But it was not a memorable sensation.

The drilling rig tipped over in an altogether matter-of-fact way, a child's toy truck suddenly lying on its side. There *had* been a distant roar, Whooten remembered, but again it was like that underground D train. The screaming came later. The flat, prefabricated roof assemblies on a few of the aluminum-sided storage buildings north of the drilling site slid sideways like lids slipping off shoe boxes. Bad stress design, Whooten thought.

The collapse of the Baraclough foundry's tall smokestack began with the sound of clattering bricks. The hubbub around the tipped-over drilling rig had increased ("hubbub," Fogle had once told Whooten, came from the old Irish cry "ub-ub," indicating contempt), and Whooten had taken a few tentative steps toward it—Fogle was over there somewhere in the midst of the confusion—when he heard the noise above him. It was almost a slippery sound, silk against some rougher fabric. Within seconds the brick and sandstone chimney was replaced by a pillar of red dust.

The meticulously rendered drawings in the Il Bisonte portfolio showed the chimney as the centerpiece of the new museum complex. Fogle planned to use an Aladdin Baraclough sketch of it in all the promotional material. Whooten had even drawn some sample logos that used its Victorian—Ruskinian? Richardsonian? Graustarkian?—Gothic detail as its key image. And now? Red dust, fallen roofs, a moaning siren that sounded as though it dated back to World War II, new sirens—more urgent ones—growing louder and overlapping as ambulances and police cars reached the waterfront.

Ghost memories, Whooten thought. Thank God Adele was spared seeing this.

"Ub-ub," he said out loud. He hoped no one had heard him. It might have sounded like blubbering. He could feel tears running down his cheeks but did not brush them away. What a silly sight that would have been, a tiny man dabbing away at his eyes like a sniveling child. Fogle, he was sure of it now, was one of the people caught under the rig when it tipped sideways.

&a.   &a.   &a.

By the time Ziza reached the waterfront, officials had taken charge. Uniforms were everywhere. Teams of policemen were stringing up yards of Day-Glo tape with the enthusiasm of a dance committee decorating the high school gym. The bark of shouted commands had replaced the screams. "Authorized personnel only" was the phrase she heard over and over again. The boys were clearly on top of things.

When she was a kid watching Saturday morning television cartoons she always hated seeing that it was the boys who were always off solving something or rescuing someone or just running for their lives. Girls held everything up by insisting on coming along and then promptly twisting their ankles. Girls tended to be more trouble than they were worth.

The activity this morning at the police station reminded her of those cartoons. Chief Malfadi returned from the radio room to announce that they were going into an Activated "A" Status Alert and that the signal had already gone over the radio net. Whatever an Activated "A" Status Alert was, it certainly impressed Wasco, who left immediately. Talk of killers and psychological profiles was forgotten. Malfadi never rushed as he headed for his car. Monty said he'd ride with him to the disaster scene. All around her Ziza could hear the sounds of policemen running, boys going into action.

Ziza headed for the howling sirens at the waterfront. She

wasn't alone. Everyone in downtown Quarryville seemed to be trying to reach the river, but when they got as far as the train station they were stopped by a crew of garbage men setting up a double line of yellow sawhorses.

Patrolling the roadblock were two men with hand-held loudspeakers. One was a policeman, but the other—in a gray business suit, paisley tie slightly unloosened, and wearing a wide "Civilian Auxiliary Police" armband—was Bob Bramer. His electronically magnified voice sounded especially whiny as he told them they were entering a restricted area. They must not cross designated police lines, he pleaded. For their own good, for the good of their neighbors, and for public safety they must not obstruct or interfere with police and rescue activity in any way. He thanked them very much for their consideration, attention, and cooperation.

The policeman simply paced back and forth shouting, "Authorized personnel only!"

"That sounds like us," said a voice next to Ziza, Ray Rickert. He was driving his Wrangler rather than the church van, and she had not heard him ease the little Jeep through the crowd. "Hop in. I've brought vats of coffee for our boys in blue." As she got in she could smell the two steaming, over-sized urns wedged behind the front seat. "Bring free coffee, you can get in anywhere," he said. "That's the secret of the Salvation Army's success. Jack Ruby's, too."

He said a few words to the policeman and two garbagemen pulled aside the sawhorses. They crossed over the train tracks on the bridge behind the station and headed south on River Road past the warehouses. Up ahead there were a lot of flashing lights, and at all possible turnoffs policemen were stringing up crime scene tapes, but they saw no sign of damage.

"I suppose you know what's going on," Ziza said. "Someone must."

"An explosion . . ."

"You're not going to tell me about terrorists."

"Underground, as I've heard it. The EPA people hit something and it blew up."

The closer they got to the Baraclough foundry, the more evidence Ziza saw of bureaucratic activity: more well-tended barricades, more Day-Glo, more parked cars with official seals on their doors, even a vacant parking area with a hand-lettered sign saying PRESS VEHICLES ONLY.

The press, of course, had driven directly to where the action was. Or had been. Camera crews were setting up in all the photogenic spots, the rubble-strewn front of the foundry building, the toppled drilling rig, the aluminum storage sheds with their tipped roofs. One crew was carefully filming cracks in the pavement as though they were earthquake fault lines. Unbroken sunshine did not stop the television people from using their high-intensity lights, and Ziza could see interviews being filmed in strange patches of unnatural brightness: Chief Malfadi, members of the rescue squad, Monty (who, she was happy to see, wasn't wearing his JUST ASK ME button), a man wearing a baseball cap who had Minor Federal Official written all over him.

Ray Rickert drove onto the faded checkerboard grid that had been chalked onto pavement in front of the foundry, and she helped him set up the coffee urns on a folding table he pulled out of the back of the Jeep. Their first customers were television production assistants, young kids just out of school, who were liberal with their thank-yous as they loaded up cups for their crews, but who also pointed out that when the Salvation Army arrives at a disaster site they always bring doughnuts and real milk for the coffee. Then the women in their white TERRA-TECH: MAKING ECOLOGY WORK jumpsuits came over. No thank-yous from them.

"You shouldn't use cups made of polystyrene foam," one of them told Ray Rickert, a low blow that hurt.

"The A&P was out of biodegradable," he said. "I looked."

"Don't be a sucker," she said, as they all headed back toward their van. "There's no such thing."

Then came Wasco.

"Coffee, regular, no sugar," he told Ziza.

"This isn't the Economy," she said. "We're self-serve, like the Mobil station."

"For the mayor," he said, as though that would have made a difference. "And the Chief." Upping the stakes.

Ziza handed him two empty cups.

"You shouldn't use Styrofoam," Wasco said. "The ladies were just talking about that."

"You'll wash the dishes?" She passed him one full cup. "Special for you," she said. "Now, tell us what's happening."

"A million-to-one shot, that's what everyone's been saying," Wasco said. He sipped the coffee Ziza had given him and didn't bother filling up the other two. "No doughnuts?"

"A million-to-one shot," Ziza prompted.

"The drill they were using to get deep samples seems to have hit something that caused a spark—that's the guess anyway—that ignited something that because of the air pockets down there—"

"Air pockets?"

"All this we're standing on down here turns out to be landfill."

"Historic Civil War–era landfill," Rickert said.

"Whatever," Wasco said, "it's landfill and it has air pockets so that in the one-in-a-million chance something burnable gets ignited it can explode, or catch fire."

"Underground?" Ziza asked.

"The Terra-Tech ladies are all excited about that possibility," Wasco said. "There's some coal town in Pennsylvania where they've had an underground fire going for twenty-five years."

"With," Ray Rickert said, "loving round-the-clock attendance from some Pennsylvania version of Terra-Tech, I'm sure."

"Damn sure," said Wasco. "Anyway, the next thing they'll be doing here is more drilling to see what's going on down there." He stamped his foot to show down where.

"And hope there's not another one-in-a-million." Ziza asked, "What about injuries?"

"At first it looked bad," Wasco said. "Damn bad." He shook his head as though it were too painful to think about. "All this stuff knocked over, the truck on its side, people trapped underneath, lots of blood, all these women . . ."

"They were a problem?" Ziza asked.

"They were here. Women and on-site disaster don't mix," Wasco said.

Ray Rickert packed up a large carton of coffee cups and took them over to the people standing around the drilling rig.

"But," Ziza said to Wasco.

"But they kept out of everyone's way, and were able to ascertain almost immediately that there were no fatalities. A couple serious-looking injuries. That Fogle's pretty banged up. Maybe lose a leg or something. One of the EPA guys was shaken up. A couple of the drillers got some cuts and bruises. But everybody'll probably live."

When Ziza heard Fogle she immediately thought of Whooten.

"Little bit of a problem there," Wasco said. "He wasn't hurt, but he wanted to ride along in the ambulance. There's regs against carrying passengers unless minors are involved, so he held his breath and turned blue until one of the drillers said he'd drive him and a couple other worried bystanders to the hospital in a van. I'm beginning to suspect that little guy might be some kind of faggot."

Ziza watched Ray Rickert handing out coffee at the rig,

talking away earnestly among the white jumpsuits, police uniforms, work clothes, and army fatigues. Picking up information of his own, she thought. A giant National Guard tow truck painted in camouflage colors was trying to pull the rig upright. At regular intervals the truck gunned its engine. There would be a whine like tires spinning on ice, but nothing moved. Another camouflaged truck arrived and the television cameramen rushed over to catch the soldiers jumping off the back and hitting the ground running, even though what they were running toward was Ziza's coffee.

Wasco watched the soldiers load up on cups, look around for doughnuts, and leave. "What did you make of all that stuff at the Chief's?" he asked Ziza. He was more at ease with her now, Ziza noticed. The afternoon they spent together seemed to have turned her into an old buddy.

"It's hard to trust a psychological profile made up by someone sitting at a computer down in Washington. They're the same guys who claim the average family is made up of two point eight children."

"Yeah, right," Wasco said. "And that business about the camera being in Monty's office all this time?"

She could see Monty as they talked. He was with a group that could only be described as a delegation. There was an army officer, several police officials, one of the Terra-Tech women, a couple of men—one of whom was taking notes— in what looked like tumble-dried wash-and-wear suits, and a silver-haired figure with a blow-dry haircut and a thousand-dollar Wall Street outfit, the sort of man who appears on Sunday morning television interview shows as an utterly un-informative Under Secretary of State.

"The county executive," Wasco said before she could ask. "Someone must have told him TV people were down here."

Indeed two film crews followed along as the group made what was obviously an Official Tour of Inspection.

"You're not serious about Monty?" Ziza said, getting back to the murders.

"My money's still on Adele, but I've a hunch the Chief's serious."

"The Chief's serious about Monty as what?" Ray Rickert said. She had not seen him return. "No one's serious about Monty."

"The Chief's serious about his FBI reports, that's what," Wasco said. He juggled his empty coffee cup and then put it back down on the table. "The Terra-Tech ladies said all these nonbiodegradable materials have to be policed up before you vacate the area."

"Don't worry about it," Rickert said.

Wasco flipped Ray Rickert a parody of a proper military salute and headed back to the toppled rig.

"So there's an FBI file on Monty," Rickert said. "Interesting."

"No," Ziza said. "Not a file. Not interesting."

"Wasco said—"

"Wasco was talking about an FBI psychological profile that says the killer was probably an unmarried, well-educated, white male, with perhaps a hang-up or two. Sound familiar?"

"No diary? Those guys always keep diaries."

"Do you keep a diary?"

Rickert did not answer immediately. He seemed to be watching the Official Inspection Tour, which had now reached the aluminum storage sheds. "Is that some sort of sly accusation?" he asked.

"Reverend Ray," she said, "I'd rather die than—"

"Careful what you say, there's been a lot of that going on around here lately." It was hard to tell from his careful, even tone just what he was really saying to her, but the hint of a threat was certainly there.

"You're right," she said, "there *has* been a lot of dying

going on around here. I've been in town for less than a month and there have been three strange deaths. What do you think is going on?"

"Someone's killing people, that's easy."

"And?"

"For once, Heavenly Roger got it right. Young ladies hired to run Sunday schools should earn their keep by running Sunday schools and not playing detective."

"Leave that to middle-aged men, right?"

"I assume you're referring to Chief Malfadi."

"There seems to be some gray hair above your ears."

"I brush it in every morning to look distinguished."

Ziza laughed. "Actually you're probably as bald as a cue ball. Why don't you just tell me what you've learned about all those deaths?"

"All I know is what Mrs. Benecosta tells me every morning after she talks to you and her grandson."

"Why don't I believe that?"

He shrugged, pulled at his hair to show that it wasn't a wig, and then carefully patted it back into place.

"As I see it," Ziza said, "the killing of Dave Spencer, the homeless man, is the easy one. He saw what happened to Dennis Morland and so the killer had to get rid of him."

"Simple as that?"

"Probably not, but simple enough for now." She paused a moment and then added, as an afterthought, "Unless, of course, we want to get into the matter of whether or not Dave actually recognized the killer from one of the Grand Central food runs."

"You're suggesting?"

"That maybe it's something you've already thought of and that maybe you've even narrowed down a little list of people it might have been."

"It would be a very long list. Just about everyone you've met in Quarryville, to begin with."

"And Dennis himself, did he ever go?"

"Dennis? Oh, sure. Not steady, but a regular. Maybe once a month, every six weeks or so. A good kid."

"So everyone says. Solving his killing is the hard one. So, I think we'll have to focus on Adele. You were there. What did you see?"

"So were you."

"But I know what I saw."

"Do you, really? What's your most vivid memory?"

"You and Monty, when it was all over, standing at the bottom of the porch steps, the two of you looking as though you'd been hit by something."

"You don't remember the others? Fogle was there. Whooten."

"Up on the porch with his model building."

"And Bob Bramer. He wouldn't shut up. He put away a couple of fast drinks and just kept babbling away."

"About what?"

"One minute it was about losing the 'soul of our community' and the next it was 'the wicked witch is dead.' A damn-fool way to carry on. Par for the course, naturally."

"You talked with Adele that afternoon?"

"I suppose. Everyone did. She was everywhere, she and Lillian Meservey. The two of them seemed to be competing for the title of Miss Conviviality."

"Inside the house or out?"

"I wasn't inside all day. I hate that place."

"You never went into the Studio at all, even to see the body?"

"That's the one thing I can remember talking to your friend Monty about, about how neither one of us could stand to go to that horrible room and see what happened."

"Monty said that, that he hadn't been in the house?"

"Of course."

"Bob Bramer, Fogle, the others?"

"Who knows? But you yourself talked with Adele that afternoon, remember? You told me she wanted to tell you something. Ever figure out what it was?"

"Maybe she wanted my opinion on when it was proper to turn in someone to the police."

"You know that for a fact?"

"Of course not."

"I'd be careful, then, about jumping to conclusions."

Another army truck had arrived, more soldiers. A van from the county Department of Health was unloading three portable toilets, but the television crews were packing up. Nothing new was going to happen. The Official Delegation had gone inside the foundry, and a few reporters waited around outside in case there was an announcement of some sort. Looking back down River Road, Ziza could see that most of the village crowd had wandered off, although Bob Bramer remained with his bullhorn to greet any newcomers.

"I know who knows," Ziza said. "Whooten. He was on that porch all afternoon showing off his model. Everyone who went inside the house passed him by."

"Good luck with that," Rickert said, as he shook the last coffee canister to see if it was empty. It was, and he began packing it away. Ziza folded up the table.

"How serious is all this?" she asked, gesturing around her.

"Very," he said. "With luck this town will never be the same again." He handed her an oversized plastic garbage bag. "Don't forget to police the area," he said. "I'm late for a meeting. *Ciao.*"

And he drove off.

Leaving me holding the bag, Ziza thought.

☙   ☙   ☙

Ziza had picked up most of the discarded coffee cups (at least the obvious ones) when she heard a voice say, "Here's a few more."

It was Miss Gatewood, and she had her arms full of neatly

squashed and folded cups. "Some of these were stuffed in very inconvenient places," the old woman said. "But I suppose there's no reason to assume that just because a bunch of men've been given something hot to drink they'd have the decency to show more consideration. Why would you? Testosterone is testosterone, am I not right?"

She dumped what she had in the garbage bag, brushed off her hands, and waited for Ziza to answer her questions.

The first thing Ziza could think of saying was, "There were women coffee drinkers, too."

Miss Gatewood's reply was a snort. "Cleaning up's woman's work, always has been, always will. The proof's in your hands. What are you going to do with all that trash? You're going to have to drag it somewhere and *then* you get to throw it away. Woman's work."

Ziza tossed the bag over her shoulder like Santa Claus and the two women walked along the factory road toward the exit patrolled by Bob Bramer. "How did you slip by the guards and get in here?" she asked. "You don't quite look like Authorized Personnel to me."

"I'm the Walker, dear. Haven't you heard? Half this burg's scared stiff of me. I can go anywhere." She had on her usual sunglasses and tweed jacket over which—in spite of the bright sunshine—she was also wearing a transparent plastic raincoat. "No one asks the village eccentric anything. Since they've never bothered talking to me, half the burg thinks I'm a recluse who never speaks. I'm speaking, am I not? Tell your friends."

"Gatewood Talks!" Ziza said, trying to sound like a headline.

"On the other hand, don't. They might start chatting me up, and then I'd have the devil's own time getting through town."

They passed Bob Bramer, who swung his bullhorn toward them and was about to announce something until he saw who they were. Then he simply smiled and nodded and waved them through as though he were directing traffic.

"Word is," Miss Gatewood said, "that that man might have made something of himself in this town if he hadn't had a horse's rear end for a wife. Not true. He's a horse's rear end in his own right. You've heard about his fence?" She didn't wait for an answer. "He put up a fancy fake-rustic fence along his property line. Very un-Quarryville. Everyone here knows to the inch where his property lines are, but no one, only a horse's rear end, would ever put up a fence along it. You can't tell me it's his wife that's kept that man from being mayor."

Ziza left her garbage bag on top of the overstuffed dumpster at the train station. "You probably know a lot about what goes on here," she said. Instead of heading up into the village they kept walking north along the river.

"I see everything. I'm part of the landscape, like a mailman. Chesterton, you know, had a mystery story in which the killer was a mailman who almost got away with it because none of the supposed eyewitnesses ever noticed him coming or going. No one sees a mailman. Father Brown, of course, made short work of that. But I'm like that mailman."

"Killed anyone?" Ziza asked.

"Not to speak of," said Miss Gatewood.

When they got to the oil tanks at the northern edge of the waterfront, Ziza was prepared to turn back, but the Walker kept walking and the twin ruts of what looked like an abandoned farm road opened up in front of them.

"But you see everything," Ziza said, repeating Miss Gatewood's words.

"You know what sums up Quarryville? The Laundromat. Very clean. You've never seen a cleaner one. All the washers work, all the dryers. There's change in the change machines. The fluorescent lights don't flicker. Signs say don't dye anything in the machines and no one dyes. No Smoking. No one smokes. The bulletin board is full of fund-raising notices for proper good-works charities. People advertise that they've *found* dogs and cats, not that they lost them. The place is always full, day or night. People come from miles around, Yonkers, all over. Even by bus. They dress up to come here. Everyone on their best behavior, everyone acting like they're Quarryville folks. But no one there's actually from Quarryville. It's a dream. Never-never land."

"You're there. I've been there."

"I may be the only one in town without a washer-dryer. And you, you haven't been here long enough to count."

Miss Gatewood set a mean pace. She wasn't an ambler who paused to identify birds or enjoy the river view, which now, Ziza thought, looked very much like the Aladdin Baraclough watercolor that sat on her mantelpiece. And her words came as fast as she walked. There was an almost jagged quality in the way she was talking, as though, having decided to talk to someone, she wasn't going to stop.

"You say I see everything," she said. "Well, I do. I know who's getting their kitchens rebuilt, who needs the exterminator once a month, who gets visits from the police, uniformed *and* plainclothes, who doesn't separate their trash the way you're supposed to. And, of course, I know where the daytime love affairs are going on (I don't go out at night, you know), who's away, what cats are at play, cats in heat. The toms, of course, were all beating a well-worn path to that Adele's door, and she wasn't pulling in the latch string, if you catch my meaning."

Ahead of them, the abandoned road they were following ran directly into a marshy inlet the river had dug into the high bank. It reemerged, Ziza saw, twenty-five yards away in high grass at the far edge of the oily backwater.

"My rule for walking," Miss Gatewood said, "is to always stick to public rights-of-way, and now's the time and place where I break the rule." She turned away from the river and the railway tracks and headed up a steep and noticeably worn path. "Kids say this is one of the River Rats' trails," she said. "If so I'm a Rat. Get down on all fours and you'll find it's easier to scramble up this thing."

Her plastic raincoat made scrambling on all fours tricky, but she tucked it up and scampered up the narrow ravine without reducing speed. "Mind the landslides!" she shouted without a backward glance, dislodging a softball-sized cobblestone that sailed past Ziza's head.

Ziza waited until Miss Gatewood got to the top and then followed, a bit slower, perhaps, but still upright.

They had come out amid the purple loosestrife at the end of the long field behind Professor van Runk's house.

Miss Gatewood had not stopped to wait for Ziza, but was striding off toward a hedgerow of quaking aspens. Ziza sprinted to catch up with her. "Have the police," she asked as she ran, "ever gotten around to question you about the morning you found Dennis Morland's body?"

"Good Lord, no," she said. "I think they have more than enough on their plates these days for that."

"It might be important," Ziza said.

Miss Gatewood suddenly stopped, so suddenly Ziza rammed into her.

"Freeze," the old woman whispered, not moving her lips.

Ziza wasn't so sure she froze, but at least she backed up, stopped moving, and caught her breath.

From out of the hedgerow of quaking aspens on the other side of the field, the one that separated the Professor's land from downtown Quarryville, came Lillian Meservey. She was followed by van Runk himself, and they seemed to be deep in conversation.

"She's able to talk to the old boy without shouting," Ziza said.

"Shhhh," whispered Miss Gatewood. The two of them were still in their frozen positions in the shade of the trees.

They hadn't been observed, although, Ziza thought, the village manager and the Professor were so intent on each other she and Miss Gatewood could have jumped up and down and waved and still gone unnoticed.

Could they, too, have come up from the waterfront on a different path? From the direction they were walking, it seemed likely, although Ziza didn't remember seeing Lillian Meservey at the accident site.

There was a sudden sharp intake of breath from Miss Gatewood. Ziza squinted to make sure she was seeing it right, but, yes, Lillian Meservey had taken the Professor's hand, quite naturally, quite, it seemed, without forethought or drama as though it were the way they usually went walking on a sunny morning, and the two of them strolled hand-in-hand toward the old homestead, bumping shoulders as they went.

"The silly fool," said Miss Gatewood, not whispering.

"Which one?" asked Ziza.

"Take your choice. Pay your money." As though the word reminded her of something, she added, "He's stone-broke, you know. That's why he's come back to Quarryville to roost."

After the couple disappeared around the side of the house, Ziza and Miss Gatewood started walking again, staying in the shadows.

"See what I mean," Miss Gatewood said. "You see everything. No one sees you."

They kept silent, though, holding their breath (at least Ziza was), as they came around the other side of the house and headed down the empty gravel driveway. No one was in sight.

"Don't skulk," Miss Gatewood said. "As the old song says, 'Hike along, hike along, hike along with a stride so free, and if you see that big old bear, just let that old bear be.' "

At the end of the driveway, they turned toward the village business district. Ziza exhaled.

"You were cross-examining me about the morning I found that poor boy."

"Not cross—"

"Of course you were. Well, besides the body I saw only one thing. As I was heading toward the grade school on the way to the Meadow, one of those funny square cars came out of the playground and then buzzed off."

"Could it have come down from the Meadow?"

"Could well have."

"See who it was?"

"Didn't. I just barely noticed it at all. Half the burg drives them. If there's two cars in a driveway, one of them's square."

"Square cars?"

"I think they're for daddies who like to pretend they're forest rangers or cowboys or something. Tarted-up Jeeps, most of them. Explorers, Broncos, Scouts, Blazers, Wranglers, Range Rovers, Cherokees, Wild West names, boys' cars for overgrown boys. Or would-be boys. It's that testosterone again. Just take a look, the street's full of them."

She took a look and the street was indeed full of them, parked all along the curb. The one heading toward them, slowing down to get a look at Ziza and Miss Gatewood before speeding up again, was driven by Ray Rickert.

Still late for that meeting, Ziza thought.

20

❧

Ziza was taken to the hospital in a square car.

"What make is it?" she asked.

"A Trooper," Rich said. "Isuzu." He was driving, but they were caught in a traffic jam, so he turned his head to look at her in the backseat.

"Yours?"

"My father's," Anne Bramer said. "He calls it his runabout, but if I don't use it, it mostly sits in the garage."

Ziza had parted company with Miss Gatewood on Main Street. The Walker's route took her up into Hillside, and even if she hadn't said Ziza's pace was a shade too slow to be "comfortable," Ziza had intended to stop off at the Economy anyway. There she could sit at the counter, sip terrible coffee, and eavesdrop on what people were saying about what happened on the waterfront.

Rich stopped her before she got there, pulling the Trooper alongside her and popping the horn just once. "Hop in," he said in his big-spender voice, "I'll take you anyplace you like. I owe you."

"How about Paris?"

"Within the confines of the continental U.S. Or at least southern Westchester."

She got in. "Why do you owe me?"

"That paper."

"On *Tortilla Flat?*"

"On the second level of meaning. You got me a B, breaking my solid record of C-pluses."

"I didn't help you."

"You told me about Peter Pan being dead. I threw in whatever bull I could think of about King Arthur and Steinbeck and then I began the last paragraph saying, 'Just as *Peter Pan* can be read as a ghost story . . . ,' and that freaked out old Smilin' Eddie."

"Mr. Stapleton, Edward Stapleton, the English teacher," Anne Bramer added.

"Footnotes by Annie," Rich said. "Anyway, Smilin' Eddie wrote on the bottom that the paper was down to my usual level. He writes notes like that"—he deepened his voice to a growling singsong—" 'Down to your usual level of achievement, Mr. Thompson.' But then he said"—he dropped his voice again—"my 'passing comment on the Barrie work was cogent and stimulating' so he was raising me half a letter grade."

"You don't know how really amazing that is," Anne Bramer said. "Once Mr. Stapleton makes his mind up what your standard grade is, that's what you always get, every paper, every time."

"So," Rich said, patting the steering wheel, "just say where."

"How about the hospital?"

"You sick?"

"The one where they took the people from the waterfront. I'd like to see Fogle."

"All Saints, in Yonkers," Anne Bramer said. "That's where emergencies always go."

"You mean it?" Rich asked.

"*You* mean it?" Ziza asked.

"Sure."

"Let's go."

It wasn't quite as easy as that. Quarryville was having one of its rare traffic jams. Since River Road was blocked off, all downtown traffic funneled onto Main Street, and with emergency equipment still arriving, TV vans leaving, and sightseers like Rich and Anne (excused from school to "round up," they said, props for *Godspell,* the fall Drama Club play), traffic was barely moving.

"Everyone says the explosion was like an earthquake," Anne Bramer said, sounding as though the earthquake had been something of a disappointment.

"What was weird was the dust," Rich said. "This cloud of red dust just blew through town after the blast."

"Fallout," Anne said.

"Like radioactive fallout after Hiroshima or something. Weird," Rich said.

"This whole town is getting weird," Anne said.

"Ever since Dennis," Rich said. They finally made it through the stoplight and turned uphill toward the Star.

"Kids are still freaking out?" Ziza asked.

"It's not just the kids," Anne said. "Even people like my father are going spaz."

"Spastic," Rich said.

"Footnotes by Rich," Anne said. "But life around our place's becoming a nightmare with my father acting as though he's going to jump out of his skin. All through dinner he fidgets around with his silverware and taps away at the table and never hears a thing you say to him."

"Thumper," Rich said.

"We've been calling him Thumper behind his back," Anne said. "Not that he'd ever notice."

"This has been going on since Dennis died?" Ziza asked.

"Not that long," Anne said. "Maybe since Adele's accident, Mrs. Bloodhorn's."

They made the turn for Yonkers at the Star, just as Heavenly Roger came down the walk from First Pres. Ziza hoped he hadn't seen her—was annoyed with herself for hoping that—and knew that he had.

"There's even all kinds of talk about Monty getting arrested," Rich said.

"That's a lot of nonsense," Ziza said.

"He's supposed to be on the FBI's wanted list," Anne said.

"Just not true," Ziza said.

"Someone said they heard Wasco say at the Economy—"

"Just not true," Ziza said.

All Saints Hospital was just over the Yonkers border. Back in the 1890s, it had begun as a Franciscan infirmary and over the years one wing after another had been added hit-or-miss to the original batten-board cottage with its vaguely Gothic windows. Rich turned down a three-lane driveway, cut across faded arrows painted onto the blacktop pointing the way to the "Emergency" and "Maternity" entrances (Emergency marked with a flashing red neon sign, Maternity with a steady blue) to the lane marked "Visitors," and pulled into a crowded parking lot big enough for a shopping mall.

"You don't need to stick around," Ziza said.

"Sure we do," Rich said.

"He's afraid he'll miss something," Anne said.

"Then we'll have to split up," Ziza said. "I'm going to be doing my Madam Clergy number, and I think it'll go over better without teenage sidekicks."

"Gotcha," Rich said. "We'll give you five minutes before we wander in. We'll pretend we don't know you."

Ziza opened the swinging glass doors marked VIS T RS in chipped white paint—no neon over this entrance—and obeyed the instructions on the wall that told her to follow the green ceiling lights to the Patient Information Desk (ALL VISITORS MUST REGISTER). The overheated corridors seemed strangely empty—where were the people from all those cars outside?—but they were bright and clean and throbbed with the sound of unseen motors and engines. Ziza imagined she was in the belly of a giant ocean liner with cement-block walls the color of pistachio ice cream.

The overhead green lights led her closer and closer to a smell of fresh paint until she reached a large square room she guessed was the original 1890s infirmary. It was being modernized. New opaque plastic screens, some still in their paper wrappers, covered the Gothic windows. Black counters as glossy as old-fashioned telephones were being installed on all sides. In the center, looking like a solid-oak altar, was the reception desk. A permanently illuminated Lucite sign read NON VISITING HOURS. Ziza noticed there was an extra switch on it to turn off the NON. She pushed a button mounted on the top.

On the gray wall behind the desk was the brighter silhouette of the huge crucifix that had hung before the painters took it down. The five holes where it had been bolted to the wall were filled with spackle and sanded down, leaving behind a dazzling white stigmata.

An electronic voice from somewhere in the desk said, "Visiting hours do not commence until three o'clock."

"Clergy," Ziza said. "Pastoral visit."

"After the tone," the voice said, "please give your All Saints registration number and the name of the patient you wish to see."

After the tone, Ziza said, "New clergy in town. Fogle."

A carefully combed middle-aged woman came out wearing a silver-gray suit that would have gone equally well on a vivacious nun or a demure airline stewardess. "Reverend Fogle?" she said.

"Reverend Todd. The patient I wish to see is named Fogle."

"First name?"

"Ziza."

"Ziza Fogle?"

"Ziza Todd. I don't actually know Mr. Fogle's first name."

"Unregistered."

"Mr. Fogle?"

"You, *Reverend*." Ziza could hear the italics.

"I've just joined with a group of churches in Quarryville. This is my first visit to All Saints."

"We don't permit unregistered clergy to roam at will."

"I have references."

"You know what happens when your car breaks down on the Thruway."

Ziza felt as though she had missed a key point. "I don't have a car," she said.

"Not just any tow truck can come and service out-of-commission vehicles. Franchised tow only. That's our principle here at All Saints."

"Franchised clergy?"

"Write to us on your church's letterhead stationery and we'll send a registration form."

"I can't see Mr. Fogle?"

"Not until public visiting hours, other requirements permitting."

"There *is* a Mr. Fogle here?"

The stewardess-nun shot Ziza a level glance, analyzed what she saw, and then pecked away quickly at a hidden computer keyboard. There was a long silence. Then more typing, even faster this time. Ziza half expected to be told the flight was overbooked.

"No."

"No Fogle?"

"He hasn't been logged in."

"He was brought to Emergency this morning."

"He has not been logged in in any fashion whatsoever. I suggest you try after three. Call first. We don't log in DOAs."

Ziza headed back down the pistachio hallway. She'd take a look inside the Emergency entrance and if she didn't find

Whooten or Fogle there she'd round up the kids and go back home.

They passed her without recognizing her.

"Rich. Anne," she called.

They paused briefly to look back at her, to look through her, and then went on. Play-acting. Drama. Ziza followed them to the parking lot.

"Zip," she said. "Nothing on the computer."

"Paydirt for us," Rich said, clasping his hands over his head like a winning boxer.

"Mr. Fogle won't be computerized until tomorrow," Anne said. "There's always a lag, they say."

"They?"

"Guys in the coffee shop," Rich said. "From the Quarryville Rescue Squad. You can see their ambulance parked over there." He motioned toward the red neon light. "We went looking for them. Found them first place we tried."

"Everyone they brought in is being released," Anne said. "Except for Mr. Fogle."

"Lucky bunch of guys," Rich said. "Cuts, bruises, one broken leg, that's all. Except for Mr. Fogle."

"Room 803," Anne said. "They said take the elevator inside the Emergency entrance and just keep walking as though you know where you're going."

"If you ask directions," Rich said, "you'll probably get thrown out."

Ziza took the elevator to the eighth floor, didn't ask directions, walked as though she knew where she was going, and never did find Fogle or Room 803. But she found who she was really looking for. Whooten was sitting in a small alcove crowded with orange Naugahyde chairs and decorated with two identical Winslow Homer prints of palm trees in a hurricane.

"I've been asked to wait outside," Whooten said. "They

seem to think this is outside." He made a gesture as though he were wiping off one of the chairs. "Have a seat. With luck you won't stick to the plastic."

Ziza sat. "How is he?"

"I'd say terrible. They say his condition's guarded and then hand me a questionnaire about locating next-of-kin."

"What's wrong?"

"Broken. You name it in the body and it's either broken or squashed. Except his head, that's fine."

"Would you like me to see him?"

"Is 'see' a way of saying 'pray over'?"

"If you want that, I can do it from here."

"Don't bother. Some sort of preacher was around earlier. Today's designated non-Catholic chaplain. He said a prayer in which he gave the name and street address of his church. In case, I suppose, God wanted to drop in."

"Or you."

"The power of advertising."

His feet, in those expensive, complexly buckled shoes, did not come close to touching the floor, but he didn't swing them back and forth. They were motionless. He held out his hand to be held, and she held it. She found herself surprised that it did not feel at all like the hand of a child.

"We can talk of other things," she said.

"Shoes, ships, sealing wax? Cabbages, kings?"

She didn't say anything.

"Did you believe me when I told you that I'd moved the boy's body? I really did, you know, even though Fogle didn't want me to. We were together when we found him down at the foundry, in a puddle of dried blood on the floor. Fogle wanted him left there. 'Let sleeping dogs lie,' he said. Can you believe he'd say a thing like that?"

She held his hand, but didn't say anything.

"You've probably figured out that he's the killer. I began to suspect as much after I called him up and told him I'd moved the boy to the Meadow. That's why I came to you for confession. I can't stand keeping all the secrets I have to keep."

"Fogle?" She was afraid to say more.

"He's dying, you know." She nodded. "I did find that camera next to the bum's body in the warehouse—that was all true—and I took his picture. Then the camera really did disappear from the car's glove compartment. Everything I've confessed is true. Who but Fogle could have taken it? Who else could be the killer?"

"You ever ask him, just right out ask him if he'd done it?"

" 'Don't worry about it,' is what he said. That's what he said about any problem I'd bring up and then he'd change the subject. Did I know that the piece of lumber they call a two-by-four is really only one and five-eighths inches by two and five-eighths? Did I know that cats never say meow to other cats? Only people. Anything but answering the question I asked. But I know."

"The camera disappeared after you told me about Dennis."

"He wasn't loyal, you know, Fogle wasn't." He looked at her as he spoke, looked directly into her eyes, young Abe Lincoln never telling a lie.

"He never told you he was the killer?"

"He'll be dead by tomorrow. I've been watching what happens in the corridors. The coming and going. I think they have a special kind of gurney that they use to move corpses. They don't wheel them around with sheets over them the way they do in movies. It has a very deep top that they put the dead body into and then close the lid down so that when they move it through the halls the tabletop looks empty. No one gets upset that way. The body's never there to see."

Ziza looked down the hall. A stainless-steel table on wheels sat next to one of the doorways. On it lay neatly stacked piles of white cloth. Sheets, maybe, towels, hospital gowns.

"Adele had something she wanted to tell me the afternoon

of the Open House, something that was worrying her. She mentioned your name. Did you ever tell her about your suspicion of Fogle?"

"Never!"

"That maybe you had begun to wonder if things on the waterfront weren't quite what they seemed?"

"Oh, no, I wouldn't have let anything slip."

"You're sure."

He didn't answer at once. "I think so, but it was on my mind."

She began again. "The day Adele died—"

"Daintily put."

"The day Adele was killed—"

"Better."

"—you were on the porch all afternoon with your model of the waterfront. You must have seen everyone who came and went."

"You know the people who had been invited to that party had seen Aladdin Baraclough's studio a hundred times. All the sightseers were long gone. It was a beautiful day, so there wasn't a lot of traffic in and out. People came up to look at the waterfront proposal but the house was old hat. Members of the committee were coming and going. Monty was hanging around, Bob Bramer, Ray Rickert, I suppose. Fogle, of course."

"Fogle went inside."

"Of course. He had to."

"Had to?"

"To do what he did."

"But you don't remember seeing him?"

"Bramer, I remember. Rickert. Fogle, I'm sure of it. He did it."

"Why did it have to be done? All of it? The boy, the homeless man, Adele?"

A nurse came out of the room next to the gurney and waited a moment, impatient, her arms folded across her heavily starched uniform. An orderly with a *Daily News* tucked under his arm ambled up. She said something to him and then held the door open as he pushed the table inside the room.

"You didn't know . . ." Whooten showed no interest in finishing the sentence. They both watched the door swing shut behind the orderly's green back.

"And you," Ziza said, hoping to regain his attention. "Of course, you could duck in and out of the house any time you wanted?"

He spoke quickly now, thankful for a diversion. "There was almost always someone there asking me questions about the new Baraclough Center. Lillian Meservey kept showing up and asking what she must have thought were clever technical questions about building on landfill, trying to trip me up. But, of course, I found the body at the foot of the stairs."

"What?"

"No one told you? I'd gone back in to get more pamphlets about the project and there she was. Dead as a doornail. I certainly hadn't expected it."

He gave her hand a squeeze and let go. The door remained shut.

When Ziza got back to the parking lot, Rich, Anne, and the square car were gone. In their place were Bob Bramer and his Ford Taurus.

"I sent them on their way," he said. "Get in and I'll take you back. Come with a Bramer. Leave with a Bramer." He held the door for her and slammed it harder than necessary. After he slipped behind the wheel he said, "Frankly, Ziza, I'm disappointed in you."

"For playing hooky with the kids?"

"I have been one of your defenders, you know. At times,

may I add, one of your few sorely needed defenders on the Community Pulpit Committee. Stunts like this with the kids aren't going to do much for your reputation."

"I'm sorry," Ziza said. It wasn't, she thought, a time to make a case for herself. "Your chores on the waterfront all wrapped up?"

"Anne called home because they'd been gone longer than she expected and my wife got the message to me. Actually Roger"—Ziza could tell he almost said Heavenly Roger—"had already dropped by my civil emergency station and told me that he'd seen the three of you joyriding around."

"Not joyriding, visiting the sick, although I admit I should have insisted that the kids go back after dropping me off. It was a bad judgment call."

"The whole town's going crazy," he said.

"That's just what Anne said."

"She did?" He drove in silence. "She say things were getting tense around the house?"

"Everyone's been pretty tense."

The sound he made wasn't so much a sigh as a long exhale. "Just between us, right?" Ziza nodded and waited. Bob Bramer slowed down so they would be caught by the next traffic light when it turned red. "Adele's death really shook me, really. I so wanted the woman out of my life."

He paused again. "She *was* out of my life, but she was still here, around, getting her name in the paper, walking down Main Street. That silly tin-plate hairdo you could spot a mile away. I wanted everything about her erased. And then, *BAM*, just like that, she was dead. Gone. Removed. All done. That's what Anne said as a baby when she finished eating, 'Aah done.' Aah done, Adele."

He had not noticed that the light had turned green until the car behind them started honking.

"And I was so happy," he said, "so happy." He laughed, but the laugh caught in his throat like a sob. "I was so happy

I began to feel guilty about it. And now that's what's really getting to me. I'm feeling so guilty I just might as well have killed her myself that afternoon."

"But you didn't."

"I found the body, you know. I'd gone into the Studio and there she was. You could tell right away she was dead by the way she was lying there. I didn't want to touch her, but I didn't have to. I just went right back outside and asked that Whooten character if he had any extra copies of his waterfront pamphlet and he toddled off inside to get them. Probably thought he had a convert. He was there a good while, longer than I expected, and I had time to get myself a drink down at the bar in the side yard before word got around about . . . Adele."

They had crossed the Quarryville village line and the church steeples around the Star were in sight. "I feel like hell now," he said, actually sounding quite relieved, "but standing on that lawn, looking out toward the river, waiting for all hell to break loose, taking that last good drink"—he caught his breath—"there was a mighty song in my heart."

21

?❧

Wasco made a halfhearted attempt to block the entrance to Monty's office, but he didn't try closing the door in Ziza's face.

"Let her in," Monty said. "If you're not going to let me make my one phone call, you should at least allow me a witness of my own choice."

"Don't talk silly nonsense," Lillian Meservey said.

Chief Malfadi said nothing at all. He didn't even bother looking up from his slow search through the coiling pages of a computer printout.

Monty was seated at his desk, and the Chief and the village manager stood on either side of him, leaning toward the mayor, balancing each other like attendant saints on a Renaissance altarpiece.

"Take a chair," Monty said. "My firing squad, here, seems to prefer standing."

"Official village business," said the Chief, still without looking up. He did not rush his words. "Restricted. Private."

"Community Access," Monty said. "Sunshine laws. Village Trustees' Ruling 1817B. The public—voters—cannot be denied reasonable access to the workings of village business."

"Reasonable access this isn't," Chief Malfadi said. "We are in the midst of a private discussion in chambers, and I doubt very much if the individual in question is even a registered voter."

"My chambers," Monty said. "The individual in question is my guest. Sit, Ziza. They're about to arrest me for a murder or two."

Chief Malfadi sighed. This was clearly a very sad business for him. "The FBI psychological profile says that when confronted the subject will demonstrate cavalier tendencies and indulge in a certain amount of exhibitionism and attempts at self-display and aggrandizement." The Chief seemed to be reading aloud from the printout.

"Sounds to me like you're talking about a flasher," Monty said.

"I beg to differ," said the Chief. "Your average flasher acts as guilty as hell and will confess to anything. Correct, Officer Wasco?"

Ziza had already sat down on one of the cracked leather club chairs in front of the desk. It smelled of antique cigar smoke.

"I believe," Lillian Meservey said, "that we are straying and straying badly, but I would like to remind one and all that the word 'arrest' has not crossed my lips nor the lips of Chief Malfadi. It's the mayor and the mayor alone who's brought up the subject of incarceration."

Monty tapped his desk. "Although I do seem to recall the words 'murder,' 'murderer,' 'suspect,' and 'the mayor' crossing a number of lips in this room, none of them mine."

"Only," the Chief said, "to point out how perfectly you seem to match the FBI profile."

"Compiled," Lillian Meservey added, "by experts whose record of success confounds, by far, the odds of chance."

"*And,*" the Chief added, "to point out that you don't seem to be able to account for yourself at any of the crisis moments."

"That means 'no alibis,' " Monty said to Ziza.

"A prudent public official keeps a log or diary that records his or her presence at all moments of the day or night," Lillian Meservey said.

"Oh, to be prudent," Monty said.

"Attitude," Lillian Meservey said, speaking over Monty's head to the Chief. "And let's not forget the camera that was hidden away in this office."

"We haven't yet brought up the mayor's reaction to the news of the discovery of the Morland boy's body. Wasco?"

"The subject," Wasco said, obviously repeating something he had earlier written in an official report, "did not seem particularly surprised that the body was found . . ."

"He'd been missing, for God's sake, for almost a week," Monty interrupted.

". . . but did register great surprise concerning its location. Not once but several times he said the body could not possibly have been found at the Meadow."

"Forensic tests," the Chief said, "have provided gravel and cinder samples that prove the crime was committed elsewhere, most likely in the waterfront area."

"And I hadn't known that someone moved my victim?"

"Exactly."

"Motive?" Monty asked.

"You are a young, unmarried male who has no record of extensive activity with members of the opposite sex, a loner. Dennis Morland, also a loner, a Boy Scout with no girlfriend, was a good-looking, athletic teenager. Perhaps something happened at a waterfront assignation."

"For Christ's sake," Monty said. "I'm unmarried, so what? Wasco's unmarried. Does *he* have to come up with an alibi?"

"I've been keeping company with Suzanne since junior high," Wasco said.

"Wasco dates," Lillian Meservey said.

"I suppose"—he glanced over at Ziza, struggling to keep

his temper, and then continued—"it's not worth bringing up Adele, my friendship with Adele?"

"Given what happened to her," the Chief said, "do you think that counts for much?"

"You're saying someone, somebody I knew nothing about, moved the body to surprise me?"

"Stranger things have happened."

"The guy in the warehouse, I killed him because he saw what happened to Dennis?"

"You use his first name, I notice," Lillian Meservey said.

"I'm not saying you killed anyone," Chief Malfadi said, "but—in theory—it follows."

"In theory?"

"It follows."

"The campaign buttons," Lillian Meservey said, lifting a handful of them from the cookie jar on the desk and letting them drop.

"Lillian," Monty said, "just what the hell are you up to?"

"The victims were all wearing them," she said.

"JUST ASK MONTY. Advertisements for myself?" Monty asked.

"The profile indicates the killer has a morbid sense of humor and a perverted desire to give himself away and be caught."

"Which brings us to Adele," Monty said. "What was on my perverted, sex-crazed, guilt-ridden mind when I shoved her down those stairs and stuck my campaign button on her blouse?" He glanced over at Ziza. "Three strikes and I'm out?"

"That's one way of putting it," Malfadi said. "Of course, you realize that once you begin something like this . . . Not that we are making any accusations."

"Then why are you doing this?" Monty asked, getting up and walking around his desk to Ziza's chair. "Why the velvet-glove third degree? Why are you keeping me under house arrest?"

Lillian Meservey prepared herself to disagree, but before she could say anything Monty cut her off.

"I *am* under house arrest, Ziza. My old high school buddy Wasco spent all evening outside my office door. Every time I've tried to leave this morning he's found some reason to stop me. He even handed over a paper bag full of breakfast from the Economy. Just like the overnight prisoners in the lockup downstairs get."

"Yesterday's explosion was a serious community disruption," Lillian Meservey said. "We've needed you here at the command post, is all."

"Is all?" he said. "What about these charges—"

"Suggestions, Monty, only suggestions."

"—that I'm a mass murderer?"

"Think of it," Chief Malfadi said, "in the context of options."

"Think about what you're doing," Monty said, dropping his bantering tone. "Lillian, just stop and think about what you're doing."

"Fogle's dead," Ziza said, the first thing she'd said since she arrived. "Died at All Saints early this morning."

"We've been expecting it," Lillian Meservey said.

"Whooten says he's the killer," Ziza said.

"Whooten confessed?" the Chief asked. "There's another loner for you, the pair of them."

"No," Ziza said. "He said Fogle's the killer."

"The first sad fatality of the explosion," Lillian Meservey said, "the only one, God willing. No one else had much more than a scratch and a bruise. You should prepare a statement, Monty. A thankful village mourns, etc., etc., the riches of a community are made manifest in the lives—and tragic deaths—its citizens, and so on."

"Fogle didn't even live here," Monty said. "I'm interested in what Whooten had to say."

"Nothing like a spate of violence to bring out weirdo confessions," Chief Malfadi said.

"Not a confession," Ziza said. "An accusation."

"You believe him?" Monty asked.

"Accusing someone of murder on his deathbed is awfully convenient," Ziza said. "Not much chance of rebuttal. Something funny's going on there, but he may just be covering up for himself."

"One of those two," the Chief said, "is a midget, isn't he? The profile clearly states that the killer may well be compensating for a gross physical insufficiency."

"I'm five eleven and a half," Monty said. "Does that get me off the hook?"

"Not all gross insufficiencies are in plain sight," he said.

"This little exercise is all well and good," Lillian Meservey said, "but as my old granny used to say, wishin' won't make it so. We have a wounded village to bind up and heal and I think we should get about that work." She pushed a stack of manila folders across the desk toward Monty's empty chair.

"Chief," she said, and Chief Malfadi remembered that he wanted to see that everything down at the explosion site was squared away. "Monty," she said, "Officer Wasco will remain to run any errands that need doing." Wasco walked over to where Ziza was sitting, winked at her, and stood as though he expected her to leave. "Ziza," she said, "I'm sure there's some way in which you should be about your Father's business."

"I'm sure you're right," Ziza said, getting to her feet, "but then my Father sometimes moves in mysterious ways." She raised her hand toward Monty. "Will I be seeing you?"

"Soon, I hope. But then Granny Meservey probably also said that hopin's no better than wishin'."

"I'll walk you out, Ziza, dear," Lillian Meservey said, ushering her toward the stairs. As they headed down, Lillian's effortless small talk touched on Ziza's running ("How much I admire all that energy") and yesterday's chaos on the waterfront ("The worst of it was that I had to be everywhere at once").

Ziza had no small talk. She just listened and then added, "This isn't the first time you've mentioned my running. You should try it yourself sometime."

They crossed the dark lobby, into the bright sunshine. Just as effortlessly, Lillian Meservey brought up her next subject.

"You seem to be an observant little thing," she said.

"I'm new in town. I have a lot to learn."

"I might guess you have a theory or two about our recent crime wave. Could you name the killer if you had to?"

"You planning on holding my feet to burning coals?"

Lillian Meservey threw her head back in an exaggerated garden-party laugh.

"Offhand," Ziza said, "I'd rule out Miss Gatewood, Mrs. Benecosta, most of the waitresses at the Economy, and myself."

"Monty?"

"I wouldn't lock him in his room without his supper."

"Whooten?"

"Maybe it's because I'm Protestant, but I find it hard to trust people who like to confess."

"Ray Rickert?"

She had no quick answer. She had more suspicions than she wanted to mention and ducked by saying, "You'll probably be asking about Bob Bramer and Wasco next."

"Forget Wasco, what about Bramer?"

"He wouldn't do it. You can't run for mayor from Sing Sing."

"Any other names you'd like to mention?"

"What about you?"

"I'd rather hear what you really think about our friend Reverend Ray but I suspect I'm not going to and I have too much else right now for a game of Twenty Questions."

For a moment Ziza thought Lillian Meservey was going to give her a friendly peck on the cheek, but she just waved a "ta-ta" and headed back up the Village Hall steps. At the top she turned. "Come back anytime, hear? We'll just kick our shoes off, put up our feet, and have a nice cup of tea."

Ziza had seen Ray Rickert the night before. She had been in front of her cold fireplace thinking through her strange conversation sitting with Whooten at the hospital when the doorbell rang. It was Ray, the first time he'd stood in her doorway since the night he arrived dragging the couch behind him. This time he brought five cans of a six-pack of beer.

"It's cold," he said, "the beer. If you invite me in word won't get around that the preacher's drinking alone."

He sat down on the couch without being asked. It was still the only piece of living room furniture. "You got the dog hairs off," he said and popped the tops of two cans.

"Brooklyn Beer?" Ziza said.

"Some magazine said it's the new great brew. They actually make it up in Utica. For all I know the same stuff's also called Albany, Troy, Schenectady, Rome, Syracuse, Rochester, and Buffalo."

Ziza took a sip. "It's beer," she said.

"What more can I say?"

She sat down on the couch next to him, and they both stared up at the only decoration in the room, Aladdin Baraclough's watercolor on the mantle.

"I've sailed past that," he said, "Point No-Point, and it's true that you can't see the damn thing when you're on top of it. You can see it coming toward you for miles, then suddenly it's behind you and you never knew when you were there."

"Good sermon subject."

"Don't think I haven't used it. Twice."

They sipped their beers. Ziza waited.

"I suppose the estate'll be asking for it back one of these days," he said. "Mine has more river traffic than yours. More sailboats, I think."

They sipped their beers. Ziza decided to nudge things a bit. "Are you here on a peace mission?" she asked.

"Have we been at war?"

"We seem to have regularly scheduled skirmishes. Yesterday morning, down on the waterfront, I kept getting the impression you were warning me about something."

"Well, I kept getting the impression that I was being accused of murder. Or should I say murders?"

"You fit that psychological profile as neatly as Monty."

"We weren't giving much credence to that, remember?"

"I know, but . . ."

"But. But I don't have a beard and I am married."

Ziza couldn't believe it. "You have a wife here in Quarryville?"

"Oh, no, it was a long time ago and she's back in the Midwest, Indiana, but we're still together. Whom God hath joined together, let no man put asunder."

"Not divorced."

"Of course not. I've provided over the years."

"Children?"

"Maybe if we had . . . But no, none." He opened two more cans.

"That's not much of an alibi, you know," she said, "having a wife in Indiana."

"I wasn't providing an alibi," he said. "I was just telling you something about myself. Something else for you to file away in that mind of yours."

Neither of them had tasted their new beers.

"Did Adele know about her?"

"Adele? Adele could be a pain in the . . ."

"A royal bother."

"A royal bitch."

"Something to get rid of?" Ziza suggested.

He didn't answer.

"You two were never joined together by God. Maybe you thought it was about time some man put the whole business asunder."

"And two other deaths before hers were just for practice?"

"Let me tell you my theory."

"Ah, theory." He laughed, and then he looked to the ceiling and said in his richest pulpit voice, "Glory almighty, the lady—dear Lord—has a theory."

"I told you yesterday that the key to solving this thing was Adele and I still believe that, but I've been thinking more and more about Dennis Morland and I've come to suspect that his death was some terrible sort of accident, that he somehow got murdered by mistake, or at least without any forethought. Then there had to be a second killing because Dave Spencer saw what happened. And then, yes, to use your word, practice was over, the killer had become accustomed to killing and Adele could be killed for the pure joy—or necessity—of it."

"Wrong," he said, "fundamentally and psychologically wrong. People just don't act that way."

"Oh, but they do. They act out of habit, and once a habit's been learned . . . No, the murderer never would have had the will, or the courage, to kill her if there hadn't been those practice sessions."

"Believe me, it doesn't work that way," Ray said. "I've studied a little bit of criminology and it's standard textbook stuff, except for psycho serial killers, that the first murder is always the important one. The ones that follow are to save the killer's neck by covering up mistakes. It's only in Agatha Christie that the clever killer knocks off A and then B to throw the cops because the real victim is C."

"I've never had much trust for textbooks," Ziza said. "Murder, here, became an unexpected habit and after two deaths that didn't really make much difference to the killer, he—"

"He?"

"Or she could finally kill someone he—or she—really gave a damn about."

They drank their beer and split the last can between them, taking turns drinking from it, while Ray Rickert cited statistics—which she suspected he made up—and historical precedent to prove his point. Her only defense was to laugh and say he was wrong in this case. And before he left, he revealed the purpose of the visit. The other ministers—Ziza assumed that meant Heavenly Roger—were unhappy about her going to the hospital with Rich and Anne. They had asked him, he said, to impress her with the fact that she should perfect a more professional manner.

"Actually," Ray Rickert said, getting up to leave, "I thought it was your finest hour. Getting those kids into a real emergency room situation . . ."

"It didn't actually work that way."

"It could've, and I say, Right on."

He gave her a quick, beery kiss on the cheek and was out the door.

And now, the next day, after that strange scene in Monty's office, after days of hints, threats, misstatements, and lies, Ziza thought she understood it all, how it all happened, perhaps even why.

She headed back to the church by way of River Road. It was again open to traffic, and on the other side of the fence squads of women in white jumpsuits were using chalk lines to section off the entire waterfront into grids for future testing. A few army trucks were parked with the Terra-Tech vans, and someone had put up a flagpole flying a Corps of Engineers pennant. The drilling rig—now circled with loops of Day-Glo crime scene tape—remained on its side. Parked close by was the huge National Guard tank tow truck, painted in desert camouflage, but no one was near it. The actual site of the explosion was the one still point on the busy waterfront.

Ziza walked through the open gate and climbed over the rubble of the fallen chimney. She went into the Baraclough foundry for one last look at the place where Dennis Morland must have died.

Wouldn't it be nice, she thought, wouldn't it be convenient to find the perfect, overlooked clue, and in a parody of discovery, as though going through the motions would make it happen, she reached down and picked up a jagged piece of reddish sandstone. It had a bit of carving on it. She examined it, sniffed it (she could smell the red dust Rich had mentioned moving through town after the explosion), and put it in her pocket.

She looked up. Outside the doorway, dressed in a variety of British tweeds, perched precariously on a shooting stick, and observing her through a pair of mother-of-pearl opera glasses, was Professor van Runk. She waved. He looked startled, as though he had not expected her to be able to see him, and then waved her toward him, welcoming her aboard.

As always when confronted with deaf people, Ziza was tempted to say something truly outrageous just to see how deaf he really was. Instead she said hello and mentioned the lovely weather.

"We'll be having you to tea," he said. "Miss Meservey and I were saying just yesterday how we must find time to fit you in for tea, although frankly when I say tea I mean something a good deal more hearty than boiled leaves."

"Miss Meservey keeps a pretty crowded social life?" she shouted.

"Her? Never. She's all business, although there for a while that Fogle kept popping up. One Sunday morning he even drove her home in her Jeep. But nothing much ever came of that, I'm happy to report." He picked up his binoculars to peer at two distant Terra-Tech women.

"Keeping an eye on things down here?"

"It's a hell of a business," he said. "Nothing's going to be set right for a good long time. Did I see you discovering a treasure inside there?"

"Just a piece of decorative stone. I thought I'd keep it as a souvenir of the tragic day."

"Yes, indeed," he said. "You might want something like that. I have at home a little stone I took from the top of the Great Pyramid in Egypt. Another from the hilltop outside Pittsfield where Hawthorne first met Melville. They met on a picnic, you see. You can sense a lot just by holding stones like that."

Ziza walked on, uphill, past the Star and Mt. Zion Methodist, where she knew there was a pile of work waiting for her, and on up, through Hillside to the grade school and the little dirt road that led to the Meadow. In the Meadow, she paused in front of the stone outcropping they called the Pulpit. The place was deserted, of course. The spot near the trees where Miss Gatewood had found the body looked no different from the rest of the little clearing. The grass had stopped growing for the fall and now was turning an almost transparent shade of gold.

Yes, she thought, it's all clear now. She just had to go home and wait for the visitor she knew would come.

22

🍂

The doorbell rang soon after nightfall. Ziza let it ring twice before she answered it. She was not surprised to see Lillian Meservey, but she didn't expect to see her dressed for a party in a smoky-blue raw-silk suit. "Take this," Lillian said, and handed her a polished metal tray holding a 1920s Art Deco cocktail shaker and two long-stemmed silver flutes.

Ziza took it and noticed she was also wearing fragile-looking antique lace gloves aged to the color of milky tea.

Before Ziza could say more than hello, Lillian brushed past her and made a quick, complete circle of the living room. Ziza closed the door but was careful not to lock it. "No coffee table," Lillian said and moved on, down the hall to the kitchen. After a glance at the kitchen table Ziza was using as a desk and at the unruly stack of papers held down by a jagged stone paperweight, she said, "Follow me."

Lillian Meservey first seemed to be headed for the back porch, but then paused before the cellar door, opened it, and flicked on the downstairs light. "In spite of appearances," she said, "the cellar is not our destination. Not another word, and don't fall behind."

Ziza had never been down there, but she propped the door open and, against her better judgment, followed Lillian into the brightest, cleanest cellar she had ever seen. Lillian Meservey went directly to a peeling red door, slid back the bolt, and pulled it open. They went through a short, well-lit cement block tunnel and then—after throwing more light switches —into a small, stale room lined with empty bookshelves. Next to a doorless closet jammed with metal coat hangers that jangled like wind chimes as Lillian brushed by was a spiral stairway.

"Up we go," said Lillian, "but mind your step with that tray, it's pretty steep. We don't want another fall, do we?"

Ziza minded her step, and they came up into a windowless room that was identical to the one below. Lillian kept moving and, with a flourish, threw open the door. On the other side was a great, round room bathed and dappled in moonlight.

"Behold," Lillian Meservey said, "St. Hubert's."

"I've always wanted to live in a house with a secret passageway," Ziza said.

"Hardly secret," Lillian Meservey said. "I was a guide here when the church was open for the Arts Club tour a few years ago. Now let's have that drink we've both earned with all this trudging around."

Ten rows of pews curved in a circle around the altar, a huge, unpolished block of marble that Ziza guessed must have come from one of the local quarries. The oddest thing about the church, though, was how much light it held. There were no ordinary windows but a glowing band maybe three feet wide of glass bricks circled the whole building at its roofline, and above was a tall cupola that caught the moonlight and funneled it down into the chancel, where the cross and candlesticks on the altar threw their crooked shadows across the uneven stone.

They sat down on the altar steps at the end of the wide aisle that led to the front door, and there was enough natural light to see mounted above it the deer's head with a crucifix in its antlers.

Lillian maneuvered the cocktail shaker and poured out two drinks.

"Miss Meservey shook," she said. When Ziza didn't say anything she added, "Social notes in small-town newspapers back home always used to end their items about ladies' teas by saying who poured. Miss Meservey poured. In this case"—she rattled the Art Deco shaker—"Miss Meservey shook." She raised her silver cocktail flute. "To dear old Quarryville" she said, and took a sip. Ziza watched. "Bottoms up," Lillian Meservey said, "mud in your eye. It's a martini, dear. Which is fast becoming a *rara avis*." She sipped again. "An antique drink in an antique vessel in a . . . I was going to say an antique building, but I suppose this place is more out-of-date than antique."

"Ray Rickert told me about the deer head," Ziza said, her drink still untasted.

"When you see it in the clear light of day it's a pretty moth-eaten affair."

"That's often the trouble with the clear light of day," Ziza said.

"Ah," Lillian Meservey said, "moral philosophy. That's what comes of drinking with the clergy. You are indeed joining me in this, aren't you?"

Ziza raised her flute, but didn't taste it.

Lillian Meservey freshened her own drink and went on. "Professor van Runk seems to think you might have made some great discovery while you were poking around at the Baraclough foundry this afternoon."

"That gave you something to worry about?"

"Hardly."

"No?"

"No, *n o* spells no."

"But you thought you'd just drop by and check me out, anyway."

"It's what you said outside Village Hall this afternoon that piqued my interest. I've long suspected that you've been spending more time nebbing into law enforcement than tending your flock."

"Well, then, shall we get right to what you want to hear?" Lillian Meservey cocked her head to one side.

"I think you're a murderer," Ziza said.

"I trust this is something you and that towering intellect Wasco came up with."

"Shall I tell you your mistake?"

"I think you should do what you seem to think's best."

"It's when I first visited you at your office and you warned me that running south from Quarryville into Yonkers was dangerous."

"Well, indeed it is."

"The meaning of what you said didn't register at the time. But this afternoon, when you mentioned my running again, it suddenly clicked. How did you know I'd run into Yonkers? I'd only done it once at that time, the first morning I was in Quarryville, the day before Dennis Morland turned up at the Meadow, the day someone took a picture of me from behind the trees at the old dump."

"Am I to be impressed with that?"

"No one saw me running that day except the mysterious photographer who was using Dennis's camera."

"This is Quarryville, my dear," Lillian Meservey said. "You'd be surprised how little goes unnoticed."

"Think about this: you had already killed Dennis at that point. I'd guess that maybe his body was in your car, and you brought him to the dump, happened to see me, took my picture, and for some reason changed your mind about leaving him there. So you just discarded his knapsack. Next morning, you went to the Meadow. But you're right about nothing going unobserved in this town. Miss Gatewood saw your car."

"My car?"

"Driving away from the Meadow that morning."

She laughed. It was a hearty, unguarded laugh, a laugh to share with old friends. "But my dear Ziza, I know you know—I know you've been told—who dropped that boy off at the Meadow that morning, and it wasn't me."

"You're talking about Whooten."

"I'm talking about Whooten."

"I suppose everyone in town knows he told me?"

"I think it's just you and I and the dear little man himself, unless you told your friend Monty about it."

"Now that Fogle's dead."

"By which you mean?"

"That your friend Fogle told you about Whooten."

"*My* friend . . . ?"

"I can't make my mind up about how much Whooten was manipulated. What would you say, how much did he do on his own?"

"Manipulated? Why I've always half assumed he was probably the killer. Who better to have killed the boy and dumped him, killed the hobo in the warehouse? (And then try to drag me in on that by arranging for me to be there when he 'found' the body.) No one had a more convenient spot for killing off poor Adele than he. He was right there on the porch all afternoon keeping an eye on her so he'd know just when to strike."

"Can it, Lillian. He was keeping an eye on her all right. He saw who slipped inside the house just before the accident. Your activities that afternoon were a study in constant movement. You were everywhere, talking with everyone, shaking hands, working the room. Ubiquitous, that's the word, isn't it? You were in so many places, so often, that you became as invisible as a mailman on his rounds."

"If I hadn't known you hadn't touched a drop of that martini, I'd say you were drunk."

A cloud must have passed across the moon. Shadows on the round room lengthened and converged.

"I suppose," Ziza said, "that it's quite a shock that Whooten, the man you were setting up as the murderer, is the one who's able to say he saw you follow Adele up the stairs. Were you carrying a film disc you wanted to tell her about in private? Had she told you that she'd come to suspect that you were up to something on the waterfront? Maybe even that she thought you were a killer? There's something she wanted to get my advice about, and I suspect it was that."

"Suspect? You have to do better than that."

"Which gets us back to Whooten. Maybe he'll be able to say that he saw the nudge—it wasn't really as much as a shove, was it?—that sent her over the edge. Maybe he can say that you followed her down the stairs, leaned over the body to make sure she was dead (you had to help her a bit at the end, didn't you, pressing down on her windpipe with all your weight?), and pinned on that JUST ASK MONTY button. It must have been a close call, getting out just before Bob Bramer wandered in to discover the body. He probably even passed you on the way, but since Lillian Meservey was everywhere that day he didn't even notice."

"Liar is an ugly word, Ziza, one I hate to use. Whooten can *say* anything, but he could have seen none of that."

"No? You're certain, aren't you? You'd checked to make sure he was busy? You were very careful? The campaign buttons intrigue me. I can't really believe they were your idea. They're all a bit too . . ."

"Pixieish?"

"Cute. If you really were trying to frame Monty you never would've done it that way."

Lillian Meservey glanced at her wristwatch, sighed, brushed invisible crumbs from her skirt, and seemed all too obviously to come to a decision. "I suppose we ought to tidy this all up. There's time. Those stupid buttons were Whooten's work. He stuck one on the boy after he moved him as some sort of joke, I suppose, a last minute hare-brained inspiration because he just happened to have a couple of them in his pocket. And he did it again with the wretch in the warehouse. I suppose he thought, what the hell, in for a penny, in for a pound. Maybe he thought it made a nice little signature piece. Who knows what goes on in that head. And since two corpses wore buttons, the third had to follow suit, although it did gild the lily. Frankly, I thought planting the film on her was enough."

"Having practiced with two almost accidental murders, you were able to strike your real enemy."

"If it makes you feel any better, everything that implicated your friend Monty was a complete accident, a little subplot that got out of hand. Thanks to Whooten, who, in the long run, has caused far more problems than he was worth. It never occurred to us that he'd take that camera from the dead tramp. (Who'd want something after being in that dreadful shoe?) We should have just let it go, but we got it out of the glove compartment, which is how it made its way to Monty's office."

"You set up the meeting at the warehouse with Whooten and Fogle, so Whooten would discover the body?"

"The tramp, you found out his name from that woman?"

"He was calling himself Dave Spencer."

"He'd seen the boy get killed, and as you guessed he recognized me from the one time I'd gone on that damn Lady Bountiful mission to the city. He wanted money, so I agreed to meet him at the warehouse."

"Where . . . ?"

"Where he went the way of the boy, of course. Then I tidied things up a bit and left behind the camera, so that anyone with half a brain would assume he'd stolen it after he killed the boy."

"And then just went off and died like a sick elephant? You

assumed no one would notice that he'd been hit on the back of the head?"

"It was an inconspicuous wound, no blood, and he was only a derelict. Maybe the River Rats got him. Who'd care?"

"And when that fell to pieces, there was Whooten to blame."

"He brought it on himself."

"You also planned to get the two of them, Whooten and Fogle, involved in a legal dispute so complex they'd never build the Baraclough project. That's why you arranged that meeting."

"Not those toadies. Adele. I wanted to get her and that Foundation Trust tax dodge of hers all tied up in legal battles. Fogle later called it a tar baby, a nice term, I thought. My plan was to save Quarryville from being harassed by every do-good governmental agency you can name, which was sure as the sunrise once they put shovel to earth around that foundry."

"Which might have gotten in the way of the project you really wanted to develop, the ten acres owned by Professor van Runk."

Lillian Meservey waved her hand as though she were shooing flies.

"The boy," Ziza said, "you said he got killed. Why don't you say you killed him, hit him with—"

"Not a piece of rock, like the one you have on your kitchen table. It was a length of pipe that was lying there. I threw it in the river."

"You hit him."

"Once. That's all it took."

"I see it as almost an accident. You saw him there and struck out in rage. I remember your telling Rich that the soccer team played as though they were afraid to get their uniforms dirty. So you'd seen him before. You knew who he was."

"I'd gone into the foundry to get a good look at the centerpiece of Adele's new empire. I wanted a nice look at what threatened to screw up all my plans, and this snot-nosed, pretty-boy kid was in there poking around with his toy camera. That bitch Adele, now she was getting the kids involved. That was my first thought. I couldn't stand the sight of him."

Her voice seemed to choke up. Ziza could not tell whether it was on tears or remembered rage. "Boy Scouts, I thought. Now she's even into Boy Scouts. Boy Scouts with cameras."

"And you hit him."

"Once."

"And threw the pipe in the river. Then you got Fogle to get rid of the body."

"Fogle?" She sounded genuinely surprised. "No, no, we talked about doing something about the body. I didn't think it was a good idea just leaving him there. After more talking than I care to remember—a day or so went by—it became pretty clear that I'd have to take care of it myself, but when I drove down to the foundry another car was pulled up to the place, Whooten's BMW. I stayed out of sight, but after he left I went in and the boy was gone."

"You hadn't expected that."

"Of course not. To do things right you always have to do them yourself. The silly dwarf left behind the boy's camera and knapsack. So I picked them up and then followed the BMW to see what he was going to do. When he took the Saw Mill Parkway for the city, I got rid of the boy's stuff."

"Off to the dump."

"How does the joke go? Where does the Lone Ranger take his trash? To the dump, to the dump, to the dump, dump, dump. And I saw you, recognized your picture from *The Weekly Spy,* and I guess for the sheer devilment of it—I was just beginning to think that I might have to frame somebody—I used up the next exposure in the camera."

Lillian Meservey glanced at her watch again.

"But Miss Gatewood saw your Jeep the next morning pulling away from the road to the Meadow."

"You want every moment accounted for? I was up early, fretting and driving around, when I caught sight of Whooten again and followed him."

"Fogle hadn't tipped you off?"

"Fogle. You keep talking about Fogle. He was one of Adele's boys, not mine. We wanted nothing to do with him, although he seemed to think he had a chance with me after that Sunday morning at the warehouse."

"You keep saying 'we.' Isn't 'we' you and Fogle?"

The warm party laugh again, the laugh between old friends.

"My dear, 'we' is me and your dear buddy Monty, for all the good that weak reed turned out to be."

Ziza froze. The gray, cloudy room seemed to shrink away from her. She felt a sick, acid taste in her mouth.

"Don't," she said, as though she wanted to ward off what she was hearing.

Lillian Meservey looked at her strangely and then reached out. For a moment of horror Ziza thought she was offering a comforting embrace but then her hands settled around Ziza's neck and she could feel the sharp threads of the lace gloves cutting into her skin. Ziza realized she was not being offered affection. She was being strangled.

Someone will come now, she thought. Someone will race up those stairs from the cellar and pull Lillian from her, save her, rescue her, put everything right. But, of course, no one would come, no one—she thought of Lillian looking at her watch—no one who would help her.

"What the hell," Ziza said out loud, rasping through the terrible pressure on her throat. She threw herself sideways. There the clatter of the silver cocktail shaker as it bounced down the three steps leading to the aisle, and she and Lillian rolled over and over again across the stone floor leading to the front of the altar. With each roll Ziza could feel the fingers around her neck tighten.

She pulled at Lillian's hands. The gloves disintegrated as she clawed at them, but the fingers stayed where they were.

She could smell the martini on Lillian's lips and taste her own blood mixing with the saliva. Holding her breath, pushing and using all the strength in her legs, Ziza sprang upright, dragging Lillian with her. The room was getting darker; the round walls whirled like a merry-go-round. She could feel the rush of heat that came just before passing out, and Ziza lunged toward the great stone block of an altar, crushing Lillian's back into its sharp edge.

She could feel warm, sweet-smelling air rush from Lillian's lungs, and a scream echoed in the rafters high over their heads. Lillian let go and dropped to the ground. Ziza grabbed the candlestick next to the cross and as she looked into the sheer terror in Lillian's eyes brought it down across her skull with all the strength she had left. Only at the last moment did she pull back so that the tarnished bronze base merely grazed Lillian's forehead.

She was carefully putting the candlestick back where she found it when she heard footsteps on the stairs. She considered hiding, but a circular room has few hiding places. If it were Monty, she wondered, would she have to defend herself again?

She waited, Lillian Meservey sprawled at her feet, listening as the steps got closer. For a second as she saw the shadow moving through the doorway she thought it was a child, and then she said, "Whooten."

"I'm a little late," he said, catching his breath. "They gave me your message at the funeral home, but I seem to have lost track of time. I followed the lights through the house to find you."

"From me?" Ziza said.

"That's what they said." He caught sight of Lillian and seemed confused about what to do next.

"It was from her," Ziza said. "She was setting you up. I was to be the next victim."

Whooten stared at her through the gray light, at the thin line of blood curling under her nose, at her sweat and tear-stained cheeks, at her tangled hair, at her torn work shirt, at the shadowy, crumpled body at her feet.

"Fogle wasn't the killer," she said. "You didn't have to cover for him. It was Lillian."

He looked at the rough marble block behind her, the uneven ashlars of the stone pavement that circled the altar, the moonlight falling upon it from the high cupola, the pale line of light caught in the circle of glass bricks.

"What a beautiful room," he said. "What a beautiful, beautiful room."

23

It was five o'clock on the first Sunday of the month and Ziza was at the hymn sing in the Undercroft of the First Presbyterian Church. Monty had been right. The long room with its brick arches and columns would have made a jim-dandy pizza parlor. There were plenty of empty seats, but the turnout was respectable enough for a December afternoon.

The new mayor was there, got there early and shook just about everyone's hand. To avoid the expense and bother of a new election, the village trustees had dusted off a half-forgotten law they could interpret to mean that the runner-up of the last election could fill out Monty's unexpired term. So Bob Bramer finally got to sit behind the big desk in the paneled office in Village Hall, and no one really seemed to mind. To show he was a good sport he insisted that Monty's picture be hung on the wall with his predecessors'.

The new, combined Sunday school had opened on schedule at the beginning of November, and it seemed to be working out better than anyone hoped. Attendance was up and growing. Heavenly Roger's fears that Reverend Ray was going to take over the whole show were—as yet—unfounded, although he did succeed in getting Ziza's office moved out of Mt. Zion and into the neutral ground of Dale DeSousa's Trinity Baptist.

Now Marge Benecosta had to walk clear across the Star whenever she wanted to share her coffee break and news (never gossip, of course) with Ziza.

This was Ziza's first Quarryville hymn sing and she was having a good time.

Mrs. Swain played the old upright with all the trills, glissandos, and chromatic runs of an old-fashioned down-home revival-meeting pianist. On a prolonged bridge between the third and fourth verses of "Rock of Ages" she managed to change key three times, and Ziza had never liked her more.

And Heavenly Roger had never been in better form. The sing was totally informal. People called out old favorites. Mrs. Swain found the place in the hymnal, and H. Roger, who actually had a pretty good voice, led the singing. More often than not he had an anecdote or two to throw in. After a call for "Guide Me, O Thou Great Jehovah!" he mentioned that its Welsh name was "Cwm Rhondda" and told about the time when he was an exchange student in Britain and attended a football game in the Rhondda Valley. Instead of a national anthem the crowd belted out—and here he broke into the Welsh first line of the hymn in the light, clear tenor—"*Arglwydd, arwai trwy'r anialwch.*" It was done with such élan that Ziza suspected the performance was repeated every month or so.

The Terra-Tech people were still tearing apart the waterfront, and it looked as though the EPA was there to stay. They'd even rented office space downtown. Whooten—who still didn't quite believe that Fogle wasn't a murderer—had been named acting administrator of the Baraclough Trust and was living in the old studio. Ziza heard he was still reworking his plans for the Cultural Center, but no one believed the place would ever be built.

Ziza had spent that afternoon on the other side of the Saw Mill Parkway (the other side of the tracks) at a motel that had been taken over as a dumping ground for homeless mothers and their children. For the past few weeks, *The Weekly Spy* had run editorials calling for the place to be shut down, but Ray Rickert and the Quarryville children's librarian had started a program of volunteers coming by to read to the youngest kids.

She had half expected it to be like a return to the chaos of Childtown, but she was wrong. The kids sat as though mesmerized as she read. Already burnt out on endless television, they were transfixed by the sheer oddity of a live person reading aloud from a book full of pictures. They watched her lips move. They wanted to sit on her lap and turn the pages for her. And they wanted the same story read over and over again. "The Three Little Pigs," with its big, bad wolf and all that huffing and puffing and stick houses and straw houses falling to bits, little pigs fleeing in terror for a new place to live. The third time through it dawned on Ziza that it was a story about homelessness and that for better or worse the TwiLite EZ Rest, with its broken neon sign and its backed-up plumbing, was a building made of bricks.

Mrs. Swain was banging through a decidedly martial introduction to "A Mighty Fortress Is Our God" when Heavenly Roger interrupted to point out what a skillful rewrite Martin Luther had made of the Forty-sixth Psalm for its lyrics. Mrs. Swain vamped briefly at the keyboard and then swung back into her mighty chords.

Ziza had talked once with Monty before they took him away. He had been allowed to stay in his office until he was booked into the county jail. "All I ever did was steal a camera," he said. He was amazingly offhanded about the whole business. "Lillian kept turning up with new stories of finding dead bodies" was the line she remembered best. That and "After Adele died I had nothing more to do with Lillian."

Killing people had never been part of the deal. They had worked out this agreement about the waterfront. Lillian would get to develop the Professor's land. Monty would get his low-cost housing as part of the multiuse development of the northern end of the old warehouse area. Adele and her boys were loose cannons who were biting off more than they could chew and were going to screw up the development of the land for decades.

Then Lillian killed Dennis Morland. Stupid move. He refused to have anything to do with hauling that body around. Then it was Dave Spencer, to cover her ass. Then Adele. Spite, sheer bitchy spite. Quarryville just wasn't big enough for the two of them. Monty said he wanted nothing more to do with the whole plan.

"Besides listening to Lillian talk, all I ever did was take the camera from Whooten's car. We knew he had the thing. Lillian said, 'Get it back.' So I started by searching his BMW, and there the damn thing was in his glove compartment. Hadn't even locked the car up."

"All that ace detective work later?" she asked. "When you were showing off how you figured out it was Dennis's old camera?"

"I guess I just didn't like the idea of Wasco becoming your Dr. Watson."

"Thanks," Ziza said.

"But if our original plan had worked," he said, "really worked, it would have been a waterfront to be proud of. A showplace for all the people."

Lillian had conned them all, Ziza thought, Monty, Professor van Runk, Whooten, all of them innocent bystanders who became her patsies.

"What I couldn't believe," Monty said, "was yesterday afternoon at my office when she seemed to be setting me up with Chief Malfadi as the fall guy. That was low, really low."

"How about money?" she asked. "Were you getting a cut of some kind, a commission?"

Monty was hurt. "Lillian had worked out a deal for herself, but I was in it only to get a good job done well. Housing for all, river access for all, a great playground, a hands-on museum . . ."

He was moving into a campaign speech, and Ziza said good-bye.

"No kiss for Monty?" he asked.

"No," she said.

He shrugged. "I didn't know she was meeting you at St. Hubert's," he said. "You don't think I did?"

"No."

"I barely knew the woman, really."

Lillian Meservey had spent several days in the hospital under observation for the mild concussion Ziza had given her with the bronze candlestick. Word was that she had hired the best lawyers money could buy.

"Good-bye, Monty," Ziza said.

"Take one of these as a souvenir," he said and handed her a JUST ASK MONTY button.

At the hymn sing, Heavenly Roger was looking around the room for the next request. " 'In the Bleak Midwinter,' " Ziza said.

"Our first Christmas carol of the year," he said, "and one of the most beautiful. A perfect choice."

He might have sounded like a wine steward, but for once Ziza agreed completely with H. Roger Swain.

Mrs. Swain began playing softly and simply, as though the winter chill was already in her fingers.

"In the bleak midwinter," they sang, "frosty winds may blow . . ."

For her, all of Christmas was in this hymn. There was something oddly primitive about it. The simple tune, the words that didn't always quite match up with the melody.

". . . snow had fallen," they sang in hushed voices, "snow on snow on snow . . ."

It reminded Ziza of lovingly amateurish, primitive paintings, of children's broad crayon sketches, of the odd little scenes that ran along the bottom of Renaissance paintings, Jesus, Mary, and Joseph on their terrible, cold journey.

"What can I give him," they sang, "poor as I am?

"If I were a shepherd, I would bring a lamb.

"If I were a wiseman, I would do my part.

"Yet, what can I give him?

"Give my heart."

She could feel the tears building in her eyes but not quite running down her cheek. On her last Easter at Childtown she had been trying to explain the Crucifixion and the Resurrection to the kids. They were confused, of course. It's a story that could confuse anyone. The last they'd heard of Jesus was only a few months before, at Christmas, and that was all about birth and presents, Wise Men and shepherds. And here he was again, being killed. Finally Ezra, the little boy whose tantrum later drove her to Quarryville, jumped up. His eyes were bright. He thought he understood. "Is God," he asked, sure that he'd come up with the right answer, "Is God a dead baby?"

It was hard to tell him no.

When they finished singing Heavenly Roger said that would be the last hymn of the day. The little congregation got to its feet. There were more hellos and handshakes. Both Swains said how glad they were that Ziza was able to drop by. Bob Bramer reminded her of the first meeting of a new village committee she had agreed to sit on. It was to solve some problem, but she couldn't remember which. Mrs. Bramer reminded her that she'd been invited to the annual Hillside caroling party. Anne Bramer and Rich had been sitting in the back. Rich shouted a "Merry Christmas!" to Ziza, the first of the season, her first ever in Quarryville.

By the time she got upstairs, the crowd had pretty much thinned out. Through the glass door of the Sunday school building she could see two cars parked in the driveway, about twenty yards apart. Ray Rickert was leaning against his Wrangler. Wasco, in civilian clothes, was leaning up against a civilian car Ziza had never seen before. They both were ignoring each other and keeping their eyes on the door, waiting.

Ziza took a breath, muttered, "What the hell," pulled open the door, stepped outside, and smiled.

AUTHOR'S NOTE

Point No-Point—sometimes written Point-No-Point—is a stretch of rock and sand on the west bank of the Hudson River just north of Nyack. Its official name, the one listed on maps, is Verdrietege Hook, *verdrietege*—according to Arthur G. Adams's *The Hudson: A Guidebook to the River*—meaning "tedious" in Dutch. Another translation, the one preferred by a Dutch-speaking river valley resident I consulted, is "sorrowful."

I'd like to thank Chris Letts, that tireless riverman and sometime keeper of the Tarrytown lighthouse, for telling me about the Point in the course of a conversation about the utter logic behind many Hudson Valley place names. It was a comment that quite literally triggered this book.

Others who should be thanked include Mary Allison and Karolyn Wrightson, for their article in the *Hastings Historian* that quoted Washington Irving's unexpurgated comments on people who try to export city ways to the country, and Robert Lescher, for his enthusiastic telling of Ray Rickert's belabored Washington Irving joke. Even though I failed to follow his advice to the letter, Jim Marshall deserves credit for his patient explanations of how federal Environmental Protection Agency toxic investigations are supposed to proceed.

Of course you will find neither Quarryville-on-Hudson on any map of New York State nor the name Aladdin Baraclough in any catalogue of Hudson River School painters. Which means, sadly, that as far as I know all those Mexican park benches didn't come from a little gringo river town after all.